FORMS
of
SHELTER

Books by Angela Davis-Gardner

FELICE
FORMS OF SHELTER

FORMS

of

SHELTER

Angela
Davis-Gardner

Ticknor & Fields · New York
1991

For information about permission to reproduce selections
from this book, write to Permissions, Ticknor & Fields,
Houghton Mifflin Company, 2 Park Street,
Boston, Massachusetts 02108.

Library of Congress Cataloging-in-Publication Data

Davis-Gardner, Angela.
Forms of shelter/Angela Davis-Gardner.
p.   cm.
ISBN 0-395-59312-3
I. Title.
PS3554.A9384F67   1991   91-16932
813'.54 — dc20   CIP

Printed in the United States of America

HAD 10 9 8 7 6 5 4 3 2 1

The passage about bees quoted on page 183 is from
The ABC and XYZ of Bee Culture by A. I. and E. R. Root,
A. I. Root Company, Medina, Ohio, 1940 edition.

To Terry and Laurel
And to the memory of
Dr. William Blackburn

Acknowledgments

I AM DEEPLY grateful to Laurel Goldman, Dorothy Casey, Peter Filene, Pete Hendricks, Linda Orr, and Peggy Payne for their fine critical insights about this book and for their unflagging support over the years.

I would also like to thank my father, Burke Davis, my mother, Evangeline Davis, and my brother, Burke Davis III, each of whom has given me so much; my uncle Alex McLennan, for his generous support; my agent, Mildred Marmur, who had faith in this book; and my editor, Jane von Mehren, who helped me bring it to a final resolution.

I appreciate the assistance of Richard Hartlage and Stephen Bambara, who patiently answered my questions about horticulture and bees, respectively, but who are in no way responsible for any errors I might have made.

For a variety of important gifts I wish to thank Don and Betty Adcock, Jean and Tom Bauso, Georgann Eubanks, Bryant Holsenbeck, Bonnie Stone, Bob Vaillancourt, and Terry Vance.

And a special thanks to my son, Heath, for his patience while I was writing.

"And yet the tree did — does — bear fruit."
TILLIE OLSEN, *Silences*

Prologue

I HAD BEEN kept awake by the tree limbs scratching on my window at night; the sound made my heart race. But then my landlord trimmed the branches and the silence has been worse.

Night after night I got out of bed and made myself stand by the window to look out at the tree. It moved in the wind, a black silhouette in the darkness; I imagined shapes crouched high in the limbs. Often I kept watch until the sky went gray and I could see the empty branches. I stayed there as the light grew brighter, looking at the deeply furrowed bark, the satiny twigs, the buds wrapped tight against Chicago's cold.

A few weeks ago I moved my desk from the living room and pushed it against the bedroom window. This was the place, I decided. I could write here looking out into the tree, just as I wrote in my tree house, all those years ago; only this time I would tell the truth.

Jack built the tree house in the Osage orange tree soon after he legally became my father. I believed I was safe there, hidden in the leaves, as I sat dreaming and writing in my journal. That was a long time ago, in North Carolina, but when I close my eyes I can still hear the sound of leaves around me like water, and I remember — with sudden shocking clarity — the goose-flesh of the Osage orange fruit, the sticky white juice inside.

In the top drawer of my desk are two relics from the Osage orange tree: a thorn and a piece of wood. I take them out and hold them in my palm. The thorn is slightly curved like an eyelash and its point is still sharp. The Osage orange wood is as long as my little finger, but thicker and wider, and whittled flat on two sides, like bone. I place the thorn and the wood on the surface of my desk: they will remind me of the price of silence.

From the bottom drawer of my desk I take photographs and tape them to the window frame. There is a snapshot of Daddy without the face — Mama cut it out — rocking a baby I think was me on the front porch of the house where I was born; a picture of me and Stevie, aged ten and six, with the snowman dressed in the Shriner's hat and fox fur; and a photograph of me at twelve or thirteen, grinning over my shoulder as I climbed the Osage orange toward my sanctuary.

I have no snapshot of Jack — Mama destroyed them all — but as I close my eyes again I can see, as I saw from my tree house, Jack, in white bee suit, helmet, and veil, with the smoker beneath his arm, move slowly across the yard to the hives. I see him close up, the veil thrown back: a face like freckled marble, pale blue eyes, one eyelid swollen from a sting. I remember, as he came toward me, his forefinger white with baking soda. And I remember what he said: "Jesus God."

I

One

DADDY WENT AWAY when I was five. My clearest memories of him are from that year, those winter mornings when he would wake me before light so we could go feed the pony, just he and I together. At least that was his excuse for waking me so early; later I thought he was telling me goodbye, over and over.

We lived in Virginia in an old house heated by a wood stove in the living room. When he woke me, those early mornings, Daddy took me out of bed still wrapped in my quilts and carried me downstairs to get dressed by the stove. After he had gone for good I sometimes jolted awake, thinking for an instant that he was about to come, that the sound of the doorknob had wakened me, but then there was only silence and the cold darkness against my face. Before he went away and he really did come to get me in the early mornings, I didn't begin to wake until my face was scraping against the rough wool of his shirt as he carried me down the steps, didn't open my eyes until he put me on the floor in front of the wood stove and said, "Be quick now, Beryl, your pony will be waiting."

While Daddy went to make our breakfast I got dressed, shivering as I peeled off my footed pajamas and the cold shocked my skin. After I had put on the jeans and sweater

Daddy had laid out for me, I sat on the sofa and watched the big window for signs of light.

At first it was so dark that all I could see in the window was myself on the sofa and the lamp beside me, but as the sky gradually lightened, my reflection began to fade. I liked the moment when I could just make out the shadowy forms of trees and then I could see them get clearer and clearer like the photographs Daddy made in his darkroom. Taking pictures used to be Daddy's hobby, but now it was his daily bread, his do-re-mi. When Mama knew I was about to be born she had made him give up his job in the dance band and go to work in the darkroom of a photo lab in Richmond. Once when Daddy took me there he printed a picture of me and Mama and Stevie, and I was so amazed to see our faces come up from beneath the water like that, I never forgot how we looked even though I didn't see that photograph again (later I thought Daddy must have taken it with him to remember us by): Mama with her pointed-chin smile and lipstick so dark it looked black; Stevie, a baby she was holding up like he was for sale; me grinning to show how all I wanted for Christmas was my two front teeth.

Daddy carried the breakfast into the living room and put it on the coffee table. "Eat up, skinny ribs," he said, pushing my bowl toward me. Daddy always fixed my oatmeal with a crust of sugar and a lump of butter so big it turned the milk yellow. Mama didn't put on so much sugar or butter and she didn't give me cocoa for breakfast like Daddy; I always ate quickly so she wouldn't come and see.

If Daddy finished eating first he would take his saxophone out of the case and polish the long silver throat until it gleamed in the firelight and made bright, wobbly reflections of our faces and the room, but he never played it then, never made a sound except when he pulled out the mouthpiece and blew on it as if he were testing a microphone. He didn't talk either, but I thought that was to keep from waking Mama and Stevie; I did not know then that he was sad. But after he went on the road with the band, leaving behind the note signed "Sadly, Daniel," and I began to relive these mornings, then I could see the sadness in his hands as he laid the saxophone back in its case and shut the wood stove door. Later I remembered asking him why he closed the stove and his saying, in the saddest voice, "So everything won't go up in smoke while we're gone."

By the front door in the hall he bent down to help me put on my jacket. Daddy's eyes were blue — Grandmuddy later told me this was so — and I know his skin was rough, I remember that myself, but his face has been harder to hold in my memory than anything else about him. I have had no photographs to help me, for Mama cut out his face from the family pictures and threw away those of him alone. Later, when we lived with Jack, and I tried to recreate in my mind that moment with Daddy in the hall, I could see his rough skin, but the eyes were harder to imagine because of Jack's eyes which were also blue. What I remember best from that moment in the hall is my jacket, the silkiness of its lining against my wrists, and then the quick sound of the zipper as Daddy did it up.

Outside there were pools of shadow where the trees were and it was very cold. The grass was a mat of tiny ice blades that Daddy's boots crunched through, but I hardly made any sound at all. It seemed a long way to the shed, where the grain was kept. One of my hands was warm in Daddy's, but the other turned pink from cold. He showed me how to make a fist with a hole in the middle and then blow through it to thaw my fingers. I liked the way my breath came out the other side in white puffs as if I were smoking a cigar.

The cold was thicker inside the shed. I stood at the doorway by the bucket while Daddy went to get the sack of feed. He came back carrying the sack on his shoulder as if it were a baby. He stood in the doorway for a moment, with his eyes smiling at me but his mouth pretending to be serious as he reached into his pocket and held out his closed fist, then dropped into my palm the lump of sugar I was to give the pony. After I put the sugar in my pocket, Daddy poured the feed into the bucket. As he tipped over the sack I squatted so that I could hold my hands beneath the grain. It felt cold and crumbly and left a fine, gritty powder on my skin.

I hated for that part to be over, because next I would have to feel the pony's awful mouth against my hand. I walked a little bit behind as Daddy carried the grain bucket to the fence. "You're not a sissy, are you?" he said, frowning a little as he looked back at me.

I peered out from between the slats of the fence as Daddy called "Ho, boy!" and banged the grain bucket against the post. "Ho, boy!" There was an answering whinny, and soon I could hear him cantering up the hill from the dark part of the pasture. I could hear his hoofs and his snorting breath before I could see him; the way he took shape out of the dark made my heart thump and the sugar go damp in my hand. As the pony came closer and I could see his eyes and big nostrils, I had to lock my knees to keep from backing away.

The pony was a Shetland, with a long black mane and bangs that nearly covered his eyes. "Give him the sugar," Daddy said. "There's nothing to be afraid of." Holding Daddy's arm I stepped up on the fence rail and held out the sugar on my trembling palm.

He sneered. There were the long yellow teeth. I held my breath and did not move. But then with just a tickle and a wash of hot breath it was over; I was safe until next time.

Then Daddy set the bucket on the ground, on the pony's side of the fence. His halter rattled against the bucket and he began to eat, a loud crunching like scissors through heavy cloth. Daddy swung me to the top rail of the fence and I snuggled back against him. This was my favorite part of the morning, the two of us quietly looking out at the pasture as the sunlight moved slowly down the hill toward the pond. The cold air made my eyes water so that I could see everything in such sharp focus: the starched blades of grass shining in the sun, the white sycamore on the far hill, the giant scribble marks on the frozen pond. When Daddy was in his slow mood we stayed long enough to see the light touch the pond. On those days Daddy smoked a cigarette, holding me tight with one arm as he reached into his jacket for the pack of Luckys. He did it all with one hand: shook out the cigarette, put it in his mouth, and lit it by striking the match on the fence post. Then he brought the other arm around me, and I settled back against his chest again. After Daddy had gone I could close my eyes and remember the warmth of him behind me, and the smells of his brown plaid jacket, a mixture of tobacco, wool, and cold air.

We were facing west, looking into the distance where Daddy was soon to go. Later it shocked me to realize that while I was looking at the line of mist on the horizon and trying to imagine, as Daddy told me to, the Blue Ridge Mountains, he must have been thinking, those last days, of the city far beyond.

Sometimes Daddy called that mist the wild blue yonder. I remember he called it that the last day. The pony was still crunching grain in the bucket, and the light was only partway down the hill. Daddy hadn't even lit his cigarette when he said, "Just think how it would be to throw your leg over old what's his name and go cantering off into the wild blue yonder. What is his name, anyway?"

I never liked that question because it meant it was almost time to leave; my deliberation about the pony's name was always the last thing before Daddy swung me up on his shoulders and took me back to the house, where Mama and Stevie would be awake and wondering what took us so long.

"I don't know," I said, looking at the pony, taking my time. "Prince? Here, Prince, Prince, Prince."

The pony munched on, not raising his head.

"Nope," Daddy said, "that doesn't seem to be it." He knew my method: if the pony seemed indifferent or snorted, he hated the name; if he raised his head, he approved. I was torn between two names, Smoky and Prince, both horses in books Daddy had read to me.

"Smoky," I said, "Here, Smoky, Smoky, Smoky."

I could hear teeth against metal so I quickly said "Prince! No, I mean Smoky!" just as the pony raised his head.

"See you later, Prince Smoky," Daddy said, lifting me by the waist and settling me on his shoulders.

"No," I cried, "Prince *or* Smoky." But we were already jouncing across the grass. I looked back at the pony forlornly watching us go. "Wait, Daddy, I didn't get to choose."

"Be quicker tomorrow," he said.

Later I wondered if he knew it was the last day. I couldn't tell, thinking back on it, from his voice, but I did remember that as he carried me on his shoulders to the house, he was humming "I Can't Give You Anything but Love" and he kept squeezing my feet one after the other as if to memorize the bones.

The next day, Mama told me he'd gone to Chicago to be with the band; then she lay on her bed and cried. I walked down to the edge of the pasture and looked at the pony with his head over the fence, but I didn't cry. Daddy had given up the band when I was born, so it was my fault he was gone. He would come back, though, or send for me when I was old enough; for a long time I believed this.

I believed it when we moved a few months later, Mama and Stevie and I, from Virginia to North Carolina. I kept believing during the years we lived with Grandpa and Grandmuddy and even, for a while, when we lived with Jack.

Two

JACK SAVED US, Mama said.

When we first lived with Grandpa and Grandmuddy, Mama worked in a department store selling perfume. Grandmuddy took me to see her once; I remember how excited I was as we rode the escalator to her floor. Grandmuddy had bought me a pinwheel, which I held high like a flag. I expected that the pinwheel would twirl with the speed of our ascent, and that Mama would see it and guess it was mine. But there was neither twirl nor welcoming smile; Mama was waiting on a customer — a man — and did not at first see us. My heart quickened as we walked toward her. How glamorous she looked behind the glass case of glittering bottles and atomizers, how unattainable. Her dark hair was in a smooth pageboy; her face was sternly beautiful. The carpet was deep, the air fragrant; in the distance a discreet bell chimed insistently, the same note over and over. That Mama was not ruffled by the bell impressed me; she understood the language of this exotic world.

I put my chin on the sharp, warm countertop and watched her move silkily about in her red and white polka-dot dress. She saw me and winked. The man — dark-haired and, if I let my eyes go slightly out of focus, a little like Daddy, though shorter —

seemed very pleased with her. As he left, he gave her a linger-
ing smile.

Mama glanced at me and reached for something beneath the
counter. It was a small, dark blue bottle; she carried it toward
me smiling, her face alight with intention. "Hold out your
wrists," she said, and opened the bottle. I stood with my arms
stretched uncomfortably across the high countertop as she
tipped the bottle against her finger and touched the sweet-
smelling liquid to my wrists and the insides of my arms where
they bend. Then she put the top back on the bottle, put the
bottle in my hand, and closed my fingers over it. "You're old
enough for this now," she said in a hushed, serious voice.

When we went down the escalator, Grandmuddy had to
carry the pinwheel because I refused to let go of the perfume;
I held it in my pocket. After we had gone out the revolving
door into the heat, I took out the perfume and read its name:
Evening in Paris.

At Grandpa and Grandmuddy's house, I spent most of that
first summer on the screened porch, holding the bottle of Evening in Paris and inhaling it like a drug. Because Daddy had
lived in Paris as a young man, playing his saxophone at the Blue
Note, I decided that Mama's giving me this particular perfume
was a message, an omen. Ever since Stevie and I had gotten
Daddy's postcard from Chicago saying he had to wear tight
shoes and a monkey suit every night, I had been sure he was
coming back; it was only a question of when. The perfume
meant he would come soon.

Between sniffs of the perfume I sat motionless on Grandmuddy's chaise and I stared at my small feet in their white
sandals and I waited. I liked to think about Mama at the store
— in my imagination she was always waiting on men, one of
whom would eventually be Daddy — but I liked even better to
think about her return. I had decided that Mama was like the
fast hand on the kitchen clock and Daddy was like the slow one;

after Mama had come home enough times, then Daddy would come, too.

I could see the kitchen clock from the chaise. At five-thirty I began to listen for the bus; the next one to stop at the corner would be hers. When I heard it, I held my breath and crossed my fingers. I could imagine the two of them walking toward the house, giggling quietly, wanting to surprise me. When I heard just one pair of footsteps coming up the drive I had Daddy tiptoe on the pavement or walk Indian-style on the grass; I could see just how he would lay one finger over his smiling lips.

It was as though I slept those long afternoons, and dreamed, and then, when Mama came back alone, awoke. The screen door made its crickety sound, and she walked in, her tired, disappointed face turned away from me. Stevie would come running for a hug; that made her smile. With a sigh she would sink to the chaise and pat my knee. If she had on earrings, she would let me try them on.

Then Stevie and I followed her into the living room where she collapsed into the brown striped wing chair by the fireplace. I was allowed to get the cigarettes out of her pocketbook, and the silver lighter. She blew smoke through her nose and closed her eyes. She liked for me and Stevie to take off her shoes and rub her feet because she had bunions that got inflamed from standing up all day. I remember that I associated bunions with onions because of the way her feet smelled.

From the dining room, where Grandmuddy was laying out supper, she would scold Mama about wearing high heels and about having taken that job in the first place. Grandmuddy said she'd be better off going back to nursing school and meeting a nice doctor. "I'm sure your father would be willing to pay for that." What Mama wanted to do was start college over and study English or art, but Grandpa had pronounced that pigwash. "You can't support two growing children on poems," he said.

Supper was an awful time. First we had to sit with our heads bowed while Grandpa said one of his homemade prayers that went on and on and usually ended with "Bless these fatherless waifs, we ask in Jesus' name and extend grace to their mother, that she may see the light and seek her strength in Thee." His voice went down at the end of the sentence and flattened out on the Thee, as if he didn't at all expect to get what he was asking for.

Grandmuddy carried the conversation by asking Stevie and me rehearsed-sounding questions. "Well, Beryl, how have you improved your mind today?" Grandmuddy would give me a brief stare, then complain to Mama about how I did nothing but sit around and mope. "Steven, tell your mother about our little adventure." And she would proceed to tell Mama how he had done something like bring a hairy caterpillar into the house and it crawled up her leg while she was reading the paper and like to scared her to death.

Stevie, who sat cater-cornered to me, in the chair beside Mama, grinned at the descriptions of his escapades. Grandmuddy's fussing only encouraged him to do something silly, like pretending his ear of corn was a typewriter; he would eat his way down each row fast, with a loud ding at the end. That used to make Mama laugh. She didn't laugh now, but she did sometimes run her hand across the soft paintbrush of his hair in a way that made me envious.

Then Stevie might ask one of his show-off questions like, "Mama, why are there twenty-six letters in the alphabet?"

"Can you believe he's only four?" Mama would say. She and Grandmuddy would shake their heads in wonder.

Grandpa heeded none of this. During the first part of the meal he was silent except for his eating noises. When he was ready for seconds he would point at whatever he wanted. Grandmuddy would see from the corner of her eye his finger jabbing toward the string beans or the cornbread and give it to him; sometimes she would rise and serve his plate.

After Grandpa had done most of his eating, he would start in on what Mama called his sermonette. Mama told me that Grandpa had been a preacher a long time ago, a missionary in Japan (she had been born there), and though he'd lost the call, he kept trying to get it back.

His text was pearls before swine. Some days the swine were the Japanese who had betrayed him and Grandmuddy and their mission at Pearl Harbor. At the time I thought Pearl Harbor was where Grandpa had cast his pearls only to have them bombed; later I came to understand that he and Grandmuddy and Mama had been safely back in North Carolina when the Japanese attacked, but the name of the place where the treachery occurred was a kind of revelation to Grandpa and had made pearls before swine his theme for life.

He had cast his pearls before Mama, too. He had warned her about Daddy, but she had not listened. She had made her bed and wallowed in it. Whereas any fool could have seen that horn player wouldn't amount to anything, that he was nothing but an atheistic bum. What kind of man would up and leave his family to go hang around with coloreds in nightclubs? Grandpa answered his own question by making a zero with his thumb and forefinger and blowing through it.

I hated Grandpa then; I wished he were dead. I wished he would go to Africa to cast his pearls before those heathen, and the cannibals would get him and boil him in oil.

What did it matter, what I wished? Grandpa just went on and on, letting more terrible words about Daddy hail down on us, while Grandmuddy played with her teaspoon and said, "Now, Beau, now, Beau," and Stevie's mouth hung open and Mama's face began to shatter. On the worst days, Mama ran upstairs and slammed the door to her room. Then I imagined the cannibals cutting pieces out of Grandpa's skin and frying them in the oil right beside him, making cracklings with the fried skin and putting them in the cornbread and making him eat it.

Sometimes I looked at Grandpa's real face, with the wrinkled, spotted skin and the thin, wet lips and the yellow teeth and the watery blue eyes that looked loose in the sockets and I wished he would really die, that while I was looking he would fall forward and hit the table with a thump.

Later I would worry about having thought such terrible things. What if Grandpa and Grandmuddy were right and there was a God who knew my every thought and motion?

My idea of God was a giant eyeball — like a picture I'd seen of Gulliver staring down at tiny, terrified Lilliputians in the cup of his hand — or a giant ear that sucked in all sinners' thoughts; after my bad thoughts about Grandpa I felt so uneasy about this possibility of the looming ear that I would go to my room and pray, just in case.

By the end of our first summer, Grandmuddy had posted rules. They were handwritten in black ink and tacked to the inside of the large downstairs closet where the maid had taken her rests, when they still had a maid, and where Stevie slept at night.

· No pets. (This includes caterpillars, lightning bugs, and any other type of insect.)

· Leave pillow on hall chair straw-side up. [The other side, which I favored, was velvet.]

· Use no more than six squares of toilet paper at one time.

· <u>Do not flush.</u>

Grandmuddy was in charge of flushing the toilets, which she did once or twice a day, depending on the season, both to conserve water and to make sure that Stevie and I were "regular."

That fall Mama got a letter from Daddy; I could tell from the way her face went white and from the Chicago postmark on the envelope she'd dropped on the floor beside her. "What did he say?" I asked, trying to peek.

Mama turned and glared at me, her eyes dark and hard, then

crumpled the letter, jumped up, and ran to the bathroom.

I followed, my heart pounding. "Mama?" I tried to open the door, but it was locked. "Tell me, Mama!"

I heard the ripping of paper, then the sound of the toilet flushing.

She came out without the letter and pushed past me. "Is he coming soon?" I called after her, even though I knew it was a stupid question. She answered by stamping her feet on the stairs. "Why won't you tell me?" I shouted.

"It's not about you," she yelled, then slammed the door to her room.

I ran into the living room and snatched up the envelope: "Mrs. Beatrice Thibedeaux, 404 Robin Hood Drive, Blacksboro, North Carolina" was typed on the front in three ragged lines. Several letters had been struck out with an *x* and then typed again. "The Drake Hotel, Chicago, Illinois" was engraved in fancy letters in the upper left-hand corner. My heart beat faster: Daddy's postcard had been from the Drake Hotel, a picture of the ballroom where he played with the band. There was nothing inside the envelope — not a picture, not a speck of dust. I ran upstairs and got into bed with the envelope under my pillow. Maybe the letter had said he'd been planning to come but he didn't have enough money just yet.

After that I started lying in wait for the postman at the bottom of the steps by the Nandina bush, but the only letter with a Chicago postmark turned out to be about Grandpa's Shriners' convention. When Grandpa found out I had steamed it open, he added one more rule to Grandmuddy's list: "No snooping in mail. Tampering with the mail is a federal offense."

———

Not long after the letter from Daddy, Mama's bad time began. She stopped going to her job at the department store and did not even get dressed in the morning, but all day wore an old turquoise chenille robe that smelled like peanuts. She did not comb her hair or put on lipstick. She wandered around the house smoking, looking at Grandmuddy's knickknacks, staring out windows. Sometimes she sat in Grandpa's den and looked at old *Life* magazines; she would let me and Stevie sit by her if we were quiet. Some days she did not even get out of bed but lay with one arm folded under her head and her body turned toward the wall; then Stevie and I were not to bother her.

Grandmuddy said Mama wasn't feeling well; Grandpa said she was lazy. In the mornings he would lean against the newel post in the downstairs hall and bellow up at her: "Beatrice, your mother has breakfast on the table! Another day, another dollar!"

Each morning he made us wait until the food was cold. Then he sliced into his fried eggs, sausage, and grits with his knife and fork, scrambling everything together. As he ate, he fumed in a loud voice — this was directed at Grandmuddy, who was trying to get him to retire from the Oldsmobile dealership, which was losing money anyway, as well as at Mama — "People work! People work!"

At ten, Grandmuddy would send me to Mama's room with coffee and orange juice. She usually sat right up, as if she'd been just lying there, not sleeping. Her eyes were puffy and crusted and her skin was unnaturally moist; I thought she must have been crying.

I began to fear that Mama's letter hadn't really been from Daddy, but someone else in Chicago who had written to tell Mama he had died and she didn't want to tell us.

One day, on the way upstairs with Mama's juice and coffee, I decided I would ask her for Daddy's phone number. If he was dead, she would have to say so.

I put the tray on the nightstand; she slowly rose up.

"Mama, are you sick? Because if you are, I could call Daddy and he could come take you to the doctor, if you would give me his number."

Mama lay back down and shut her eyes.

"He's not dead, is he?"

"Good riddance to bad rubbish," she said.

I backed out and walked downstairs, holding myself very carefully upright, and shut myself in the bathroom. I sat on the cold tile floor a long time and stared so long at the cardinals printed on the wallpaper that when I shut my eyes I could still see the red blots.

That night Grandmuddy, Grandpa, Stevie, and I sat in the living room and listened to Mama sobbing upstairs. I had never heard her cry like that, a terrible kind of crying, with moans mixed in. I had the cold feeling in my bottom again and I was afraid I might go to the bathroom on the sofa, but I could not move. None of us moved, or spoke.

Grandpa with his newspaper and Grandmuddy with her Bible sat frozen in the wing chairs at either side of the fireplace. Their gazes did not meet, I noticed, but intersected above the coffee table and then drilled into the wall of either side of the sofa, where Stevie and I sat. The two of us edged together until our shoulders touched.

Finally the crying stopped and we got up and went to bed. Stevie wanted to sleep with me, but Grandmuddy said no.

"Is Daddy dead?" I asked Grandmuddy when she and I and Grandpa were in the hall upstairs.

"No, honey. He's not dead. Go on to bed now," she said, giving me a little push. Each of us went into our rooms then and shut the doors.

Later Stevie came up to my room; he brought with him some green grapes he had stolen from the kitchen. We got under the covers and ate all the grapes; then we curled up together and slept.

In the morning Grandmuddy asked who had taken the grapes; when we did not confess she said she felt sorry for whoever had eaten those grapes because Japs had picked them and they hadn't been washed yet.

I began to feel sick. I went to the bathroom and locked myself in. Burning brown water came out of my bottom. I was very scared, because it kept on coming and coming out of me. I was sure I had gotten a terrible disease from the grapes and everything was coming out of me and it was me who was going to die without ever seeing Daddy again.

Three

In late November Mama went to the hospital — to have her appendix out, Grandmuddy said, though even at the time I did not believe this. Stevie and I were not allowed to visit.

There was nothing to give thanks for at Thanksgiving. I remember staring at the salt and pepper shakers — two Pilgrims, male and female — while Grandpa prayed: "O Lord, I beseech Thee on this day of Thanksgiving, teach the mother of these precious children who sit here before me today to humbly give thanks for all the riches she doth enjoy. Guide her, O Lord, through this dark and perilous time, take her hand that she may stumble the less, and show her, I ask Thee in Christ Jesus' name, the straight and narrow path to salvation."

Grandmuddy pretended to blow her nose, but really she was wiping away tears. Stevie stared at her, terrified. I felt so sick I could not eat. I shut my eyes and promised God that if He'd save Mama I'd believe in Him and be good forever.

When Mama came back a few days later — and so transformed — I thought my prayer had been heard. It was a miracle: God had saved her.

She returned in a taxi. There was a misty rain. I watched out the living room window as she came up the front walk in a belted raincoat, with the collar turned up, like a glamorous spy.

Her private smile made me think she had a secret, and my stomach swooped like it did on a fast elevator: maybe Daddy was coming too. There was only the uniformed taxi driver, following at a respectful distance with Mama's bags, but Daddy might come later.

Grandmuddy opened the front door, and Mama walked in grinning. Stevie tackled her. "Whoa!" she shouted, laughing, and picked him up. He wrapped his arms and legs around her. "Mama, Mama, Mama," he wailed. Mama jiggled him up and down. "Poor little boy, did your Mommy go off and leave you? Well, I'm back now, everything's OK." And she kissed and kissed the top of his head.

"Stevie broke a glass, meaning to," I told her.

"Right on my clean kitchen floor," Grandmuddy added.

"Did he? Well, that naughty boy." And she kissed him again.

Then Mama bent down to me and stroked my head with both of her hands. I can still remember how thick and warm that made my hair feel. She pulled my braids one at a time and said she had something exciting to tell us at lunch. I begged her to tell then, but she wanted to wait for Grandpa to get home.

Daddy was coming: I knew it. He hadn't written because he wanted me to be surprised. I put on my best dress, the blue dotted swiss Grandmuddy had made for me.

Mama was late coming down to lunch. We sat waiting a long time after Grandmuddy had rung the bell.

Grandpa kept moving his silverware on the tablecloth — spoon to the right, knife to join it; knife to the left, followed by spoon — reminding me of the sullen way boys in my ballroom dance class did the two-step.

When Mama finally entered — unaccompanied, breathless — she was dressed up, too, in a dark red wool dress and pearls.

Grandpa said a short blessing that did not include Mama.

Then Mama told us that she was going back to school in January. She looked around the table, smiling.

"What about Daddy?" I blurted out.

Mama's smile froze. She and Stevie, big-eyed beside her, and Grandpa at the end of the table with his mouth open looked like statues. I bit the inside of my mouth hard to keep from crying.

"That's nice, Beatrice," Grandmuddy said. "Tell us about it." And Mama went on to explain that while she was in the hospital she had met a wonderful writer named Bernie Hoffman, who thought she was a wonderful writer, and he'd talked to a friend of his at the college — a very influential man, head of the classics department, a former dean, blah blah blah — who'd gotten her a scholarship. As she talked on, my chest drew in so tight I could hardly breathe. There wasn't any God.

"What does that high-priced head doctor of yours have to say about this scheme?" Grandpa demanded.

"Ssh, Beau," Grandmuddy said, looking at me and Stevie.

"Did you have a headache, Mama?" Stevie asked.

"Sort of." She pulled him from his chair and into her lap. "Dr. Becker thinks it's a terrific idea. And he thinks I can do more with my degree than just teach English — he also thinks maybe I really can be a writer."

"And while you twaddle around with poems," Grandpa said, "I presume I'm to go on feeding and clothing the passel of you?"

"As a matter of fact, Bernie said he could get me a part-time job as well as the scholarship. I can pay rent and board."

"When hell freezes over, maybe." Grandpa reached for the cane that was hooked over the sideboard and hauled himself upward.

"Beau!" Grandmuddy cried. "Where are you going? There's pie for dessert!"

Across the room Grandpa stumped, coming down so hard on his bad leg that dishes rattled in the china cabinet. "I am going," he said, glaring at Mama, "to try to sell a few more Oldsmobiles before I die."

The door banged shut. Grandmuddy fled to the kitchen.

"Don't worry, kids, we'll be out of here soon," Mama said,

"I promise." She hugged Stevie so hard I could hear him wheeze and she smiled at me, but I didn't smile back. I looked at her — the front tooth that stuck out too far, the shiny, wrinkled skin at the corners of her eyes — and thought the meanest thing I could: Daddy had left because she wasn't pretty enough.

————

We lived with Grandpa and Grandmuddy two and a half more years.

The first year, Stevie and I got another card from Daddy, this one with a bird's-eye view of Chicago and Lake Michigan on the front. "Isn't this some big city?" he wrote. "And what about that lake? I wish you could see it. Be a good girl and boy and help your mother."

I was sure there would be more cards. When months went by and none came I decided Grandpa must be intercepting them; he was always home for lunch when the mail came and got to look through it first.

The second winter there was a big snow. Mama helped me and Stevie build a snowman. We used Oreo cookies for the eyes and buttons and one of Grandpa's cigar butts for the nose. Then Mama said, "Let's go root around in Grandpa's closet for a hat." Grandpa was in his den, so we tiptoed upstairs. Mama tried on Grandpa's tasseled Shriner's hat. It looked funny, like an upside-down flowerpot on her head; when we laughed, she looked into his mirror and stuck out her tongue. Then, while Stevie and I waited in the hall, Mama crept into Grandmuddy's room and came out with a fox fur piece draped around her shoulders. "Won't our snowman look fetching in this?"

"Mama, no!" I said. "What if she catches us?" Grandmuddy was at the store, due back any time.

"Just long enough for a picture." Mama ducked into her room for the camera, and we tiptoed back down the stairs.

I didn't know Mama could be so much fun. We put the

Shriner's hat on the snowman — Mama tilted it to one side with the tassel dangling over an eye — and arranged the stole around his neck so that the two fox mouths appeared to be biting the tails. Stevie and I lined up on each side of the snowman and Mama backed up with the camera.

It occurred to me that Mama might send this picture to Daddy, to show him how much we'd grown. Just before the click I pointed at the Shriner's hat to warn Daddy about Grandpa — a clue about the stolen mail.

Though the photograph was never mailed it did come to Chicago with me years later; it is taped to the window frame above my desk.

In this picture I am ten years old. I have on the pea jacket I hated and a striped stocking cap pulled low on my bangs; my long braids shine in the winter light. With a wry smile, I am pointing to the snowman's hat: a hopelessly inscrutable gesture, I should have known, even had Daddy tried to read it. Stevie is turned slightly away from the camera and staring solemnly into the distance. Though four years younger, it is he who seems to understand our situation; indeed, his expression seems almost clairvoyant. For what compels me now about this photograph is the invisible presence of Jack.

Jack was there when Mama swiped the hat and fur and dressed the snowman: I can see his hand in the rakish tilt of the hat and in the positioning of the furs. And he was with us the next day, as we rode to church with Grandpa and Grandmuddy, as the voice in Mama's ear.

Grandpa and Grandmuddy were in the front seat; Mama and Stevie and I were in the back. Grandmuddy had the foxes arranged importantly on her shoulders. Poker-faced, Mama stroked the pelts, then whispered in my ear: "If foxes could talk! Pass it on." I passed it on to Stevie and we got into one of those giggling fits where you laugh until you feel sick. As I remember riding all the way to church like that, Stevie and I giggling, Grandpa glaring in the mirror, Mama winking at us about our secret, it chills me to realize she had a deeper secret still.

I look back at the picture of the snowman. Now I see in him a fore-ghost, an effigy: Jack Frost.

That December Stevie and I finally heard from Daddy again: a Christmas card with no return address — this was how it had slipped past Grandpa, I decided. "Merry Xmas, Yr. Dad" was all the card said, but he had also enclosed two five-dollar bills and a postcard, written earlier, with a picture of a polar bear on the front.

"Dear little girl and boy," he wrote, "It's the right weather for polar bears up here. You wouldn't like that. You would like this zoo tho. I wish you could go there with me sometime. With love, your dad."

I ran upstairs and burst into Mama's room, waving the money and the card. Mama was sitting at her dressing table, getting ready for a party; she had on the corset-like strapless bra that is called a Merry Widow. I remember that the bra had lace cups I could see through, and I remember how she held the postcard up in one hand and kept on brushing her long hair with the other.

" 'Dear little girl and boy,' " she read. "Guess he can't remember your names." Mama flung the card on the dressing table; I picked it up.

"Can we go visit him?" I said, but my heart was already beginning to sink.

"Of course not."

"Why?"

She did not answer, but began to pin up her hair, turning her head this way and that, looking at herself in the mirror. A little smile appeared at the corners of her mouth.

I felt a chill across my ribs. "Who are you going to the party with? That writer from the hospital?"

"No."

"Who, then?"

The smile widened. "You'll know soon enough," she said. But it was the next summer before she spoke his name.

———

Stevie and I were in the back yard squeaking back and forth in the glider. I was telling him one of the stories from our ongoing series about a little old man and woman pepper and salt shaker. They used to be human — the Reverend and Mrs. P. U. Quimper — but they were so mean to children that a witch had shrunk them into porcelain figurines with holes in their heads. But every year on Christmas Day, they came back to life. They would awake on a doorstep and knock, begging to be let in. Each time they were asked to prove they were Christians; each time they failed. Then they met various cruel fates: freezing to death, being eaten by a hungry cat, being flattened by a hurled newspaper.

But on this Christmas, things were looking up. A fat woman who collected dolls had let the Quimpers into her house. She even had a miniature table and chairs, where they had been invited to sit.

The Reverend Quimper said grace. Then the meal was brought out: Brussels sprouts, slimy okra, hominy grits. The Quimpers said they weren't so hungry after all, but the fat lady said they must eat: think of all the trouble she'd gone to; think of the starving Armenians.

I heard a sound and looked up. There stood Mama in her tennis dress, laughing through her upheld racket.

"They died," I concluded, "choked to death on okra slime, but they were made honorary members of the clean plate club in heaven."

Stevie hooted and clapped — he was always an enthusiastic audience. Tucking her racket under her arm, Mama clapped too. She was still grinning. "I know someone who's going to love your sense of humor."

"Who?"

"Jack. You'll meet him one of these days." Then, as if she'd said more than she meant to, Mama turned and walked quickly toward the house. I watched her go, noticing how pretty the backs of her legs looked with the tennis skirt twitching back and forth across them. She let the screen door slam, and I heard again, in that sound — I can hear it still — his name: Jack.

The name echoes through the years.

Jack: Grandpa's word for money.

Jack: the steel rod that props up a car, or the foundation of a house.

Jack: I think of the sound of a tennis ball hitting the racket at dead center.

Jack: our savior.

Four

I FIRST MET JACK on a street downtown where Mama and Grandmuddy had taken me shopping for school clothes. I was to enter the seventh grade in September; it was now only July but Grandmuddy said the early bird gets the worm. Worm was right, I remember thinking. I hated all the clothes that had been picked out for me: a Black Watch plaid dress that Mama had chosen, a gray pleated wool skirt that Grandmuddy said would last for years if only I'd quit growing like a weed. I did grudgingly like the blouse chosen to go with the skirt: an odd print of small gray oak leaves and straight pins on a white background. But what I really longed for was the flared pink skirt with the black poodle on it (I especially admired the clever way the leash led up to the waist and became a belt) and the ballerina shoes that I hadn't even been allowed to try on. I was now clumping sulkily along in new brown oxfords identical to last year's.

Mama and Grandmuddy were walking ahead, talking about me. Grandmuddy said she would have counted herself fortunate if she'd had such fine new clothes as a girl; young people today didn't know the meaning of hard times.

"Beryl is going to be a clotheshorse, I'm afraid," Mama said.

Grandmuddy agreed by shaking her head from side to side and clicking her tongue.

I'd never heard the word *clotheshorse* before, but I knew it was no compliment. I glared at their backs, imagining Mama as a brown mare mincing along in a navy blue suit and spectator shoes and Grandmuddy as an old gray nag with a huge rump that bobbled back and forth beneath a shapeless print dress.

Mama and Grandmuddy stopped so suddenly that I bumped into Grandmuddy's soft bottom. I heard Mama's voice go high and gushy.

She was shaking hands with the strangest looking man I'd ever seen. He had red hair and a beard — the only bearded men I'd seen up to that time were department store Santas — and he was wearing a white hat, a lime green suit, and tennis shoes.

Grandmuddy backed off, holding up her purse as if she might use it as a weapon.

Mama introduced him: Dr. Jack Fonteyn, head of the classics department. Her favorite professor, she added, blushing.

He made a funny little bow and held out his hand to Grandmuddy. She nodded but kept her gloved hands tightly on her purse. He then offered me the rejected hand, which was, I saw, covered with ginger-colored fur; I put both hands behind my back.

"Beryl!" Mama gave me a look so hot I could feel it on the side of my face. "She's been a real pill all morning," she said to him. "Whining about an absurd poodle skirt she claims she'll die without."

I was outraged: I had never said I would *die.* Mentally, I stuck out my tongue.

Hands on his knees, he bent to inspect me. I stared at the frowning faces of my shoes. "She doesn't look like a pill," he said. "I think she's been taking pretty pills though, just like her mama."

This was the first time anyone had suggested I might be

pretty; it gave me a pleasant little shock. And then, too late, after he'd straightened up and begun talking to Mama, I wished I'd smiled at him. I kept my eyes on him, waiting for a chance to smile, but he was fixed on Mama. She kept touching her hair and smiling in the way that showed her dimple.

He had the funniest way of standing, like he had rubber bones, one leg crossed over the other and that foot laid on its side. His arms hugged his chest. Occasionally he put back his head and scratched the hair on his neck in a way that made me think the beard pained him. Maybe he had burn scars there, or a terrible case of acne.

Grandmuddy made several noises with her throat. "We'll miss our bus," she said finally. "Come along, Beatrice." She started off down the sidewalk.

Jack bent down to me again. "You like honey?"

I nodded and gave him my stored-up smile.

"Good, you'll have to come out and rob my hives. You and your mama and your brother. OK?"

"OK," I said.

He stood and touched Mama's wrist; his fingers lingered there. "Goodbye," he said softly, and stepped back.

Mama took my hand and squeezed it. She seemed to have forgotten she was mad at me. We went down the sidewalk swinging hands.

"Buy that girl a poodle skirt!" he called after us.

As I glanced back at him, he took off his white hat and waved it. For several steps I kept on looking back. I remember so well my chin against the waffle weave of my collar and the grain of the sidewalk that connected us, for I date from the moment of that semaphoric message Jack's entry into my life.

I looked up at Mama. She was grinning.

"Will you?" I asked.

"Will I what?"

"Buy me a poodle skirt."

"We'll see."

Grandmuddy was at the bus stop staring into the far distance. There was no bus in sight.

Mama still held my hand. None of us spoke.

Finally the bus came around the corner and stopped in front of us. Mama gave me a boost up the steps.

"I hope you're not fixing to get mixed up with that beard," I heard Grandmuddy say.

"Jesus had a beard."

"Don't be sacrilegious, Beatrice," Grandmuddy hissed, scanning the bus to see if anyone had heard. "If Jesus had come to Blacksboro, North Carolina, in 1956, He wouldn't have worn a beard; He has too much respect and common decency."

Mama started humming — strangely, the tune was Daddy's "I Can't Give You Anything but Love" — and I saw her smile at herself in the mirror as she dropped our tokens in.

Five

GRANDMUDDY never missed church, Sunday school, or prayer meeting, yet I often heard her say that gardening was her salvation.

Every day after lunch, no matter what the season, Grandmuddy went to work outdoors. I remember thinking how funny she looked in her old blue straw hat, the sagging hose, the long-sleeved Japanese apron with grimy eyelet-trimmed pockets, where she kept clippers, envelopes of seed, and the Clove gum she chewed half a stick at a time. But I also noticed how her foot in its old-lady tie shoe could slice the shovel down through hard earth, how her fingers yanked out weeds and powdered any inhospitable clods of dirt to fine soil.

Grandmuddy's front yard, and part of the back, was a conventional lawn bordered with perennials, but beyond the boxwood hedge in the back yard was a tangle of trees, shrubs, and vines with a path twisting through it; along the path were ferns and wildflowers. At the end of the path, in the far back corner of the yard, was what Grandmuddy called her winter garden; it was an open space with a brick wall at one end and a collection of plants that are fragrant in winter. Sometimes on a sunny February or March day she took me there, me alone; together these moments form an oasis in my memory of that time.

Along the base of the wall were several brass plaques. Four of the plaques had nothing but dates inscribed upon them — October 19, 1919, is the only one I still remember; on the fifth were a date and the words "Robert Lee lives here." Grandmuddy told me that the nameless plaques commemorated the children she had lost through miscarriage; Robert Lee, who had been stillborn, she named for the famous Confederate general her father had served under.

I liked to think that in bringing me to this shrine for her lost children Grandmuddy was implying that I, being alive, was doubly precious. I believed this even though Mama said Grandmuddy cared more about her dead children than the survivors. (Mama had just one brother, a dentist named Paul, who lived in Seattle and rarely visited.) I believed that Mama was not aware of how much Grandmuddy loved me.

On warm winter days Grandmuddy and I sometimes sat on the bench in front of the wall, basking in the sun; even in February, reflected heat from the wall warmed us. Sometimes we played a game called Nose Quiz. Grandmuddy liked to have me break off fragrant twigs and blossoms and bring them to her to identify with her eyes shut. She was vain about her sense of smell, which she claimed to have kept intact by using her nose as God intended and by keeping it out of other people's business. In the garden, though, Grandmuddy didn't seem to mind talking about private things, so it was there that I one day dared to ask about Daddy.

Grandmuddy told me that Mama had met Daddy when his band was playing for a dance at the King Cotton Hotel. Mama had gone to the dance with Allan Miles, the boy she was supposed to marry, but he had done something to hurt her feelings and she'd gone out on the porch to cry. That's where Daddy had found her and brought her home in a fancy black Packard that he told Mama was his but turned out not to be. Next day he was back to take Mama to church, Grandmuddy said, "acting like butter wouldn't melt in his mouth. They went for a long walk that afternoon, and that was that."

"That was what?"

Grandmuddy sighed. "She was head over heels. Two weeks later, they were married."

"When was I born?"

Grandmuddy leaned her head back against the bench and shut her eyes. "About a year later."

"Did he love me?"

Grandmuddy was silent a moment; then she reached for my hand and squeezed it. "Of course, honey. Now go fetch me a flower."

I went to a small bush, broke off a small white flower and brought it to her. I remember so well that moment when Grandmuddy held the flower to her nose, her whole wrinkled face smiling as she breathed in and then exhaled her answer: *"Daphne odora."*

—————

In summer I went less often to the garden: it was buggy and hot there, and Grandmuddy would set me to weeding if she saw me outdoors. But I sometimes liked to lie in the deep, tangy shade of the boxwood hedge — the far side, out of sight — and read.

One Saturday in August, not long after the day I had met Jack downtown, I was behind the hedge rereading *Honey Bunch: Her First Trip West.* This was my favorite book at the time because it helped me imagine riding a train all alone, just like Honey Bunch, only my trip would end in Chicago instead of California. I was also waiting for Stevie to come tell me Grandpa was asleep; we planned to further investigate his desk that afternoon.

Recently we had found a framed picture, in the lower right drawer, of Mama as a bride. I thought we might find even more pictures of Mama, maybe even one with Daddy without his face cut out, though I hadn't much hope of that. But what I really longed to find, perhaps stuck in the back of a drawer, was a postcard from Chicago that Grandpa had forgotten to throw away.

Stevie came to tell me the coast was clear; Grandpa, who had sat down in front of the TV after lunch to watch a baseball game with the sound turned off, was now asleep. We crept along the boxwood hedge, keeping low and quiet so Grandmuddy, who was weeding the daylily bed on the other side, wouldn't see us; then we went through the back door into the kitchen, and down the hall to Grandpa's den.

Grandpa's den was a small windowless room with two doors, one to the hall and one to the living room. These doors were always kept shut, whether Grandpa was in the den or not; Grandmuddy had made this rule to try to keep the cigar smell closed in. Of course it didn't work — the entire house smelled like cigars — but the odor was strongest in the den.

I could hear Grandpa snoring in the living room, but I eased open that door to peek at him, just to make sure he wasn't playing possum. He was in his wing chair and looked convincingly asleep, his middle covered with newspaper, his head slumped down, and his mouth hanging open in a way he wouldn't have wanted anybody to see.

I shut the door and Stevie eased open the rolltop of Grandpa's desk; he liked to poke around in the cubbyholes first for cigar rings and spare change. I took the picture of Mama out from its drawer and knelt against the red leather couch to study her. She wore a lace veil and a shiny white dress that rippled way out behind her on what looked like a stage. Her head was cocked to one side and there was a distant smile on her face which I associated with the picture's having been made a long time ago. It gave me a shivery feeling to realize I had not existed then. Had she wished for me, or someone like me? What if I had died and was only a plaque in the garden that said, "Beryl lives here." Would she have loved me more?

Suddenly I heard her voice through the closed door, in the living room.

"Daddy?" Her voice sounded like a little girl's. "I'm sorry, but I wanted to tell you right away. Oh, Daddy, guess what — I'm engaged!"

"Hah?" went Grandpa. Stevie scrambled over to the couch and knelt beside me; I gripped the picture tighter in my hands.

"What's this?" I could hear the crumple of Grandpa's paper as he sat up.

"I'm engaged — to Jack Fonteyn. You remember, that brilliant, brilliant professor I told you about, the one who helped me get the scholarship? He's wonderful, Daddy, and very well off, but the best part is, he *adores* me. We're going to have just a quiet wedding, since we've both been married before. . . ."

"No!" I cried. Stevie grabbed at me; I shouldered him away so I could listen better.

"This that commie beatnik your mother told me about?"

"He's as patriotic as you are. He is an intellectual, however."

"Aha, that's him."

In the silence that followed I stared at the picture frame: it was painted gold and carved in narrow ridges, like tiny steps you could walk down into the picture.

"Well, Daddy, say something. Are you going to give us your blessing or not?"

"I would of thought you'd learned your lesson by now."

"You've never understood me," Mama shouted. "You've never even tried."

"I understand you're a fool. Horn players!" There was the sound of Grandpa hauling himself out of his chair. "Communists! I wash my hands of the whole shooting match! You're no daughter of mine!"

"Daddy, no!"

I heard Grandpa start across the floor, heard the swish of his slow foot punctuated by the cane.

"Daddy!"

The door slammed. I heard Mama fall onto the sofa and begin to sob. Stevie buried his face in the couch beside me and cried too. Above their crying I could hear the sputter of the car as it pulled away from the curb, then its screech at the corner. I listened to the car go down the hill, the noise of it smaller and smaller, until the distance finally swallowed it up.

When Daddy went away, I had been asleep. He was there, and then not there. He never said goodbye; I did not hear him leave.

In the den, I kept hearing Grandpa's car long after the sound of it had faded. And always, after that, I filled in the silence of Daddy's leaving with the sound of Grandpa's car going down the hill.

Six

DURING THE TIME I lived with Grandpa and Grandmuddy, I kept my lucky charms in the secret compartment of
my jewelry box: Daddy's postcards and Christmas card, the
Drake Hotel envelope, and a gold bangle he had given me on
my first birthday. These objects were arranged in a special
order, each of them touching the envelope on which I had
written the Girl Scout slogan, "Do a Good Turn Every Day."
Inside were descriptions of all my secret good deeds: righting
an upended beetle; giving dandelions to a crippled lady; taking
the smaller piece of pie; agreeing, for Grandmuddy's sake, to
be the flower girl on Confederate Memorial Day. I liked to
think that when I had accumulated enough good turns, I would
get my reward: reunion with Daddy.

The night before the first visit to Jack's house I could not
sleep. I tried Grandpa's solution, counting sheep and goats. I
drank the warm milk Grandmuddy brought me. Finally, after
staring up into the dark for what seemed hours, I got the bangle
from my jewelry box, climbed back into bed, and holding the
bracelet tight in my hand, began writing a letter to Daddy in
my mind. This worked like a spell.

I told him everything: that my mattress was too soft and
smelled like cat pee even though Grandmuddy would not allow

a cat or any other pet in the house; that we had nothing to eat at her house but fried chicken and beans cooked in fatback, the greasy food he disapproved of; that Mama said she had to marry a Communist named Jack, who looked like one of the bearded men on the Smith Brothers cough drop box, only uglier; that Grandpa had washed his hands of us and Mama had cried; that I had seen Mama on her knees in her bedroom, praying for Daddy to come back; that tomorrow Stevie and I were being forced to go to this man's weird house that Grandmuddy didn't like the sound of at all, for a picnic.

The next morning began with the apparition of Mama in a flowered dress and big straw hat, shaking me awake.

Then there was a ride in a limousine (actually a hearse, Grandmuddy said) that Jack had rented for us. He had sent flowers too — a spray of small green orchids for Mama and a corsage of pink carnations for me. The flowers thrilled and unsteadied me. I had decided to wear my Brownie uniform, even though I wasn't a Brownie anymore, because Jack might be impressed by all my badges. I even had a beekeeping badge that I'd earned by reading about bees in the school library and serving SueBee honey to go with Grandmuddy's biscuits.

As we rode into the country, Mama sat like a queen in the middle of the back seat; Stevie and I were on the jump seats. Stevie kept swiveling around in his seat, but I sat still, frightened by the thick, silent neck of the driver and by the hearse's refrigerating hum.

We drove for what seemed like forever, past the houses at the edge of town, then between mile after mile of fields and woods, with only an occasional farmhouse or trailer to suggest that other people lived out here too.

When we turned off the main road onto a smaller one, Mama said we were getting close, but out the window I still saw nothing but trees.

"Who are we going to play with out here?" Stevie asked.

"I'm sure there are other children nearby. Besides, you always have each other."

"You mean you have me as a babysitter," I said.

"I don't need a babysitter, stupid." Stevie kicked his foot against mine; I kicked back.

"We're here!" Mama cried.

I stared. There on a hill was a gray cement box with porthole windows near the roof. How did he get it up there? was my first thought; it reminded me of a stranded battleship.

"That's a *house?*" I said.

"It looks better on the other side," Mama promised. "This is the back — he made it that way to hold in the heat."

"He must be crazy," I said in a voice to let her know I might not put up with this. I tried to start another letter to Daddy but could not keep my eyes from the house: I felt it tilt toward me as we went up the hill.

The driver helped us out, and Jack came walking toward us. He had on tennis clothes — I felt stupid to have gotten dressed up — and he was grinning like he had a secret.

"You've shaved your beard!" Mama cried.

"The metamorphosis of Jack Fonteyn, family man!" He held out his arms and stood frozen for a moment. I stared at the smooth, freckled face, then at the freckled arms and legs covered with red hair. "Will your mother have me now?" he said to Mama. "What do you think?"

"I think you'll be easier to kiss," Mama said.

"Really? Let's see." And right there in front of us, he put his arms around her and kissed her on the mouth. I looked down at my Brownie badges so I wouldn't have to watch.

"Hey," Stevie said, "where's the picnic?"

"Hold your horses, pardner." Jack stepped back from Mama, then pretended to do a double take when he saw my badges. "What regalia is this?"

Mama laughed. "That's her Brownie uniform — she insisted

on wearing it for you." I crossed my arms over my chest and felt my face burn. "She's a Girl Scout now, though, a Tenderfoot."

"Well, Tenderfoot." He smiled and pulled at one of my braids. "Let's go investigate the premises." And with one arm around me, one arm around Mama, Jack began walking us toward his house.

I was watching my brown oxfords move across the patchy grass when suddenly we stopped.

"That's where the bees live." Jack lifted his hand from my shoulder and pointed across the yard.

The four of us stood silently looking at the row of square white boxes at the edge of the woods. I hadn't known there would be so many hives; even at a distance I could see bees darting around them. I slipped my arms down to cover the bottom part of my sash where the beekeeping badge was, hoping now that Mama wouldn't mention it.

But no one spoke, not even Mama. Then Jack put his hand back on my shoulder and steered us to the house.

This side of the house was mostly glass, huge windows along the living and dining rooms. Only at the far end of the house was there a wall — that same gray cement — and a normal window.

The floors of the living and dining rooms were white marble; when we stepped into the living room, the light pouring through the window onto the floor was so brilliant I had to shade my eyes.

Jack laughed. "It's like the light in Greece. The first time I went there I squinted for a week. You'll get used to it." When he pulled the sheer draperies the sunlight slanted down in a filtered way that reminded me of being under water.

"Where's the furniture?" Stevie said. There was only a sofa and an ugly metal and leather chair in front of the fireplace.

"The last lady to come through sort of cleaned me out, buddy. But we'll get it fixed up when you move here."

When you move here: I could feel the words sink into my skin.

"At least we have one good piece," Jack was saying. He patted the back of the ugly chair. "Mies van der Rohe. Now let me introduce you to these folks."

Mama and Stevie followed Jack across the room to look at a row of statues on pedestals, but I did not move.

"This lady is Minerva, goddess of wisdom," Jack said. "Found her at a garage sale in Chappaqua, New York. The gentleman is Ovid, the great, irreverent Latin poet."

"Remember I told you that Jack is translating Ovid's *Metamorphoses* into English," Mama said in a too loud voice. "Beryl, you ought to come see this."

"Yeah," Stevie said. "There's a naked man without a head. And a hand all by itself."

"If you come here, Tenderfoot," Jack said, "I'll show you a trick."

My legs carried me toward them. I stood beside Stevie and looked at the marble hand mounted on a steel rod. It was a woman's hand, gracefully cupped upward, broken clean at the wrist. From the corner of my eye I could see the naked man Stevie had been talking about: a headless, armless torso.

"OK, kiddos." Jack moved his hand in a circle above the hand. "Abraca-zebra. Now look inside."

Stevie stood on tiptoe. "Hey!"

"Help yourselves," Jack said, winking at me. "One to a customer."

"Look, Beryl," Stevie said, "a silver dollar!" He held it up for me to see. "There's one for you too."

Mama gave me a nod that meant move, so I reached inside the hand and took out the coin without looking at it.

"Cat got your tongue?" Mama said.

"That's all right," Jack said. "Maybe she'll like some of the other surprises better."

"What surprises?" Stevie said.

"We'd better go see." Jack started off across the room with Stevie and Mama close behind. I put my silver dollar back on the edge of the pedestal, then picked it up again, thinking he might not let me have anything else if I didn't take this. Before I left, I stole a glance at the statue of the naked man. It ended just above the interesting part, but still, I thought, Grandmuddy would die.

In the next room, Mama was standing beside a table with her hands over her mouth and what I thought was a fake thrilled-shocked expression on her face while Jack talked about where he'd gotten her the table and how much it cost. There was nothing else in the room but a mirror on the far wall. I stood beside Stevie and waved at his reflection; he waved back, then we stared at ourselves, hands upraised but motionless as if we were posing for a picture. I imagined Daddy there, camera to his eye, looking at me with the flowers pinned to the Brownie uniform he'd never even seen, looking at Stevie in the too large sports coat and bow tie that made his Adam's apple stick out.

"OK, kids, your turn," Jack said, waving us to follow as he walked to the corner of the dining room and started up a winding metal staircase. Stevie ran after him, and Mama shooed me along, too; our feet made a racket on the steps.

We went first into Jack's study, a large room on the porthole side of the house. The longest wall was lined with bookshelves; above them, the round windows let in poles of light but were too high to see through. The only view was out the side window in front of Jack's desk.

Jack called us over to the window. "See anything interesting?"

"A tennis court," Stevie said, in a disappointed voice. "We already knew about that."

"Well, I bet you didn't know about that tree right beside it. You notice anything unusual about it?" When Stevie shook his head no, Jack said, "Well, I suspect that tree used to be a girl — a Kappa Kappa Gamma, maybe, who was jilted for a Tri

Delt. Every year she cries big green tears of envy — they're all over the tennis court. I'll show you later if you don't believe me."

Stevie leaned forward, squinting hard.

"Jack's teasing you, honey," Mama said, "those are really Osage oranges. That would be a good job for you and Beryl, to keep them picked up."

"I bet your sister can see it. She seems like a girl with imagination. Look," he said to me, pointing, "there in the leaves. Can you see the outline of a face?"

"I guess so," I said, looking down at the tree.

"What a relief, we have a poet in the crowd. I'll have to get you to help me with Ovid's book, since it's mostly about pretty young girls who get turned into trees and stones and things. You could help me with the pretty young girl perspective, OK?"

"Yeah." I could feel myself blushing.

"I already have the beautiful woman perspective," he said, smiling and putting his arm around Mama; she giggled and put her head on his shoulder. Stevie made a face at me like he was going to throw up.

"OK, any children who want surprises, come with me." Jack and Mama started out of his study and down the hall; Stevie and I followed.

The hall reminded me of a hospital, it was so white and empty, with the doors all closed. Jack opened a linen closet and we stood for a moment looking in at neatly stacked white sheets and towels. Then we went farther down the hall, and Jack opened another door. "This will be your room, Tenderfoot," he said.

"My name is Beryl," I said. "My father named me that."

"Beryl!" Mama said with a scowl.

"That's OK," Jack said. I could feel him and Mama looking at each other over my head. "Well, Miss Beryl, come in and tell me what you think."

Mama gave me a little push, and I followed Jack into the room. I saw a dressing table with a mirror, a four-poster bed, and — from the corner of my eye — a poodle skirt lying on the bed. I ran over to the dressing table as if it was that, rather than the skirt, that most interested me. I wondered if Mama had gotten the skirt for me, or Jack; I guessed Jack but was embarrassed to ask.

Jack brought the skirt over to me and held it to my waist. He and Mama were grinning. "Oh, no!" I said, trying to sound surprised.

"Most fetching," he said. "Pun intended. Do you want to try it on?"

I shook my head no, but I did touch the poodle's ear. The loops were fuzzy, just as I remembered.

"Well, no hurry."

Mama silently mouthed "thank you" at me.

"Thank you," I said.

"You're highly welcome," Jack said, but from the way he swung the skirt away and walked quickly to put it back on the bed I knew I had hurt his feelings.

Stevie's room was to the right of mine, with a connecting door between. When we went in and Jack showed Stevie the lamp, the toy soldiers, and the Book of Knowledge encyclopedias that had all been his as a child, I tried to make up for my earlier silence.

"Gosh, isn't this great?" My voice sounded so off-key that I tried again. "Those are the greatest soldiers I ever saw."

Stevie picked up one of the soldiers and chipped at the paint with his fingernail. "I want something new," he said.

"Steven!" Mama frowned at him, but not in the mean way she had at me.

"Well, I've got something out here that might interest a boy of your type." Jack walked to the sliding glass door and stepped out onto a balcony.

We all followed him out.

"Don't you think it's just like a tree house?" Jack said. "I'd have given my eyeteeth for something like this when I was a boy. Or a girl," he added, winking at me.

"Isn't this wonderful?" Mama said. "You kids are going to love it here."

Jack hugged Mama sideways; she giggled and held her hat as if it were about to fly off.

I leaned against the railing and shut my eyes. There had been a balcony like this at a hotel where I'd once gone on a beach vacation with Mama and Daddy. Daddy had carried me out to the balcony wrapped in my quilt and sung "Mr. Moon" before he put me to bed. I felt a sudden stab of homesickness for that small, plain room with its metal beds and the picture of the sailboat that Mama said was ugly. But it wasn't ugly, it was beautiful. I wanted that picture, and I wanted that night back. I bent down to pick up some acorns from the balcony so no one would see me crying, but they wouldn't have noticed anyway because just then Stevie put his head through the railings and got stuck. By the time Jack got him out I'd stopped crying and wiped my eyes with my braids.

"Look, kids," Jack said. "The thing to do out here is give speeches." He raised one fist. "Friends, Romans, squirrels, give us your nuts. As if we weren't nutty enough already. How about you, Miss Beryl, do you have a statement to make? What do you think of your new home?" Down to me swooped the fist, now a microphone.

"It's OK," I whispered. My eyes filled up again.

He bent closer. "I bet you miss your father," he said in a low voice. "Is that right?"

When I nodded, he said, "Well, you're getting a better deal this time. Look at your mother — isn't she happy now?" I could see from the corner of my eye Mama leaning against the rail. She was smiling out at the view and pretending not to listen. "You're going to be happy, too, I promise." When my gaze moved to his eyes he gave me a wink: freckled eyelid, short golden red eyelashes. Then he jumped up and turned to Stevie. "What about you, sonny?" he said, holding out the microphone fist again. "Think you might want to shimmy down from here sometime?"

"Good Lord," Mama said, "don't give him ideas."

"Pooh, he's got ideas, don't you, bud? What's your comment on the setup here?"

"Well, the soldiers are pretty good, but I'd like to have an electric train and a model airplane."

Jack staggered back a few steps, pretending to look shocked, then said into his fist, "Folks, did you hear that? This is an amazing lad, a young man possessed of extrasensory powers, for how else could he have known that exactly one week from today, an electric train and a model airplane will be on the premises?"

"Yea!" Stevie said.

"And maybe something special for our little poetess." Jack added. I noticed how his face softened when he turned to look at me.

"Jack, you'll spoil them," Mama said.

"That's what they need, a little spoilage. Don't you, sweetheart?" He held out his hand to me, and I took it.

We walked through my room past the dressing table, past the bed with the poodle skirt lying on it, and then went down the winding stairway, Jack still holding my hand.

———

We had the picnic in the back yard, midway between the tennis court and the beehives. Before we sat down, Jack showed us what he called his honey plants, clumps of flowering herbs that were full of loud, darting bees. Mama made me and Stevie stand way back, but Jack told us not to be frightened. These were friendly bees, he said, pets, practically members of the family. Between the herbs and the patio were rosebushes from which Jack picked a full red rose for Mama and a pink rosebud for me. Mama put her flower behind her ear, but I just held mine, thinking it would look funny above a braid. Jack — misunderstanding — told me I shouldn't worry, bees didn't like roses, so I tucked the rosebud into my corsage of carnations. Then we walked across the yard to a blue-and-white quilt that had been laid out ahead of time and set with wine glasses and china plates that were warm from the sun. Each plate had a different wildflower on it. Mine was decorated with forget-me-nots, Stevie's with wild ginger, and Mama's with a cluster of yellow, dark-centered flowers that Jack called black-eyed Beatrice.

Before lunch Jack poured our drinks — dark red wine for him and Mama, red Cheerwine for me and Stevie — and toasted each of us, linking arms first with Mama, then me, then Stevie. I was afraid I would do something wrong in the toast, but Jack pulled my arm through his, nodded when it was time to drink, and as we drank he gently squeezed my arm in his.

Then he served us food I'd never heard of before: pâté, avocado sandwiches, artichokes, duck in aspic. Everything tasted strange and wonderful, and I remember that with the warmth of the sun on my face and legs I began to feel a little dizzy. I also remember — when I close my eyes, I can hear this still — the low, sleepy mumble of bees.

After lunch, Jack gave us presents. There was a slingshot for Stevie, an aquamarine pendant for me (because, he explained, aquamarine is a form of the beryl stone) and for Mama a ring of dark blue lapis lazuli set in gold.

"Thank you, darling," Mama said, throwing her arms around Jack and giving me over his shoulder a sudden brilliant smile. When she sat back down, I kept looking at her, at her face spangled with sunlight that filtered through her hat, at the soft, deep glow of her eyes, and it struck me that what Jack had said was true: Mama really was happy. I felt a sudden thrilling vividness. Maybe we were all going to be happy. For a moment everything around me throbbed with that possibility: the blue sky, the leaves of the trees, the stars in the quilt, the remains of the picnic on the china plates, even the artichoke leaves marked by our teeth and mingled together in one bowl.

Jack went into the house and brought back dessert, a raspberry torte sweetened with honey.

Bees came to investigate, one or two at first, then several.

"Shoo!" Mama said, flapping her napkin at a bee on Stevie's plate.

"Careful, Joanne," Jack said, "these are not flies."

"No," Mama said, jumping up, suddenly furious, "not Joanne — that's the other lady, the one who cleaned you out, remember?" Although her face looked angry, I could tell she was about to cry.

"Oh, come on, honey," Jack said, "don't be so darn sensitive. You know very well — "

Mama turned, her dress whirling out, and started toward the house.

"Beatrice!" Jack called, but she kept on going, went inside, slammed the door.

Jack sighed and, without looking at me or Stevie, jumped up and ran to the house.

Stevie and I sat for a few moments in shocked silence, then he said, "I didn't like him anyway."

"Me neither," I said.

They were gone a long time. Stevie and I went over to the court and found the Osage oranges Jack had told us about, lumpy green balls that didn't look at all like tears. We pitched them at the trunk of the trees and at the tennis court posts. Stevie and I kept count of which of us got the most hits, but I was playing my own private game: every hit I made was yes, every miss no. If there were more nos than yeses, they would come out and announce it was over: the picnic, the afternoon, the whole deal. I didn't know what I wished for. I did hope I could keep the poodle skirt; I was sorry I hadn't thanked him better. I didn't care as much about the aquamarine; if the answer was no, I would hide it in the grass and then some day Jack would find it and feel sorry.

But when Mama and Jack finally reappeared they were holding hands and smiling. Mama had put on her tennis clothes, too; I didn't remember her bringing them. I was shocked when I realized they must have been there all along.

Jack put me and Stevie in a rope hammock that was stretched between pine trees on the far side of the court. He had pillows there and some books he'd bought just for us — *The Secret Garden* for me, *The Swiss Family Robinson* for Stevie. He gave us a big push.

I wanted the hammock to stop swinging, but it kept going back and forth. I began to feel sleepy; I put down my book and closed my eyes. I remember the hypnotic rhythm of the ball as it bounced and was hit, bounced and was hit. I remember, in the silences before I slept, Jack's voice: Fifteen-Love. Thirty-Love. Forty-Love.

Seven

THE WEDDING was not announced ahead of time.

All through June, Mama had been staying out late, sometimes until daylight, and sneaking back in through the kitchen window. The day she wasn't there for breakfast, I went into her room, and — as I'd been instructed to do if the need ever arose — arranged the pillows and covers to make the bed look occupied. Then I went back downstairs and told Grandpa and Grandmuddy that Mama wasn't feeling well, she wouldn't be down for a while.

After breakfast I went to my room and sat by the back window so I could see when she came walking up the drive. I wished for Stevie, who was away at Baptist Bible camp, to keep watch out the front.

The clock on my bureau ticked loudly; I watched the minute hand make its little jerks forward. When Mama hadn't returned by ten, I began to fear something had happened to her. At eleven, I thought of telling Grandmuddy, but then she'd know everything, including my lie.

Finally the doorbell rang. I crept out of my room onto the landing and peered down as Grandmuddy opened the door. When I heard Mama's voice my legs went weak. I walked down the stairs quickly, holding the banister, and stood by Grand-muddy.

There, on the front steps, were Mama, Jack, and a curly-haired man I hadn't seen before. They were all grinning.

"We did it!" Mama said, holding up her hand for us to see the gold ring.

"In that?" Grandmuddy said, looking at Mama's sundress and sandals.

"I can attest to the fact," the curly-haired man said, holding up a paper bag that seemed to have smoke coming out of it. "Hel-lo," he said, winking at me, "you've got to be the lovely daughter I've heard so much about."

"This is Bernie Hoffman, my writing teacher," Mama said.

"And the matchmaker," Jack added. "The cause of it all."

"Now, I wouldn't go that far," Bernie said.

"Well, Mother, are you going to let us in?" Mama said.

Grandmuddy didn't move. "Your father isn't here," she said.

"I'm sorry if we shocked you, Mrs. Taylor," Jack said as he opened the door. "But we didn't know ourselves until about two hours ago." As they came in, Jack said, "Hello, Tender-foot," and bent down to give me a kiss. I backed away just in time.

"Hello, Tenderfoot," Bernie echoed, and pulled one of my braids. He had nice brown eyes that looked right at me.

Mama gave me a hug and whispered fiercely in my ear. "Don't look so glum, Beryl. This is a happy day." Then she said out loud, "Since Daddy isn't here, we can have a real toast."

"Not in my house," Grandmuddy said, following them to the kitchen. I followed too.

"Not in my house," Grandmuddy said again as Mama got five juice glasses, and Bernie poured champagne in each one. Jack handed out the glasses; Grandmuddy put hers on the counter.

Bernie lifted his glass. "To their wedding day, which is not long."

"It's not over yet," Mama said. "Here's to us," she cried, holding her glass high.

"It was a quote, darling," Jack said. "Spenser?"

"Spenser," Bernie said, winking at me as if I'd known the answer, then we all — except Grandmuddy — drank.

The champagne brought tears to my eyes; I put my glass on the counter by Grandmuddy's.

"Mrs. Taylor," Jack said, taking a box from his pocket. "Here's a small token of my esteem — something I'd have wanted you to wear if there had been a ceremony."

"Reverend Taylor isn't going to like this one bit," Grandmuddy said, but she opened the box anyway. "My land," she said, as she pulled out a long strand of pearls.

"They're real," Mama said.

"Just like us," Jack said, giving Mama a hug. Then he looked at me and said, "Better start getting your bags packed, Tenderfoot. We're a family now."

"We are not!" I said. Looking at Mama's startled face, I yelled, "I fixed your stupid bed like you said to," then turned and ran out of the kitchen and up the stairs.

———

Mama and Jack's honeymoon was a weekend at the beach. On the way home, they picked up Stevie from camp, and the next day we moved to Jack's house.

Jack had borrowed a pickup truck for the occasion: it was dark green with slats in the back which held in our possessions. I remember a hat rack, a wrought-iron floor lamp, a rose armchair that sank in the middle (this ended up in my room), Mama's big trunk stuffed with clothes and manuscripts, and my things and Stevie's in grocery bags from the Piggly Wiggly.

Jack drove; Mama sat in the middle, with Stevie in her lap.

I was by the open window with my head tilted out so I would not have to listen to Jack.

With the wind in my hair and eyes, I pretended to be riding my pony on the shoulder of the road; I had Daddy following close behind, as he had always done the few times I had actually ridden, in the white, wood-paneled station wagon we called Saddle Shoe.

I closed my eyes and went back to where I had been that morning, in the space between sleep and wakefulness, remembering the winter mornings when I had gone with Daddy to feed the pony.

I skipped over the part when I had been a sissy about holding out my hand with the sugar and went to the time when Daddy sat me on the top rail of the fence and, with his arms around me, we watched the slow movement of sunlight down the hill to the pond. I remembered how I fixed my eyes at the edge of light and tried to see its exact inching forward but could not because my eyes kept forgetting where the starting point had been. When I told Daddy, he understood; playing jazz was something like that, he said.

Jack made a sharp turn off the highway onto his road and we all fell toward him. I struggled up and stared, unseeing, out the window. For as long as I could — even when I felt the truck go up the drive — I tried to keep the pond and pasture in my mind.

The truck jounced across the yard to the back door and stopped. Mama pushed me, and I got out. I leaned against the truck's warm fender and closed my eyes.

Jack was unloading furniture. "Hey, Tenderfoot," he called, "I'll bet you a double dip ice cream with fudge sauce that you can't find all the new things in your room. You too, Steveo," he added.

"Hot dog!" Steve said, and ran inside.

"Does Daddy know where we are?" I said to Mama.

She stared at me, her face shocked at first, then angry. She was holding the big wooden radio with cutouts in the front which reminded me of a cathedral window. It had been in her room at Grandpa and Grandmuddy's house and before that in the living room of the house where we had lived with Daddy. "You can have this," she said, shoving it into my arms. "Now move."

As I stamped upstairs I decided I would just get in bed and listen to the radio and go back to sleep. If Mama expected me to help unpack, she could just go jump.

Going down the upstairs hall I heard a clattering sound. When I peeked in Stevie's room I saw him kneeling in the middle of a huge oval track with a long train going around him. He looked up and grinned. "The engine makes real steam. And look," he said, holding up a box, "a model airplane!"

"Big deal," I said. I went into the room that was supposed to be mine and stood holding the radio. There on the bed was the poodle skirt and above it a pink sweater set. Arranged below the skirt on the floor were the black ballet slippers I'd wanted. "Big deal," I said again. But I sat on the bed with the radio in my lap and touched the sweaters. They were wonderfully soft — angora and lamb's wool, the labels said. One was a short-sleeved pullover, the other a cardigan with mother-of-pearl buttons.

I put the radio on the floor, pulled off my shirt, and put the sweaters on. They smelled new and expensive, and I liked the way the cardigan covered my wrists; most of my sweaters were too short.

On went the poodle skirt (over my jeans, in case Jack should come in); off came the clunky brown shoes, the socks, the jeans. I stepped into the slippers and twirled in front of the dressing table mirror: it all fit perfectly. Then the glittering objects on the dressing table caught my eye.

I held my breath. There were a silver hand mirror and brush, each with a fancy *B* raised on its surface, and a tortoise shell comb with a silver edge.

I sat on the stool in front of the dressing table and undid my hair. The braids had made my hair wavy; I brushed it into a rippling blanket of reddish gold. It felt heavy and warm on my back, especially with the sweaters underneath. I leaned forward to look at my face made radiant by the surrounding hair. Even my eyes glowed: I was for that instant, beautiful. I wished Daddy were here to see.

I stood up and walked out onto the balcony. Leaves had fallen since we had last been here. They were all over the yard and on the balcony, red and brown drifts against the railing posts and up against the house.

I picked up some acorns; they had smooth green or light brown skins and tips on the ends like nipples. When I lined them up on the balcony railing they looked like a row of breasts in saucers. With my thumb and forefinger I shot them into the air. Some fell on the truck. I heard a ping on the roof and the duller sounds of acorns hitting the truck bed.

"The sky is falling!" I heard Jack exclaim.

I leaned over the rail and looked down. I saw Jack's eyes widen when he looked up at me in the pink sweaters, at my bright hair hanging down. I stood up straight and gazed off into the distance a moment, then walked slowly back inside.

We had lunch in the kitchen, cream cheese and date nut bread sandwiches and some brown soup I wouldn't have eaten if I'd known what it was — oxtail, Jack said after we'd finished. Stevie made some noises that sounded like he was pretending to throw up, and Jack sent him outside. Jack told Mama that she let Stevie get away with murder, but when I went outside later I found him crouched shivering near a tree beside his vomit. The sight of it, yellow streaked with brown, made my own stomach lurch, but I squatted down and put my arm around him. I stared at the raked, sparsely grassed ground, letting the terrible unfamiliarity of this place seep into me. This was it; this was where we had to live.

Jack won the bet: Stevie and I had not found everything. He

was glad I liked the fripperies, he said, when I thanked him for the sweaters and shoes and brush and mirror set, but there was something more, something cosmic. He would show me and Stevie at bedtime, if we would be good children and turn in early.

That night I was lying in my new bed listening to "The Great Pretender" (a song that always brought tears to my eyes) when I heard footsteps coming down the hall. I turned down the radio: four feet in uneven rhythm. I was relieved; that meant Mama was coming too.

They went first into Stevie's room. The crack beneath our adjoining door went dark and the murmur of Jack's voice began. It went on and on: a storytelling rhythm.

Then they filed into my room, Jack first. He was carrying a candle and looked serious; Mama looked like she wanted to smile but knew she wasn't supposed to. She came to the side of the bed next to the wall and sat down. Jack put the candle on the bedside table, turned off the light, and sat by my knees.

"Look up," he said. He turned my head with his hand so that I was looking at the ceiling in the middle of the room. "What do you see?"

I did not say because it sounded like a test question, and "stars" seemed like the wrong answer. But that's what they were, glow-in-the-dark stars pasted on the ceiling.

"It's the constellation Pegasus," he said. "He's the muse of poets, a beautiful white stallion with wings who belongs to Minerva, but she lends him to mortals who are especially imaginative. Can you make out his shape? That curving line at the top follows his head and neck, and that rectangle — the Great Square of Pegasus, astronomers call it — is his body. Can you see him?"

"Yes," I said, though I couldn't. It was like a connect-the-dot puzzle without numbers and I could not tell where to start.

He began to tell one of his made-up stories about Pegasus, I do not remember which one. I remember that when I closed

my eyes I saw my black pony instead of the white, winged
horse.

"Wasn't that a nice surprise?" Mama said, patting my arm as
she stood up.

"Yes."

"What do you say, then?"

"Thank you," I said. "Thank you for everything."

He touched my face with both hands, holding my forehead
as if he were checking my temperature. "Good night," he said,
and started to kiss me but did not.

Sometimes Jack came alone to tell me stories. Then I could
hear his feet going *squee squee* on the stairs and in the hall. Those
were the shoes with soles like art gum erasers; I think of them
now as erasing his footsteps as he came and went.

"Once upon a time there was a lovely young girl named
Beryl, who lived way down south in North Carolina. One
spring day she was out in the pea patch picking peas when she
noticed a peculiar cloud in the sky. It kept shifting and changing
shapes — a bull, a tiger, a coiled snake, finally a white horse that
glided down from the sky and landed beside her, one hoof in
the pea vines. When he said, 'At your service, Miss Beryl,' she
didn't hesitate, just put her foot in the stirrup and . . ."

I liked Jack's voice; it made me feel sleepy all over. But I did
not like his story. I did not like to see the white horse, did not
want to put my foot in the stirrup. Sometimes as Jack's voice
washed over me, I sank like a stone and thought hard about my
black pony, shrinking it and the white horse to the same size,
very small, like the black and white dog magnets I'd gotten at
a birthday party a long time ago in Virginia, and lost in the
grass.

————

Jack saved us. Mama said this over and over, and she made me
agree.

Once she said it to me in the bathroom while Jack was downstairs in the living room waiting for my right answer. Stevie had already said yes; why wouldn't I?

Mama was braiding my hair to get me ready for school; we were both facing the mirror. She reviewed the case against Daddy: he had left us without one thin dime when he ran off to Chicago; he had not sent an iota of child support; he was irresponsible, selfish, and craven. He did not give one royal goddamn, apparently, whether we lived or died. "Not one royal god-damn," she repeated in a furious voice, pulling and tucking in a strand with each syllable, as if she were braiding the evidence into my hair. "He said he just *had* to go, that he was so *sad*. Poor *thing*.

"Beryl, do you remember that summer we were at Grandpa and Grandmuddy's and I stayed in bed all the time?"

I nodded. Mama locked eyes with me in the mirror as she fiddled with the rubber band, twisting and snapping it onto the fresh braid.

"Do you know what I was *doing,* while I lay there in bed?"

I shook my head no. I didn't want to hear. When Mama was saying something I didn't want to hear and we were standing face to face, I would look at the reflections of myself in her eyes. I couldn't do that in the mirror, no matter how hard I stared.

"I was trying to decide how to kill myself — by taking pills or cutting my wrists. Not *whether,* but how. The main thing that held me back was how you or Stevie would feel, finding me."

It came upon me before I could stop it, an image of Mama lying motionless in bed, her eyes rolled back, and my hands shaking so that coffee splattered all over.

Goddamn you. Goddamn you. I thought this as loud as I could. She would not look at me now. She was pushing against the side of my head with the heel of her hand as she brushed with short, hard strokes.

"I also worried a lot about leaving you and Stevie at the mercy of your grandparents. I even thought about taking you with me, putting arsenic in your ice cream. . . ." She glanced at me quickly, to see how I was taking this. I looked, too: my face was amazingly normal. "I tell you that just so you'll understand how bad off I was, and what Jack saved us from. . . ."

She waited for me to say something; I did not. I thought of the time she'd asked me to hold out my wrists at the perfume counter. I thought of sawing my wrists back and forth on the sharp edge of the glass until blood spurted and she screamed, "No! No!"

"When Jack and I fell in love, I thought: we're saved, me and Beryl and Stevie. We were about to be goners, but now we're saved." Mama snapped a rubber band onto my second braid. "I knew everything would be all right, and then it was, wasn't it?"

Her eyes sought mine; I nodded. I watched in the mirror as my head went up and down, up and down. Sometimes before I went to sleep my head got a strange, stretched feeling, as though my brain were way up near the ceiling; that was how I felt now.

She began tying bows on my hair; the ribbons were red plaid, I remember, to match my dress, because I was going to have my school picture taken that day. But I also remember thinking she was dressing me up for Jack, for when I gave him the right answer.

"Anyway, here we all are." Mama smiled at me in the mirror until my lips turned up, too. "A family again, or almost. Jack really wants us to be a family, Beryl, and so do I. Don't you?"

"I guess so," I heard myself say.

Mama frowned. "He's so *nice* to you."

This was true. I thought of the poodle skirt and pink sweaters.

"And he really likes you, you know. Stevie too, of course, but especially you. He told me he likes to pretend you are his real daughter, his biological daughter. You could be, he said, because of the color of your hair."

"Jack's hair is plain red. Mine is Titian blond — Daddy said so. He said I got it from his mother."

"Beryl, your so-called daddy deserted us. He doesn't deserve to be called your daddy. But Jack is generous and kind — *he saved us* — and he really wants to be your father."

She turned me toward her and lifted my face by the chin. "Don't you care anything at all about me?"

Her dark eyes held mine.

"Yes," I said.

"Then let Jack adopt you. How do you think I would feel if he adopted Stevie but not you?"

I found myself in the blacks of her eyes and began to travel in.

"Do you know what adoption means? It means you'll take Jack's name legally, it means he'll be your father, and you his daughter, for *life*. He'll give you the best. He's already talking about sending you to an Ivy League college. Isn't that wonderful? Aren't you a lucky girl?"

I had journeyed deep into the small black tunnels of her eyes, but I could still see myself up on the surface. I saw the reflections of two tiny braided heads nodding, saying yes, saying yes that is wonderful, saying yes I am a lucky girl.

"That's great, honey. Go tell him. *Thank* him." She gave me a little push. "You'll make him very happy. Me too."

I walked out of the bathroom and down the spiral stairs to the living room, walked to where Jack our savior sat cross-legged in his Mies van der Rohe chair. I remember that he was pretending to read, and that he had on a corduroy suit the same color as his freckles.

He looked up.

"OK," I said. "Yes. Thank you." In my mind I could see my words, like hard shiny marbles, roll randomly about.

"Beryl," he said, and reached out his hand to claim me.

II

Eight

JACK HAD ALREADY transformed Mama. She'd been a sad sack, a shopgirl, a bright but untutored mind. He'd gotten the hair off her neck into a sleek bun; bought her clothes that didn't look small-town; persuaded her that one Tolstoy was worth a thousand Edna Ferbers. He'd put a desk and her typewriter in their bedroom, and she worked there every day from nine to twelve, the same hours he worked in his study on his Ovid translation; she was on her way to becoming a writer. And not just one of those lady writers the local woods were so full of either, but the genuine article, the real thing.

Jack set out to make something of me and Stevie too. He was going to get our teeth straightened, improve our postures and manners, send us to first-rate schools. Though I was only in the seventh grade and Stevie in the fourth, he wrote off for college catalogues: for me, Radcliffe, Bryn Mawr, and Mount Holyoke; for Stevie, Harvard, Princeton, and Davidson College, Jack's alma mater.

On Sunday mornings we went on hikes in the woods behind the house. Sometimes Mama came with us, but usually it was just me and Stevie following Jack along the path he had cut through the trees. Stevie carried the army surplus canteen of water and I the tree identification book. Jack was empty-handed, because it was his job to instruct.

"*Liquidambarstyraciflua,*" he would say, breaking off a leaf and holding it up for us to memorize.

"*Liquidambarstyraciflua,*" we mumbled in unison.

"Sweet gum," Jack said.

"Sweet gum," we replied, then followed Jack to the next tree, where the same rhythm — *Acer rubrum, Acer rubrum;* red maple; red maple — would be repeated.

One day there was a quiz. "Genus and species," Jack said, holding up a leaf and pointing at me.

"*Cornus florida,*" I said. "Dogwood."

"Good girl!" He winked at me, then walked to another tree. "Steven?" he said, holding up a slender leaf.

"I don't know." Stevie shrugged. "Oak or elm."

Jack sighed. "An elm," he said, "is mainly a city tree nowadays. We haven't seen an elm in these woods." He turned and walked on.

"I don't care," Stevie said to his back. "This is stupid anyway."

Jack whirled around. His face had gone cold and hard. "Names," he said, "are the basis of knowledge."

———

Daddy's name was Thibedeaux, a Louisiana Catholic name alien to North Carolina. After Daddy left, Mama changed us to Taylor, her maiden name.

I became a Fonteyn at the Blacksboro County Courthouse, the same place where Jack had married Mama. Of the proceedings inside the courthouse I remember nothing; my memory of the event has largely been defined by a grainy black-and-white snapshot — taken, no doubt, by a passerby — that is now above my desk. We are standing at the top of the steps, Jack between me and Stevie, his hands grasping our shoulders as though to keep us from falling forward; Stevie in a lopsided raincoat and bow tie; me tall and skinny in a too short sailor dress, my long face made even longer by the clumps of permanented curls on either side (the awful new haircut Mama had insisted on). All three of us are staring straight ahead. Mama, in a dark coat and sunglasses, her feet arranged in a model's pose, is standing slightly apart and smiling off to the side as though it was not in this photograph, but some other, that she belonged.

After we left the courthouse Jack took us to a delicatessen for Nesselrode pie and, while we tried to eat it, told me and Stevie our name was now Fonteyn.

"No," I said.

"Beryl!" Mama gave me her nastiest look.

I stared down at the smooth green tabletop, the sugar bowl with the hinged silver lid. Daddy had no idea what was happening. I imagined him in Chicago, gazing sadly out at the frozen lake.

"You are lucky children," Mama said. "This is a wonderful day."

When neither Stevie nor I spoke, Jack got up, scraped back his chair, and walked to the men's room.

"You hurt his feelings," Mama hissed. "He doesn't have to be doing this, you know."

"We already have a father," I said.

"Where?" Mama held out her arms and looked around the restaurant.

It suddenly came to me why I'd had no letters from him. It wasn't Grandpa's fault, it was Mama's; she had told Daddy not to write.

I opened the sugar bowl and shut it, opened it, shut it. Beside me Stevie was playing church and steeple fast with his hands: church steeple people church steeple people.

Mama didn't say anything else, but I could feel her glaring. I hid my face from her with one hand and looked out into the parking lot at the hood ornaments and the sharp silver fins shining in the sun.

Jack slid back into the booth beside Mama. I could smell the bathroom soap on his hands. "I just had a great idea," he said in a starting-over kind of voice. "I'm going to build a tree house for you kids."

"I don't want one," Stevie said.

"OK by me," Jack said. "But I bet your sister does."

When I glanced at him, I was surprised by how sad he looked — for me, I thought. It was almost as though he knew what I'd been thinking, almost as though he could see in my mind that picture of Daddy by the lake and knew that I missed him.

My eyes watered as he reached for my hand. "Don't you?" he said, in such a kind, soft voice that I couldn't help it: I whispered yes.

Jack built the tree house that spring in the Osage orange that hung over the tennis court. On a small block of wood nailed to the trunk (my first step upward), he painted in small black letters the Latin name for Osage orange: MACLURA POMIFERA. On the second step he painted BERYL'S TREE, and on the third, NO TRESPASSING.

———

The Osage orange was a huge tree for its kind, some fifty feet tall, and fierce thorns quilled its branches, keeping other people out. Once the tree house was finished, Stevie wanted it to be his too. He tried to come up once, but I screamed at him to keep out and he got scratched and went wailing to Mama. She asked Jack to build Stevie a tree house somewhere else, but he said it was too late; he bought Stevie a bicycle instead. The very day he got the bike Stevie rode it under the tree and was so badly cut over one eye by a thorn that he had to have stitches. Then Mama started a campaign to have the tree cut down. It was just too dangerous, she told Jack: Stevie could have lost that eye. Even after Jack trimmed the lower branches Mama continued her argument. The limbs would grow out, Jack would forget to cut them, and someone else would get hurt walking under the tree. A tennis player, on the way to the court: Jack could be sued for all he was worth. Let 'em, he shrugged, I ain't worth much. But there were other perils, Mama said. If I fell, for instance (she always said "for instance"), I could get cut to ribbons on the way down. Jack said I knew what I was doing — I'd never have been fool enough to ride a bike under a thorn tree, and I wasn't going to fall either. As insurance, however, he added horizontal boards on two sides of the platform — crib railings, he called them — in case I ever went to sleep there or daydreamed too hard.

At first I didn't like the railings — they interfered with spying, which I liked to do belly down, my head over the edge. But I soon learned I could get almost as good a view of the yard by putting my feet against the trunk and dangling my head over the unboarded end. And when I lay flat on my back, the railings made the platform seem like a boat; if I closed my eyes on a breezy day I could even make the sound of leaves into water.

At supper the day Stevie got his stitches out — leaving a small lightning-shaped scar through his right eyebrow — Mama said the doctor agreed with her that the tree should come down.

"I can just imagine how you must have described it to him," Jack said. "Hysteria is no reason to fell a tree, especially one," he added, winking at me, "with a resident dryad."

"What's a dryad?" Stevie asked, in a tone of disgust.

"A lovely young nymph said to inhabit trees — that's what the Greeks and Romans said, anyway."

Mama went off to her room and slammed the door.

"Isn't this romantic?" Jack said in a voice meant to be funny. "Our first big scene."

I stared past Stevie at my reflection in the mirror behind him: the pimpled face, the frizzy curls that made my long face look even longer. "I'm ugly," I burst out.

"Don't be silly," Jack said. "Remember the duckling to swan story. You're at least halfway there."

I had on shorts, and as I stood up, his glance appraised my legs. "You're going to be a knockout," he added.

Face burning, I ran from the dining room out the door, across to my tree. After I scrambled up, I sat on the platform with my back against the tree and looked at my outstretched legs. I was amazed to see they were pretty: it was almost as if he had made it happen.

Everything else about me, however — now that Mama had ruined my hair — was awful; I knew that for a fact.

———

The Osage orange, too, was unsightly; had my tree house been in one of the large oak or maple trees in the yard, I might not have taken up what Mama called full-time residence in it. I cherished the tree for its untidy growth, its ridged greenish bark, and especially for its peculiar fruit, the Osage oranges that in late summer and early autumn fell onto the tennis court, where they split open and bled sticky white liquid.

The Osage oranges were chartreuse, pimpled, and irregularly shaped. Though the size of lopsided softballs, they more resembled brains because of the encircling lines that cleft the lumpy surface of each one. The unevenly pebbled skin of the Osage orange reminded me of a geographical relief map, like the one at school; that first autumn, as I sat in my tree house, stroking an Osage orange with my eyes shut, I liked to imagine the hand of Mr. Snow, the handsome young science teacher, guiding mine over mountain ranges, continents. But when I inspected the fruit closely with my eyes open, I thought this was like looking at an organ in my own body, the poisonous color, the infected-looking swellings, all deliciously confirming my worst suspicions about my insides.

I was glad the Osage oranges were useless, good only, Mama said, for producing more of their kind. They could not be eaten raw, their odor alone would guarantee that. They smelled like horse manure doctored with perfume, I thought, a lady's idea of horse manure. When I held my nose and tasted an Osage orange, the fruit's milky, stringy pulp made me gag. And it couldn't be transformed into anything edible, either. Mama pointed out that even sour persimmons could be made into pudding and quince into jelly, but Osage oranges were nothing but a damn nuisance.

Since I was dryad of the Osage orange, Mama said, I could darn well clean up after it. Although I grumbled about picking up Osage oranges from the tennis court, it was a chore I secretly enjoyed, relishing the pungency and texture of each fruit as I gathered it and laid it gently in the wheelbarrow up on the grass. Poor unloved wretches! Unappreciated, misunderstood! I wished I had some fine white papers to wrap them in, like the thin-skinned oranges at Mr. Medlin's store. I imagined laying the wrapped Osage oranges in the drawers of the Japanese tansu chest Mama used as a dresser; how uniquely this would scent her underwear!

Jack and I formed an Osage Orange Appreciation Society. He told me that although the pumpkin-colored wood of the tree wasn't prized now, the Indians had used it for bows — hence its familiar name, bois d'arc, or as hicks in the South pronounced it, bodark. And when white men first came they used the wood for fence posts, and, out west, planted Osage oranges in thick hedges to keep out the wind and unwelcome visitors.

He also told me that the Osage orange was of a higher evolutionary order than most trees because of its method of reproduction — dioecious, with female flowers on one tree and the male on another. His bees carried the pollen from stamen to pistil. He showed me the male tree, an inconspicuous, thorn-less specimen, at the edge of the woods beyond the hives. He joked that I shouldn't tell Mama because she'd hold the male responsible for all those Osage oranges on the court and might sneak out with a hatchet some dark night and do it bodily harm. I promised to keep mum, and we shook on it solemnly, hooking little fingers; this became the Osage Oath (O.O. for short), and after that whenever we had any kind of secret from Mama, like a birthday or Christmas present for her, we referred to it in public as "the O.O."

———

Not long after he nailed the crib railings onto my platform, Jack attached a flat tin roof to branches directly overhead. Mama was sorry that Jack had put on the roof, for this made it possible for me to be in the tree house any day, even when it rained. Not only was I going to catch my death up there in the damp, she said, I wasn't doing my share of housework. But Jack said leave her be; he gave me his old army slicker to keep me dry and his Boy Scout knapsack to put my books and lunch in.

It was the rainy days I came to like best — the raindrops drumming on the tin, the leaves rustling green and wet around me — as I lay on my back with my eyes shut and dreamed myself elsewhere.

I was in Virginia, floating on the pond with Daddy in a rowboat. He poled us along with one oar that made a sucking sound when he pulled it up to show me its sock of slick mud and algae. It began to rain, big drops that made dimples on the water, so Daddy carried me on his shoulders to the house and we went through the living room and up the stairs and he tucked me in bed for a nap. Mama and Stevie would be there when I got up — he didn't say this, but I knew it. He went back down the stairs and soon I could hear him playing his saxophone, a lullaby like he'd played for me at bedtime, years ago. The sweet sad notes and the rain on the tin roof made me sleepy, made my pillow get softer and softer, and then, both in Virginia and in my tree house, I was asleep.

Nine

I HAD THIS RITUAL for ascension to the tree house: keep to the right on the first three steps (segments of sawed-off broom handle, these were no more than toeholds), shift to the left up the next three, inch sideways across the top step and pull up onto the first big limb, whispering *"Illigitimis non corroborundum"* (Don't let the bastards get you down). Climb four limbs counterclockwise, not looking down, until Spit Point. Spit (hitting the tennis court sideline was a bull's eye), climb two more limbs, and step sideways through a gap of air onto the platform: then I was safe.

When I was in my fortress in the leaves, nothing, no one, could touch me; or so I thought. And even now, when I think *home,* what comes to mind is that green solitary space, me with my eyes closed as I leaned against the trunk and thought about Daddy; me with my eyes open as I peered down through leaves, Osage oranges, thorns, a spy with a superior point of view.

Sitting in the tree house, I could see the tennis court and the back yard all the way to the beehives at the edge of the woods. To my right was the west end of the house, a stucco wall with the windows to Stevie's bedroom and Jack's study above me — I could make out nothing there unless one of them appeared at the window — and below me, the window of Mama and Jack's room. I could look into their room when I lay with my head hanging over the unboarded edge of the platform. In this position I could also see anything that moved on the tennis court and in my part of the yard.

At first, Stevie was the main object of my surveillance. I liked to watch him roam the yard — alone, or with the Latham boys — in the red Superman cape Mama had made for him. The Lathams, Ronnie and Tim, were rough black-haired boys who looked like twins but weren't. They were both older than Stevie but clearly tolerated him at least partly for the sake of his new bike. They had only one bike between them, an old rusted clattering thing with missing spokes, and they would sometimes borrow the red bike Jack had bought while Stevie, who was forbidden by Mama to go on the road, waited forlornly at the bottom of the drive.

When the Lathams played with Stevie — always at our house, because Mama wouldn't let him go over there — it was usually some variation of Master and Slave. Stevie was the slave, a role perhaps suggested to the Lathams by the gold *S* Mama had embroidered on his cape. He followed several steps behind the older boys, carrying whatever they told him to carry — the baseball bat, glove, and ball, for instance, or, if no grown-ups were around (and at these times I watched very carefully), an armload of sticks. It made me uneasy to observe that procession winding across the yard: King Ronnie, the oldest, followed by Sir Tim, then Stevie with the sticks. When Ronnie called "Halt!" by the oak tree and said "Make the fire, Slave!" I would begin to feel a little sick to my stomach, and think about going down, but I never did. I told myself that Stevie didn't seem to mind his part in the drama; even so, I watched with my heart in my throat as Stevie arranged the sticks and then let Tim tie him to the tree. When an imaginary match was dropped on the kindling, Stevie was supposed to begin wailing. One day Ronnie took a stick from the make-believe fire and, lifting the front of Stevie's shirt, said, "We're going to brand you with the red-hot poker, Slave. You better say your prayers!"

"No! No!" Stevie screamed in a high voice, looking up, I thought, in my direction, so I cupped my hands around my mouth and yelled, as loud and deep as I could, "Unhand that boy, you sniveling Latham scum!" Ronnie dropped the stick, and he and Tim fled, terrified by the disembodied voice from the leaves.

———

I knew from this incident with the Lathams that Stevie was often aware of my silent presence, even when he played alone. The settings for his private dramas were within view of my tree house — the same oak tree that the Lathams tied him to served as the telephone booth in Superman — and he said things aloud that I would merely have thought. "Here goes the mild-mannered Clark Kent into the phone booth!" he'd yell, disappearing behind the tree, and then, emerging, call, "Watch out, Evil Empire, here comes SUPER-man!" As he zoomed across the yard, holding his red satin cape wide open behind him, he'd make at least one pass by my tree, though he wouldn't look up.

But there were times when Stevie clearly had forgotten that I might be in the tree: when he picked his nose, or grinning, peed on the lilac bush that Jack had transplanted from his mother's yard in New York State after she died and that was so hard to keep alive, Jack was always saying, in the South. And sometimes when Stevie played alone, I could tell he was in an entirely private world, as he went sleepwalking around the yard, making sudden strange gestures, his lips moving silently. Though his actions might be mysterious to me, I knew I was seeing his naked self; that would have been pleasure enough, even had I learned no secrets.

I did learn secrets, however.

I learned that the *S* on Stevie's cape, besides standing for

Superman and Slave, could also mean Christ the Savior. I figured this out from watching him stand against the oak tree with his arms outstretched, mumbling up at the sky. At some point he would fall to the ground, lie there motionless awhile, then rise and bow. This was hard to decipher until one day I made out the words, "Father, forgive them . . ." This made sense of certain other of his acts, too — parading around with his hands folded in front of his chest; standing on the tennis court steps and handing out what I now realized were loaves and fishes to people who passed before him.

One afternoon when he was below me on the steps, distributing this miraculous food, sometimes pausing to partake of some himself, I became aware of the silence all around him and above him. He and I were enclosed in the same silent space, only he didn't know it. I pinched an Osage orange from its stem and let it drop. When it hit his shoulder and bounced onto the court, he looked up at the sky, dazed at first, then said, "Beryl?" I quickly drew my head back from the edge of the platform. I lay still — no sound but the leaves — and when he called "Hello? Hello?" his voice uncertain and embarrassed, I had to dig my teeth into my arm so as not to laugh out loud.

————

In the afternoons Jack was often in the yard, pruning and spraying his roses or working with his bees. Resting from the labor of metamorphosis, he called this; it looked like work to me. When he was digging and planting I focused my spyglass (a rolled-up comic book) on his face, just trying to figure him out in a general kind of way, but I learned very little except that he had a curious lack of expression when alone. That freckled face, so animated when he was laughing or talking, in his solitude reminded me of a speckled stone egg. It was, oddly enough, when he appeared in his beekeeping costume, his face obscured by the veil, that I began to form a notion of his private character.

The long-sleeved one-piece suit he wore was white, as were the long heavy gloves and the helmet and veil. I could not make out eyes behind the veil, nor any other feature, except, from the inhalation of his breath, a suggestion of a mouth. Beneath one arm, held forward like a snub-nosed rifle, was the gleaming metallic smoker; from one gloved hand swung a bucket. It was a ghostly, alien figure that advanced across the yard to the hives.

Sometimes Mama was watching, too, from her reading chair on the patio; I remember how she leaned forward, the muscles of her legs tensed as Jack took the lid from the first hive and set it on the ground. She feared that he would stir up a swarm of bees that would head toward the house. Together we watched as Jack pulled back the steel rod of the smoker and pushed it in, sending a white billow into the hive. He slowly lifted out a frame of honeycomb and held it up to the light. If the honey was not ready, he replaced the frame; if the combs were full, he cut them with his knife and dropped them into the bucket. Then he went on to the next hive, and then the next, lifting, smoking, inspecting, moving with a dreamlike slowness that I shiver to recall.

When he had visited all the hives, Jack pulled up his veil and walked back across the yard. If Mama was in her reading chair he went to her; I watched through my spyglass as he bent to kiss her neck or the top of her head. Then he stood behind her and massaged her shoulders. I remember thinking how uncomfortable it looked — his hands seemed inattentive and rough — and I felt with Mama the intensity of his eyes upon the page as he silently encouraged her forward.

If Mama could write a good book, Jack would love her more: or so I believed at the time. Years later when Stevie and I began to have our talks about Mama and Jack, he said he had believed it, too.

We remembered how Mama sat in the lawn chair with those assigned books, studiously turning the pages whenever Jack was in the yard, but when he was not, sometimes closing her eyes and putting her head against the plastic webbing of the chair to sunbathe.

In the mornings from my tree house I could hear Mama typing in her corner of the bedroom; she was getting her chapters ready for Bernie to see in the fall. Though she wasn't letting anyone read these new chapters, Jack had seen her first one and agreed with Bernie that it had promise.

Usually all I could see, looking into Mama's and Jack's bedroom, was a patch of wood floor, the southwest edge of the bed covered with the brown-and-yellow spread Grandmuddy had woven, the profile of Mama's writing chair, and sometimes, depending on how close the chair was to the desk, Mama's hunched back.

Once she surprised me by pushing her chair away from the desk and leaning out the side window. I froze, thinking she had sensed my gaze. But she put her elbow on the windowsill and, chin in hand, looked straight out into the yard. Then she smiled, a strange and private smile; it made my heart beat faster to see her thus exposed.

What did not occur to me was that Jack, working in his study, might have paused to look out his window and seen, through a gap in the leaves — like an illustration from his book, half girl, half tree — my intent face looking down.

Ten

JACK CALLED my tree house the second house that Jack built, the first being the glass and stucco house, which was known locally, I soon learned, as "Fonteyn's Folly."

In September I entered the eighth grade at Blacksboro County Junior High. I was miserable at first, especially on the school bus, where the girls shunned me and some of the boys taunted me about Jack: he was an atheist, an egghead, a nigger lover. Fonteyn's Folly looked like a Russky sub because he was a commie spy; probably we were all commie spies.

I began to develop stomachaches, sometimes such bad ones that Mama let me stay home from school. Jack didn't approve of this; I learned not to complain of the stomachaches before he left for his school because he dosed me with what he called "Jack's Tonic" (a mixture of paregoric and honey) and sent me on my way, saying — even though I'd never described the school bus problem — "Remember *illigitimis non,* Beryl — they're just a bunch of hicks." I hated him for understanding, and I hated his stupid house.

That fall Mama came to hate the house too, but for a different reason: she decided it was haunted by the ghost of Jack's first wife, Joanne.

Jack told visitors he had designed the house himself — a

marriage, he liked to say, of the pure forms of ancient Greece and the Bauhaus. But one day Bernie let it slip that the framed blueprint on the dining room wall had been drawn by Joanne's father, a world-famous architect who had helped Mies van der Rohe design New York's Seagram Building (a photograph of which also hung in the dining room).

Mama told me she'd never understood before why anybody would want to look at a skyscraper while they ate, but now of course she did; it just confirmed what she'd known for some time, that Jack hadn't gotten Joanne out of his system.

Mama now saw traces of Joanne everywhere in the house: those ugly ocher Jugtown pots that gathered dust on top of the kitchen cupboard, the cookbooks heavily stained on the egg and cheese pages (this explained, she said, Jack's tendency toward vegetarianism), that damn Mies van der Rohe chair in the living room. There were even personal items of Joanne's in the bedroom, for God's sake; she should have gotten rid of them long ago.

One weekday morning in October I was home with one of my stomachaches. Jack was at his college, and Stevie — after a last-minute attempt to convince Jack and Mama that he was sick, too — was at his school, the county elementary. I was at my dressing table brushing my hair and lip-synching in the mirror as Doris Day sang "Que Sera Sera" on the radio.

"Well, this is an amazing recovery." I turned and saw Mama leaning against the doorjamb, smirking. She had on navy blue shorts and an old white shirt of Jack's rolled up at the sleeves; her hair was in pin curls because she and Jack were going that night to a toga party (a Halloween event he staged annually for his classics students). "Turn off that noise now. I need your help."

"But I don't feel good, really," I said, thinking she meant dusting, or vacuuming.

"Oh, come on. We're going to get that woman out of this house."

That sounded interesting, so I followed, though with a groan or two along the way, as Mama led me down the steps to her and Jack's bedroom. I had visions of going through drawers and boxes I'd never seen before; I even hoped that Mama might throw a thing or two of Joanne's my way.

Mama waved me to the bed and started with the closet, whistling as she examined Jack's side, hanger by hanger. I could see in the closet door mirror that she was smiling, which cheered me up even more. This was actually going to be fun.

I watched as she pulled out and threw onto the floor a pair of black-and-white check pants, a crumpled white silk blouse with mother-of-pearl cuff links, a soft black wool skirt with the cleaner's tag still on it, and a silky red jacket I could not resist trying on: it felt and smelled expensive, and it almost fit.

"She was a lot smaller than you," I said.

Mama spun around. "Take that damn thing off."

"Well, *gollee,*" I said. I had only been *playing.* I slid the jacket off and dropped it onto the pile of clothes.

No longer whistling, Mama began rummaging on the floor of the closet. "I guess Jack would've let this stuff rot in here," she said. She flung behind her one mildewed black suede shoe, then another. "We've been living here four months and her junk is still here. I call that pretty peculiar, don't you?"

When Mama went for a trash bag I lay back on the scratchy coverlet and remembered I was sick. I felt my forehead: hot. Probably I really was sick.

Mama returned with a large cardboard box, put the clothes, shoes, and a hatbox into it (what a shame, I thought, that I hadn't been able to look into that hatbox), and went into the bathroom, where she poured ammonia into the tub and turned on the water.

"I really wonder about Jack sometimes," she yelled over the sound of the water. "Have you ever noticed how he stares at other women when we're out in public? I don't think he's an active womanizer, he just likes to get my goat. Same thing with all this Joanne business, Joanne this, Joanne that, plus all her goddamn junk around. The worst thing is — I don't know if I ought to tell you this — he actually calls me Joanne in bed sometimes. You know what Dr. Becker says about that?" Mama came out of the bathroom with an armload of jars and bottles from the medicine cabinet and stood looking at me, waiting for me to answer.

"No," I said.

"He said it wouldn't surprise him if Jack ran Joanne off by doing the same kind of thing, like calling her some other woman's name in bed."

"Why don't we just leave, then? I hate this stupid place."

Mama glared at me, her nostrils going out and in. "I'll tell you what else Dr. Becker said — Jack is still a thousand percent better than your father."

"I hate you," I said between my teeth, not quite loud enough for her to hear.

"What did you say, young lady?"

"I'm sick!" I shouted at her. "Leave me alone!" I shut my eyes and turned my face away. There was a silence. I breathed in the smell of ammonia from the bathroom, suddenly feeling really sick to my stomach.

There was a huge clatter of glass as Mama dropped the jars and bottles into the box; then she stamped away and slammed the door.

I opened my eyes. My legs felt strangely heavy. Maybe I was coming down with polio, like Eugenia Holderness in elementary school who'd had to be in an iron lung. I imagined the bed where I lay as an iron lung, me unable to move anything except my head when Mama brought me soup. My tears would dribble down into the bowl; she would cry, too. A lot of the time I'd have to lie here in the silence, though, looking at the bookcases on the walls, and above Mama's writing desk the Japanese Noh mask of the angry demon woman with a big grimacing mouthful of teeth and horns sprouting from her forehead. The marble-like eyes of the demon woman seemed to be fixed on me right now, each eye circled in black and with a black dot in the center like a sting mark.

The wool coverlet Grandmuddy had woven rasped at my bare arms and legs. I closed my eyes again and wished for Grandmuddy. Maybe I could go back there to live. She'd be sad if she knew how I felt now, and she'd be so sorry the coverlet scratched my arms. I'd watched Grandmuddy weave this cloth, watched her throw the shuttle and pull the beater again and again until very slowly there emerged a row of what Grandmuddy called blooming leaves. Blooming Leaf was a very old pattern, she had said, an heirloom pattern. I'd thought at the time but hadn't said, because Grandmuddy was proud of her hand-dyed wool, that the leaves didn't look like flowers at all. They were the wrong colors, dark, ugly brown leaves against a vomit yellow ground. But if I told Grandmuddy how much I hated these colors and how I had to lie here and be scratched and smell the ammonia, she'd wish she could weave the coverlet over in soft green silk, two shades of green, like the upperside and underside of the leaves on my tree.

I turned on my side, wrapped the coverlet over me, and with my eyes still shut, imagined myself in the tree house. I could almost hear the sound of its leaves stirring around me. It was raining, there was that cool green smell, and a drumming sound on the tin.

———

It was afternoon when Mama woke me.

"I thought I should let sleeping dogs lie," she said, as I sat up and she put a tray in my lap. She was smiling, cheerful again, and she had brought my favorite lunch: a cream cheese and jelly sandwich and chocolate milk.

"Eat up," she said. "I need your help in the storeroom —

then we're going to the dump. By the way," she said over her shoulder as she left the room, "I found something wonderful for you up there."

I ate quickly and hurried upstairs to see the wonderful thing: a Japanese silk kimono, orange, with white and blue flowers and birds. Mama put it on me, and I stood holding my arms out straight like a scarecrow. "What will I do with this?" I said.

She looked hurt. "Wear it. It was mine when I was just about your age in Tokyo."

I must have looked dubious because she said, "Well, you could wear it to your school Halloween party. I could fix your hair up with chopsticks, like a geisha. Nobody else would have a costume like that."

That was what worried me. "No thanks," I said, sliding it off.

"Well, suit yourself. Let's get to work, then. Here's the throwaway pile." Mama pointed her foot at a small mountain of stuff — cardboard boxes, a flowered sewing box, a dressmaker's dummy — then picked up one of the boxes and started downstairs.

I picked up another box and saw that it contained doll clothes, my Brownie scout uniform, an old scrapbook of mine. "Hey," I called after her, "these are my things."

"There's a lot of old stuff in there we might as well get rid of at the same time."

"You can't throw my things away."

"It's a fire hazard to have all that junk in there, Beryl," Mama shouted. "I knew I shouldn't have asked you to help. Pick out what you want and put it in your room, then, but hurry up."

I sat down by the box and looked deeper: mine and Stevie's things mostly — old toys, clothes, books. At the bottom, beneath Stevie's old baby blanket and a paper bag of birdseed tied with red string, I found the records. They were old, scratched seventy-eights without covers, songs by Artie Shaw, Glenn Miller, Lucky Thompson. They had to be Daddy's; the Lucky

Thompson record even had "I Can't Give You Anything but Love" on one side.

I heard Mama coming back up the stairs so I quickly stuffed the things back in the box with the kimono on top. I was carrying it out of the storeroom as she came in. "I'll be right there," I said in my most helpful voice, and hurried down the hall to my room, where I pushed the box — it just did fit — far underneath my bed.

Then together Mama and I carried out everything of Joanne's — clothes, hatbox, cosmetics, shampoos, linens, kitchenware, cookbooks, wildflower plates, dressmaker's dummy — and put it in the trunk and back seat of the car. The only things that did not go were the Jugtown pottery, the blueprint of the house, and the photograph of the office building; Jack would kill us if we threw them out, Mama said, so we carried them up to the storeroom and then drove to the dump.

The dump was in a wooded area by the side of a road. Everyone in the surrounding countryside took their trash to the dump and some went there to pick through it. Besides the mounds of garbage, there were old refrigerators, tires, bedsprings, occasionally even a couch or chair.

Mama and I carried the boxes to the edge of the dump, a slight hill from which things could be pitched, and set them down. Then she reached into her pocket, pulled something out, and held out her hand to me. "Here," she said, smiling.

I opened my hand; she poured into it some dried black-eyed peas.

"What's this for?"

"Exorcism," she said. "This is a ritual I learned in Japan — I was writing about it just the other day. I was amazed that I still remember the words to use: *oni wa soto.* Say that: *oni wa soto.*"

"*Oni wa soto,*" I repeated.

"Good. Now say it and throw the peas."

"*Oni wa soto,*" I said, and flung the peas into the dump.

"Can you guess what it means? Devil, get out. OK, let's get rid of this junk."

Mama picked up a wildflower plate and winged it toward a pine tree. It missed, but the next one hit. "Bull's eye," she cried. "Your turn."

I picked up one of the plates, aimed at the tree, and missed, but it did shatter nicely on an overturned sink.

We threw the other plates — Mama got three bull's eyes, I got one — then everything else, piece by piece. We pushed the dummy over the edge of the hill; it gradually picked up speed as it rolled, bouncing over heaped-up garbage, and finally lodged against a wrought-iron bedstead.

Mama handed me more black-eyed peas and took some herself. "*Oni wa soto!*" she shouted, flinging the peas. "Devil, get out!"

I threw in a handful. "*Oni wa soto!*" It felt wonderful. Mama handed me more peas, and I threw them as far as I could, shouting so loudly that a passing car stopped, the woman and the girl in it stared and then slowly moved on. The girl, it happened, though I didn't recognize her at the time, was Eunice Whitaker, who rode the school bus and who thereafter, out of curiosity, pursued my friendship.

On the way home, Mama told me that Grandmuddy's Japanese housekeeper at the Baptist Mission in Tokyo had taught her the ritual. On New Year's Day in 1930, Mama got to purify the Japanese house by throwing beans out of the north, south, east, and west windows because it was the Year of the Horse and Mama had been born in the Year of the Horse, twelve years earlier. That year of the Chinese calendrical cycle, the obasan told her sadly, was the most inauspicious for the birth of a girl, and though Grandpa, when he got wind of it, said this was the kind of superstitious poppycock he'd come there to wipe out, Mama said she'd always half believed there might be something to it.

Eleven

My FRIENDSHIP with Eunice began when she sat down next to me on the bus one morning. She didn't introduce herself; she expected me to know who she was — a Blacksboro County Junior High cheerleader and homecoming queen runner-up, whose blue-eyed, blond cuteness evoked comparisons to Sandra Dee.

And she knew who I was. Is your stepfather really a commie? and What were y'all doing down at the dump? were her first questions to me.

I told her my stepfather was not a commie but an eccentric millionaire who was always buying so much stuff he had to throw a lot of it away: that's what my mother and I had been doing.

"What happened to your real father?" she asked, fixing me with her round blue eyes.

"He died in a car accident."

"You poor kid," she said. "You want to come over this afternoon?"

The Whitakers lived down the road on what Eunice called a dairy farm, although their herd consisted of three cows, one of which was too old to milk. Because Mrs. Whitaker did all the work with the cows (Mr. Whitaker was a railroad engineer and away most of the time), Jack called her "our local Europa." A plump, gray-haired woman in a housedress, Mrs. Whitaker bore no resemblance to the beautiful maiden whom Zeus, disguised as a bull, had seduced, but Jack said she'd been good-looking in her younger days.

"I used to get all my milk there," Jack said, waggling his eyebrows at Mama.

"You're lucky you didn't get brucellosis," she retorted.

"Brucellwhosis? Your mother," he said to me, "is a walking encyclopedia of diseases."

I didn't like the way Jack made fun of Mrs. Whitaker. I thought she was just what a mother should be, always baking, ironing, sewing, and completely devoted to Eunice. As Eunice's friend, I received some of that warmth. "Hello, honey," she would greet me at the door. "Come on in. I bet you're starved." That first visit, when Eunice and I sat at the kitchen table eating doughnuts and drinking milk while her mother cooked fried chicken for supper, I began to wish I lived there, too.

Upstairs in her room, Eunice showed me her closetful of clothes (including a multitude of starched crinolines), her dressing table with its lighted mirror and horde of perfumes, lipsticks, and nail polishes, her Elvis Presley record collection, the framed pictures of her boyfriend, Wayne, and — the thing I coveted most of all — her diary. This was a pink leather book with "My Diary" embossed on the front in gold; it also had a gold lock and key. Eunice kept the key in her locket next to a picture of Wayne — appropriate, I thought, since the diary was mostly about him. That first day she read me some of the tamer parts — the first meeting, the first date, the first kiss — and showed me, on the wall behind her bed, where her mother wouldn't see, the penciled X's that recorded Wayne's kisses, fifty-seven up to that point.

She also told me why I wasn't popular: I didn't laugh enough. The most I ever did, she said, was smile; boys liked girls who laughed out loud. She sat me beside her in front of the dressing table and, while I watched, threw back her head and went haw haw haw. When I tried, Eunice thought I looked so funny that she laughed even harder, and then I finally really laughed, too, until tears came to my eyes.

"There," she said, looking at me in the mirror. "Not half bad. Your laugh could actually be one of your good points, if you'd work on it." She showed me in the diary her assessment of her own good and bad points. The only debits were thick ankles and eyebrows that had to be tweezed, but the asset list was long: dimples, peaches and cream complexion, hourglass figure, long eyelashes. She even included the mole on her chin as a beauty mark, though in my opinion it was no such thing.

"Let's do you," she said, and, turning to a new page in the diary, wrote "Beryl, Pluses and Minuses." On the minus side she wrote "complexion, hair, personality (too quiet)." The plus side went "Laugh?, hair (color, not style)," and when I pulled up my skirt and raised one leg she added "legs."

"Smart," I said.

"Yeah," she said, in a tone that meant this was no asset, but she put it down anyway. "Mrs. Bannister liked a poem I wrote so much she's going to have it published in *The Bugle,*" I told her, but Eunice didn't respond. She was doodling in the margin. "She said I have great talent," I added, though it was actually Jack who had said that.

"Hey, I know what," Eunice said, her face brightening as she looked up at me. "I'll help you with your hair and stuff, if you'll help me with my English themes."

"OK," I said, shrugging, but secretly I was thrilled. I had visions of myself in the group that always gathered in front of Eunice's locker before classes each morning. Maybe I could talk Mama into getting me some more crinolines; I could imagine my legs (much prettier than Eunice's) beneath a rustling mass of taffeta and net, as she and I sashayed down the hall together to homeroom.

Eunice walked me halfway home, the two of us scuffling through the leaves on the side of the road.

"Tell me about the accident," she said. "Did he linger?"

"I don't know. I was a baby."

"Aw, that's sad. Did your mother rush to the scene?"

"She couldn't. It happened in Chicago."

"Chicago!" She stopped and grabbed my wrist. "What an amazing coincidence. My father goes to Chicago on the train all the time."

"He does?" I had a sudden wild thought of asking to go along. "Do you ever go with him?"

"Naw." She turned and walked ahead of me, her ponytail swinging. "Mama went once, though. She said there wasn't anything to it."

———

For dinner that night we had calves' liver and Brussels sprouts. Stevie poured ketchup all over his food, which Jack said was a desecration, but I said I didn't blame him.

"Why can't we ever have fried chicken?" I asked.

"Fried chicken!" Mama made a face.

"Well," Jack said, "this *is* the South."

"I wish I had a diary," I said, glancing toward Jack. He was always more willing than Mama to get me things.

"Good for you! I've been trying to persuade your mother to keep a journal. All good writers keep journals."

Mama looked up — a quick angry glance that included me and Jack — then picked up her plate and walked toward the kitchen.

"For God's sake, don't throw that one out!" Jack called after her.

"Where are you going, Mama?" Stevie said, as Mama clattered her plate on the kitchen counter and headed for the back door.

"To call a man about a dog."

"Really?" Stevie twisted around in his chair. "Really, Mama?" When she didn't respond, Stevie looked at Jack. "I wish I had a dog."

"That was just an expression, son," Jack said. "Go on, eat that mess on your plate."

———

The journal Jack gave me was a disappointment. A handmade book with a marbled cover and watermarked pages, it seemed too beautiful to write in. And it had no lock and key.

"It's from Italy," Jack said, watching as I opened and shut the cover. "I thought you could use it to record impressions for your poems."

I glanced at Mama, reading *House Beautiful* on the sofa; she did not look up.

"It's great," I said, "thank you." I stood, feeling awkward, and hurried from the room.

It was a Saturday and I was going to my tree house, anyway, so I decided I might as well take the journal. I went to get my fountain pen and ink, put them and the journal in my knapsack, and went outside.

I climbed the tree, leaned back against the trunk, and flipped through the book. Nothing but empty pages. Eunice's diary had dates and special sections for "Pet Peeves," "Groovy Hits," and "Heartthrobs." This paper had sharp edges and faint horizontal lines that reminded me of fingerprints. I cracked the book open in the middle and held it to my nose: at least it smelled good. Turning it sideways, I wrote in tiny letters next to the hand-sewn seam: "Hi! If you're reading this, you ought to be ashamed." Then I turned back to the first page and wrote "My Diary" in curlicue script.

On the following page I wrote out Joyce Kilmer's "Trees," which we'd had to memorize in school and I thought was the most beautiful poem ever written. I illustrated it with a drawing of my tree, the Osage oranges hanging from the branches like

Christmas tree ornaments, the small limbs bristling with thorns.

Next I recorded all my poetical works up to that time: a verse about trees I had written in fifth grade, two poems about flowers, and several about horses. The most recent horse poem (the one Jack and my English teacher had liked so much) began: "O gallant dusky steed of night / Now thou art gone and dimmed the light."

Then I began in earnest. "Dear Diary, What a glorious, ethereal day it is! What a thrill to breathe the air with the sky so blue, the birdsong so gay, and the leaves of the trees resplendent in nature's finest handiwork."

I stopped and looked out at the few remaining brown leaves clattering around me. Suddenly sad, I leaned back against the tree trunk and closed my eyes.

The next day I began by writing out, like Eunice, the "Top Ten Tunes of the Week," but I decorated my list — the book seemed to call for it — with an elaborate border of hearts, flowers, and moons. All of Elvis Presley's songs — "Jailhouse Rock," "Teddy Bear," and "All Shook Up" — I embellished with stars.

Then I wrote out my own list of pluses and minuses. On the asset side were "Intelligent, sense of humor, talented (writing, etc.), hair — Titian blond, eyes — mysterious hazel, legs — gorgeous, face in general — going to be not just cute but a knockout (some day)." On the debit side, I put "Complexion (improving tho) and "Braces (coming off soon)."

At the top of a page I wrote "Heartthrobs." Closing my eyes, I summoned up, and slightly revised, the face of Bob Banner, a football player who sat across from me in algebra and always copied off my papers.

"He is Robert," I wrote, "tall, dark, and enigmatically handsome. He hasn't said much to me in words — but O! His eyes! I know that when the time comes he will be much more eloquent than W., boyfriend of a certain E."

I closed my eyes again. Hugging the journal to my chest, I leaned back against the tree and developed Robert.

I decided that Robert Thompson was his full name; he would be new at Blacksboro Junior, would have moved here from Chicago, in fact. Though he was a football player, he was very sensitive and even liked to read poetry; he had liked my poem so much he cut it out and kept it in his wallet, though I didn't know this until later. He played in the band and during halftime at football games he quickly changed from his football to band uniform and marched onto the field playing his trombone. It was he who encouraged me to try out for cheerleader — he just walked up to me in the hall one day and said this — and I did and was picked, much to my amazement. I became very popular after that — and he was already popular, though a lot shyer than I realized. It was not until the night we were crowned home-coming king and queen that he got up the nerve to ask me on our first date.

Throughout November and into December I continued to spend hours in my tree house, even though most days I shivered in my heavy jacket, cap, and mittens. I liked to look at the last few curled leaves hanging stubbornly onto the branches and to breathe in the aroma of fallen Osage oranges, composting beneath a thick layer of leaves.

I reread my poems from the journal, aloud, if no one was around; they sounded fine in the frigid air. I wrote very little except for — over and over — "R.T. + B.F."

I had made the mistake of telling Eunice about my diary; during her first visit to our house she asked to see it. I told her I didn't know where it was just then, to which she replied, "Ha, I bet. What do you have to write about anyway, since you don't have a boyfriend?" When I said I had important thoughts to put down, she rolled her eyes. I could tell this was going to be gossip material, like the statues she'd giggled over in the living room; as soon as she left I took my journal out of my underwear drawer, went to the tree house, and wrote, "Eunice Phewnice, ugh, she stinks!" then leaned back against the tree and thought hard about Robert.

Robert would invite me to a dance, a fancier one than Eunice had ever been to in her life. I would have on a gorgeous blue dress and matching high heels. It didn't matter if the heels made me tall because Robert was even taller. I discovered during the first slow dance that I could easily rest my head on his shoulder. I shut my eyes as we swayed back and forth to the music. There was a real band playing a beautiful song, "Stardust." I could hear the saxophone solo. Then — we happened to be right next to the band at that point — I opened my eyes and saw it was Daddy playing the saxophone. He had on a tuxedo, and the saxophone shone in the light of the chandelier. This was the Drake Hotel Ballroom in Chicago. It turned out that Robert's grandmother had invited me to come there for a holiday. Robert and I hadn't been getting along very well, though. Actually, I had been crying; when we danced up close to the band again, I could tell Daddy felt sorry about how sad I looked, even though he didn't quite recognize me. I turned my head away, but I could feel his eyes following me as Robert and I danced across the floor.

When the band took a break, Robert went to get me a Coke. I walked out onto the porch, and Daddy followed. He stood near me at the railing, took a cigarette from his tuxedo pocket, and lit it. He offered me one.

I shook my head. "I'm not old enough."

"Yes, I can see that now. You know, you remind me of someone. Down South, I have a — wait, miss, please don't go."

But I had turned, hurried across the porch and the ballroom, went through the revolving door and onto the street. Daddy came after me but made the mistake of stopping to tell the bandleader he was leaving. By the time he went through the spinning door, I was nowhere in sight. It was raining and cold, but Daddy stood waiting a long time before he sadly walked away.

When I finally moved inside for the winter, I hibernated in my room, reading, studying myself in the mirror, listening to the radio. I kept the radio tuned to WSKY, broadcast from the Sky Castle Drive Inn; they played golden oldies along with the top ten, and people could call in requests and dedications. "Love Me Tender" always went out for Eunice and Wayne, along with a lot of other people. Once when Mama and Jack weren't home, I called in "Why Do Fools Fall in Love?" for Eunice and Wayne. Eunice called and said, "Did you hear that?" and I said, very innocently, "What?" Then I called in "Stardust" for "Robert and a certain someone." While it played I danced in my room with my eyes shut, my right hand held up to clasp Robert's, my left hand and my head on his shoulder.

One day I took out Daddy's records and spread them on my bed: Glenn Miller's "A Million Dreams Ago," "Sleepy Town Train," "Melancholy Baby," "Always in My Heart," and Lucky Thompson's "I Can't Give You Anything but Love" and "Don't Blame Me." It thrilled me to think about Daddy touching them, putting them on his record player and humming along, maybe even playing his saxophone as he listened. On one record was a clear fingerprint to which I touched, very lightly, my own fingertip. The print on the record was larger than mine, so it had to be his.

For Christmas that year I asked for and received a three-speed hi-fi record player. Jack also gave me a small collection of classical records — *Swan Lake,* the *Peer Gynt Suite,* Chopin waltzes — to offset what he called "that chain gang music" emanating from my room.

I was careful to play Daddy's records when Mama and Jack were in some other part of the house and when Stevie wasn't around or was asleep. Late at night was the best time, when everyone was in bed. As I lay in the dark listening, it was Daddy I heard and saw, his head back, his eyes shut, thinking of me as he played "Don't Blame Me" and "I Can't Give You Anything but Love." "Don't Blame Me" was slow and melancholy; in the middle he even lost the tune for a while, but at the end it came back, a message that I should not blame him. It wasn't that he wanted to leave me and Stevie, and he was glad we'd been born; it was just that he couldn't go on working in the darkroom. He wished Mama would let him write to us; he would give anything to see me.

As I listened to the records, I imagined meeting after meeting with Daddy.

My glee club teacher, I decided, would discover that I had extraordinary singing talent. I would take lessons in Blacksboro for a while and then, because there weren't good enough teachers here, in Chicago. My teacher there would be an old woman a little like Grandmuddy, only with a Russian accent; when she felt I was ready to sing in public she got me a gig at the Drake Hotel.

The Drake was a tall marble building with ornate windows and a doorman out front. We walked through a red-carpeted lobby and into the ballroom, which was full of glamorous people in evening clothes. Madame led me up to the bandstand, where the musicians were just getting ready to play. "Here she is," she said to the band leader, Lucky Thompson, "see what you think."

I had on a blue net dress and a gardenia; my hair was long and smooth. My braces were off now, and my smile dazzled Mr. Thompson, and also — as I happened to turn that way and much to my surprise saw him — Daddy.

Daddy was just getting his saxophone out of its case. He had a funny expression on his face. "You know 'Anything but Love'?" he asked me. I nodded and we began. Our harmony was perfect. He watched me as I sang. I could see the light of recognition spread gradually across his face; by the middle of the song, he was sure. He led me onto the floor and we danced.

———

It was in early spring that I wrote the letter. One night I awoke from a dream and sat up, not knowing at first where I was. Then I saw the moonlight on the balcony outside and the familiar shapes of my furniture. I turned on the light, took out my journal, and turning to the last page, so I could tear it out later, I wrote,

Dear Daddy,

Hello, it's me! Can you believe it?
Stevie and I are growing up. I look the same I guess except tall and skinny. My hair is still the same color of course but Mama made me get it cut and have a permanent which she said would look great but doesn't. I can't send you a picture, I look too awful.

I would like one of you though. Do you have one you could send?

Do you still smoke Luckys? What's your favorite song now? How is the band? Fine I hope.

Please write to me and visit if you can. Or maybe I could come visit you. I have this friend who could maybe get me a ride on the train.

Sincerely,
Your daughter Beryl (age 13)

On the envelope I wrote "Daniel Thibedeaux, c/o Drake Hotel, Chicago, Illinois. Please forward if necessary." In the upper left-hand corner, I wrote my name, care of Jack and the address, then at the top added "Stepfather," with an arrow pointing down to Jack's name.

Twelve

IN APRIL Jack painted Greek letters on each of his seven beehives: alpha, beta, gamma, and delta from the beginning of the alphabet, and chi, psi, and omega from the end. Jack said his reasons for this were purely educational; besides teaching me and Stevie a little Greek, he was going to show us how bees recognize and come home to particular markings. Right from the start, however, Mama said Jack's ulterior motive was to impress Mackey Tull, his new female colleague in the classics department.

I knew from dinner table conversations that Jack had hired Mackey Tull from Athens (Georgia — he joked about this) and that he felt sorry for her (though Mama did not) because she was divorced and all alone in the world. But I did not see her until the Saturday afternoon when she and Bernie came to play tennis.

Jack had finished painting the hives that morning — just in time for Mackey's arrival, Mama said. Each had two fresh coats of whitewash and a sky blue Greek letter on the top and one side of the hive body. I hadn't done any of the painting, but I had gone to town with Jack to get the paints and the fingernail polish he was going to use for the homing experiment. I had been glad to go along because I got to pick out the nail polish

(Hound Dog Orange, like Eunice's, which I would get to keep afterward), but Stevie didn't want to go. Jack said that was OK by him, he only wanted enthusiasts in on this deal.

I was in my tree house when Mackey and Bernie came. Fixing her in my spyglass as she walked across the yard, I was surprised to see that Mackey was just a regular old schoolteacher with glasses and straight, mousy brown hair. Her legs were pretty nice but too white. Nothing for Mama to worry about, I decided. She did have on a tennis dress I envied, with a scoop neck and green piping around the edges.

Jack and Mama came out of the house to greet them, Mama already looking like a sourpuss. When Jack led Mackey and Bernie near the hives to show them the Greek letters on the tops and sides, Mama stood on the patio hugging herself and scowling. On the way back from the hives, Jack glared at Mama and when they started to play tennis he chose Mackey for his partner.

I leaned way over the edge of my platform to watch the game. Mama kept missing shots even I could have made and she looked madder than ever: her face reminded me of the demon woman mask over her desk. Mackey Tull kept smiling and laughing. She didn't seem to know that her white thighs jiggled when she ran or that the kind of hits she made, high and soft, were what Jack called marshmallow shots. I didn't see how Jack could stand to play with her (she even screamed every time she got a ball over the net), but he acted as if she were doing great. "Way to go, Mac!" he said after every one of her pathetic little hits. "That was a beaut!" But I noticed that as the game went on, Jack ran for most of the balls, even when they were on Mackey's side, and kept aiming them at Bernie's weak backhand. Jack and Mackey won, 6–1, 6–love.

After the game the four of them sat drinking gin and tonic, Mama and Bernie on the tennis court steps, Mackey in a lawn chair right below me, Jack on the grass beside her. I had a bird's-eye view right into the top of her dress — there'd been a big booby hatch, as Eunice would say — but I didn't see that Jack was doing any looking.

Jack was telling Mackey about the experiment, how he was going to mark the bees from the chi hive and track them to make sure they always returned to the same place. He'd chosen chi for the pivotal hive because he wanted to mark the bees with the same letter, and an X would be almost as easy to do with polish as the usual dot would be. To make it challenging for the bees — and these were very gifted bees, he told her — he was going to keep moving the chi hive. That would not only confirm previous experiments on bees' visual perceptions, but he'd have the only Greek-literate bees in America.

Every time Jack took a breath, Mackey said — in this drawl I would have thought would make him sick — "That's fascinating, Ja-ack."

Mama and Bernie sat on the tennis court steps talking about her novel. Every once in a while I caught the words "editor" and "agent." She was pretending not to be listening to Mackey and Jack, but I knew she was; she had a talent for following two conversations at one time.

Suddenly Jack looked straight up into the tree. "Come on, Beryl," he said, "let's get this show on the road."

"My word," Mackey said as I came down from the tree. "I didn't know anybody was up there."

Bernie whistled. "Look who's growing up," he said.

I felt my face turn red.

"Isn't she, though?" Jack said, and winked at me.

I looked at Mama; she was frowning.

"How old are you, dear?" Mackey Tull said.

When I said, "Thirteen," she said, "My goodness," and looked surprised. I couldn't tell whether she'd thought me younger or older.

"Come on," Jack said, "I'll get suited up, and you get the polish. Also find out what's happened to that brother of yours. He ought to at least see this."

"They're not going near those hives," Mama yelled after us as we went to the house. "Jack, do you hear me?"

"Yes, dear," he called back in a pretend sugary voice.

I found Stevie on the balcony, shooting rocks at the maple tree with his slingshot. He had on his Superman cape, which was tattered now and comically small. He looked embarrassed when I stepped out next to him, so I figured he'd been talking to himself again.

"Jack's going to do the bees now," I said. "He told you to come watch."

"I can watch from here if I want to." Stevie took an acorn from his pocket, put it in his slingshot, and aimed toward the hives.

When I went into my room to get the nail polish, I checked in the mirror to see what Bernie had been whistling about. My complexion was clear today, and my hair had worked out better than usual; not half bad, I decided. I let my hair fall over one eye and tried out a new smile. Hearing a noise behind me, I turned and saw Stevie in the doorway, grinning. "Primper," he said, a word Jack sometimes used against me.

"Get out of here, you stupid sissy."

"I am not a sissy."

As I leapt up and went down the stairs, he followed, yelling, "I am not either a sissy."

"Says who?" Jack called from the bottom of the steps. He had on his bee costume with the veil rolled up on the helmet. As we came down, he held out his hand for the polish and took it, then pulled down the veil and went outside.

Stevie and I followed him out. Stevie hung back by the door, but I walked to the patio, where Bernie, Mama, and Mackey were watching Jack walk across the yard to the hives. I stood by Bernie, but casually, as if by chance. He smiled down at me. "Quite a production, hey?"

"It really is quite dramatic," Mackey Tull said as Jack took the cover off the chi hive and set it on the ground. He took the

polish from his pocket, held it in the air, and with a flourish —
as though this were part of a magic act — opened it, then bent
over the hive.

"What's he doing now?" Mackey Tull said.

"Painting the goddamn bees," Mama answered. I didn't
blame her: it had been a stupid question. Then she added: "This
is his he-man act."

Suddenly Stevie was running across the yard toward the
hives, slingshot poised, cape flapping behind him.

"Come back here, Stevie," Mama yelled. Jack jerked his head
up and gestured him back.

"Stevie!" Mama shouted again, panic in her voice.

"Stevie!" we all yelled, and Mama started toward him.

Stevie stopped, pulled back his slingshot, and let go. I could
hear the thunk of the acorn against the chi hive, but I didn't
realize what had happened next — I didn't see the bees fly up
— until Jack grabbed Stevie by the arm and propelled him back
across the yard. Stevie was crying; he had dropped his slingshot.
Jack still had on the veil but I could see, beneath it, as he came
closer, his features turned to stone.

Mama ran to him. "Did you get stung, darling?"

"Of course he did," Jack said, dropping Stevie's arm and
pushing him toward us. "And he damn well deserved to. He
ought to have his hide tanned."

Stevie wailed louder and clutched his arm.

"Let me see, sweetie," Mama said.

"I'll handle this, Beatrice," Jack said, prying Stevie's hand
away. With his thumbnail he dug out two stingers; Stevie
yelped. "Come on, Steven, buck up. They're out, and look how
small they are. He held one out on his fingertip, about the size
of a short eyelash. "OK, we'll go get some soda on these. Carry
on with the revels. Bernie, would you refresh the ladies'
drinks?"

Stevie looked so pathetic as Jack led him away that I tried to pat his arm, but he knocked my hand away. "Gosh, Stevie, it's not my fault!"

Jack and Stevie went upstairs to put soda on the stings. Bernie went into the kitchen. Mama, Mackey Tull, and I stood at the bottom of the steps long after Jack and Stevie had disappeared.

"He's sensitive to beestings," Mama said.

"He'll be fine," Mackey Tull said. "Jack knows what he's doing."

"Is that so?" Mama gave Mackey her iciest look.

I followed Mama and Mackey to the living room. They faced each other at opposite ends of the sofa as if it were a seesaw. I sat in the Mies van der Rohe chair.

There was silence until Bernie and Jack came into the room. Bernie was carrying the tray of drinks — more gin and tonics for the grown-ups and what he called the virgin version, lime and tonic, for me; Jack had a fistful of mint.

"Where's Stevie?" Mama said to Jack as Bernie handed her a drink.

"Nursing his wounds. He's fine," he added, waving her down. "Let's not let him spoil this too." He went around the room putting a sprig of mint into each glass.

"Home grown," he said when he got to Mackey. "*Mentha gentilis variegata.*"

"*Mentha gentilis variegata,*" she repeated, as if this were part of a ritual. Then she added a sentence in Latin that made Jack laugh.

Mama took the mint out of her glass and flung it on the coffee table, then took several big swallows of her drink.

Stevie came partway into the living room. "Mama?" he said.

Mama didn't notice him at first. She was staring gloomily into the fireplace.

"Mama?" He came closer. He was pale and sick-looking, what Grandmuddy called green around the gills. "I don't feel good."

Mama looked at him and jumped up. "Give me the car keys, Jack."

"Where are you going?" Jack had just gotten his new book on Greek sculpture from the shelf to show Mackey and Bernie.

"I'm taking Stevie to the hospital."

"What for?"

"He's having a reaction."

"For God's sake, Beatrice, we have guests. And he is not having a reaction."

"Give me the keys, dammit."

When Jack glared at her, she turned to Bernie.

"Bernie?" she said. He stood up.

"Oh, for Christ's sake." Jack took the keys out of his pocket and threw them toward Mama.

She snatched them off the floor, grabbed Stevie by the arm, and hurried out of the room. "Mama, do you want me to come?" I called after her, but she didn't hear me.

"You're being absurd, Beatrice," Jack yelled.

The talk went on, but I could feel everyone listening to the sound of the car starting and going down the drive.

———

It was dark when Mama and Stevie got back. I was in my room, and Jack was in the dining room eating alone; Mackey and Bernie had gone.

I tiptoed out to the top of the stairs.

"Where'd you take him?" I heard Jack say. "The Mayo Clinic?"

"He had a very close call," Mama said. "The doctor wanted to watch him."

"I've been around bees and beestings all my life. He didn't have any close call, except in nearly getting his fanny warmed. What's that?"

"Adrenalin. The doctor said we should have some on hand just in case."

"If Stevie'd needed Adrenalin, he'd have been dead by the time you got there. That idiot doesn't know what he's talking about."

"He's a doctor," Mama shouted. "He said we ought to have Adrenalin."

"Sounds like he already gave you a dose."

There was an explosion of sounds: the bang of the front door, the clatter of dishes as Jack pushed up from the table, the pounding of Stevie's footsteps as he came up toward me.

———

Stevie and I have often talked about the day he shot the acorn at the beehive and got stung; it marks the beginning of the time that everything began to go wrong between him and Jack.

But I never have explained to Stevie — not even last year, when I told him the worst — what changed for me that spring and summer.

Thirteen

EXCEPT FOR sleep, breakfast and dinner, and occasional visits to Eunice's house, I spent the early days of that summer in my tree house.

I added furnishings: a yellow flowered curtain draped over a limb on the tennis court side; a small oval braided rug that Grandmuddy had made and that just covered the platform; a triangular bolster pillow for greater comfort when leaning against the tree. A three-legged stool served as my table for meals; in my knapsack were salt and pepper, a tin cup and plate, and a setting of Mama's best silver (she never missed it). Also in the knapsack along with my journal were a comb, mirror, eyelash curler (Eunice had given me her old one), and books: a picture book about Chicago that I had stolen from the library, several books that Jack had recommended, and one — *Gone With the Wind* — that he had not. On the trunk of the tree were a larger mirror and Daddy's picture postcard of Chicago, a section of lake and a curve of tall buildings beside it like a backward *C*. I put the postcard away at the end of every day; the first thing I did in the morning was remove its protective layers — rain slicker, knapsack, waxed paper — and thumbtack it back to the trunk. Then I would take out my journal.

Beyond a "Thought of the Day" — if I were feeling profound — and reports on the weather and nature, I still wrote very little in the journal. I remember what I did not write, however, as I sat holding the journal on my knees or clasped to my chest; for it was what I did not write that mattered most.

I had read in a magazine about World War II soldiers lost for years in Japanese jungles because they had amnesia. Daddy could have amnesia; he could have been hit on the head and robbed on one of those dangerous Chicago streets. When he came to, his wallet was gone, so he had no way of knowing who he was. Finally he made up a name and got a new job as a dishwasher; he was miserable without knowing why.

Jack and Mama had died in a car crash. There was a story in all the papers about it, with a picture of me and Stevie. "Orphans Seek Father," the caption said. That day Daddy stopped to buy a paper at a newsstand; pictures of me and Stevie lay in full view on the counter. Our faces suddenly brought back his memory, and he was so happy to know about us that he didn't know whether to laugh or cry. He got in touch with us right away, though, and there was another news story about our tearful reunion.

One day Jack loomed over the edge of my platform. Shocked by the sudden appearance of his face, I snapped the journal shut and put it beneath me.

"Sorry, didn't mean to scare you." His neck emerged, thick and muscular, then his freckled, hairy arms and his chest, a tuft of red hair sprouting from the top of his shirt. I leaned away from him and held to the far limb.

He reached into his shirt pocket and pulled out an envelope. One arm reached across the platform as he leaned in and put the envelope on my knee. "This came today."

I stared down at it: the letter I'd sent to Daddy. His name had been slashed with a big black line; "Return to Sender" was scrawled beside it. I burst into tears.

"Why doesn't he ever write to me?"

"Maybe he's doing you a favor."

"He is not!"

"It's time you put him aside. You'll be a lot happier girl when you do. Beryl, there's something you ought to know."

A chill went through me as I looked at Jack's serious face. My crying slowed.

"What?"

"Not long after your father left, your mother wrote to him begging for reconciliation — this was for your sakes. She even offered to move to Chicago with you kids. But he turned her down cold."

My crying had stopped completely. I thought of the day Mama got the letter at Grandpa and Grandmuddy's and had gone running up the stairs. She'd said it had nothing to do with me.

"I don't believe you," I said. "She never told me that."

"It would have hurt her pride to tell you. He already had another woman, Beryl. That's what he told her." Jack looked at me, his blue eyes steady. "For all we know, honey, he has another family now."

A family. I had never thought of that. Everything froze inside me.

"I'm sorry," Jack said. I saw the muscles of his arm tense; for a moment I thought he was going to pull up into my tree house. But he moved jerkily, one step downward; half of his chest was gone. "Why don't you come on in, honey?" he said. "Dinner's almost ready."

I nodded quickly up and down to make him go. Another step, and his chest had disappeared. Then his face slid out of sight.

———

That night I lay sleepless a long time, staring into the dark. Mama and Jack had gone to bed, and Stevie had been asleep for hours. There was no moon. The whole house was dark and silent. Even the ticking of my clock, as loud and fast as a racing pulse, was nothing but a scrap of sound floating on the silence.

I felt sure Mama had told Daddy not to write to me but that did not explain why he didn't. If he cared at all, he would have sent me some sign — a present on my birthday, at least a card. Even if he had another family — the thought seared my chest — I could not understand how he could forget me so completely. Maybe he really was dead. It was certainly possible. People did get killed in car wrecks, or just walking across the street. Maybe it had happened long ago and all this time I hadn't known.

It could have happened just after he sent that last card from the Lincoln Park Zoo. He would have been absentminded that day, thinking of me and Stevie; maybe he had stepped off the curb even though the light had turned green. The taxicab tried to stop but too late.

I could see him lying on the street in his brown plaid jacket, his rough face turned to one side, his mouth open just a little as if he'd been about to speak. "Dead." I whispered it out loud; tears burned my eyes. I thought of the scrape of his shirt against my cheek, the cold grain running through my fingers, his last words — "Be quicker tomorrow" — and began to cry harder, burying my face in the pillow so I wouldn't make any noise. He was dead, it really was true; I cried myself to sleep.

———

The next day when no one was around I went into Jack's study, picked up the phone, and asked for Chicago information.

There were clicks, and static. Then a woman's nasal voice leapt into my ear. "Chicago."

"Hello? Could you tell me — is there a Daniel Thibedeaux?" I spelled it for her.

"That's T as in Tom, H as in Henry?"

"Yes."

"One moment please."

There was a brief silence; my heart pounded.

"The only Thibedeaux I have is an Earl on Pontiac."

"No D. B.? Or Daniel?"

"No. Sorry, dear." She did sound sorry.

I hung up the receiver. That was it, then; he was dead.

Jack never mentioned the returned letter, but I knew without his saying so that he wouldn't tell Mama. It would upset her too much. I also knew his sympathy for me was the reason for the new books — novels by Jane Austen, the Brontës, Dostoyevsky, Tolstoy — and for the offers of lessons in Latin, chess, and tennis.

———

In late summer Jack went to New York for a Greek and Latin teachers meeting. Nothing but two long days of boring academic papers, he told Mama when she proposed going along.

Mama looked cheerful and pretty in her new sundress when she went to pick up Jack from the airport. She came back in a bad mood.

Jack had brought gifts, which we opened in the living room. He had brought me a tennis dress with a scoop neck and full skirt, and to go under it pants trimmed in lace. I ran to the downstairs bathroom to try it on, standing on the toilet to admire the full effect in the mirror. On the hem of the skirt was an insignia of twin laurel leaves that set off my leg like a beauty mark.

When I went back to the living room, Jack whistled and said, "Now you don't have any excuse not to play," but Mama glared at me.

"Why didn't you bring Stevie anything from that fancy pro shop?" she said. Stevie's present was a T-shirt with a picture of the Empire State Building on the front. It was much too large, coming almost to his knees.

Jack fished in his suitcase and pulled out a white terry cloth visor. "Here you go, bud," he said, putting it on Stevie's head.

The visor fell over his eyes, and Mama snatched it off. "Nobody wants an afterthought," she said.

"Okeydoke." Jack shrugged and tossed the visor aside. Then he brought out Mama's present.

"Books," she guessed, ripping off the brown paper. She stumbled a little as she read the title aloud, *"A la recherche du temps perdu."* "In French?" she said, making a face as she flipped through one volume.

"I know a lot of people who would give their eyeteeth for these books."

"Why don't you give them to her then?" she said, and marched off to the kitchen. I could hear her flinging things around, slamming the refrigerator so hard it rattled.

The whole evening was going to be ruined; probably she wouldn't even make baked Alaska like she'd promised. "I don't see why she has to be like that," I said.

"The green-eyed monster," Jack said with a sigh.

I thought he meant she was mad because I had gotten the best present; I did not think of Mackey Tull. But then during dinner Mama asked how Mackey had liked all those boring papers. When Jack shrugged, Mama said, "Maybe you talked about something else on the plane."

"Don't be absurd. She *is* my colleague."

"Why didn't you tell me she was going?"

"It never occurred to me."

"That's why you didn't want me to go, isn't it?"

"That's crazy. You're being completely childish."

While they argued, Stevie's head jerked back and forth as if he were watching a tennis match, and his mouth hung open. "Shut your mouth," I yelled at him. "Flies'll get in."

He looked at me, startled. Mama and Jack fell silent. Jack looked down at his plate as he started eating again, but Mama continued to glare, her nostrils flared out in a way I found totally repulsive.

Mama did make baked Alaska, but burned it. She set it down in front of Jack and went to her room — to cry, I could tell from her face.

Jack sliced through the charred crust and fixed plates of the dessert for me, Stevie, and himself.

Stevie ate fast and left. Jack and I sat in silence, except for the sound of his fork against the plate; I had taken one bite and quit.

"Thank you for the tennis dress," I said.

"You're welcome."

"It's a beautiful dress — and I really would like to learn how to play."

He looked up and smiled. "Thatta girl!"

"You know what?" My heart was pounding as I said this. "I'm glad you're my father."

His face grew serious; I thought tears came to his eyes, but I couldn't be sure. "Thanks, honey," he said. "I needed that."

Jack and I were doing the dishes when Mama came out of her room. She had washed her face and put on fresh makeup and perfume. "Need some help?" she said, putting her arms around Jack's waist as he reached up to put a bowl away. He turned around and kissed her.

I tiptoed out and went up the stairs. Stevie was lying on his bed reading a Spiderman comic. "Now they're kissing," I told him.

"I wish he'd make up his stupid mind."

After a while Jack called us down to play Scrabble. He and Mama and Stevie and I sat around the coffee table in the living room. "This is more like it," Jack said. "My happy family." But it was me he winked at; and I winked back.

———

I rarely thought about Daddy after that, but I dreamed of him at night, dreamed he was coming to wake me so we could go feed the pony. Sometimes, shifting my long legs beneath the covers I would half wake, feeling that my bed was facing the wrong way or that I was in some unfamiliar room. Only as I opened my eyes in the early morning would I remember — the realization seeping through me like slowly changing light —

that I lived with Jack now, that Jack was my father, yet the dressing table mirror had, as I dropped back toward sleep, the luminescent sheen of the pond Daddy looked toward as he banged the grain bucket against the fence and called, "Ho, boy!" his voice faint in the distance, and so lonely, that I pulled the pillow over my head to keep from hearing what it meant: that I had betrayed him.

III

Fourteen

THAT FALL Jack began what Stevie and I called the "Bee Lectures." These were inspired not only by an unusually large honey harvest but by Jack's growing alarm over our educations. He thought we weren't learning anything in the county schools; neither of us had enough homework to shake a stick at, and what we chose to read on our own horrified him. I was to start reading the books he had given me. Stevie was to read the Hardy Boys to ease him off comics, and to learn five new words every day from a book called *Vocabulary Made Simple.* And — our home nature course — Jack was going to teach both of us everything he knew about bees.

We learned, mostly during dinner, about the organization of labor in the hive (females did all the work, while the males got to loll about until mating time); the amazing industry of the bees (one thimbleful of honey represented six thousand visits to flowers, so we mustn't be greedy gluttons); the miraculous architecture of the hexagonal combs (the wax for which was extruded from the bees' abdomens and then chewed into workable lumps — not dinner table conversation, Mama protested). But the subject that most fascinated Jack, and the one we heard most about, was the dancing of the bees. With these dances — the round dance, the wagtail — the bees told each other about the presence and location of a particular honey source; it was, Jack claimed, a language at least as precise as our own.

I remember particularly the night Bernie was there for one of these talks. He sat across the table from me; Stevie was to my left between me and Jack. Though I was intensely aware of Bernie's tanned, smiling presence — he looked, I decided, like a curly-haired Rhett Butler without a mustache — I hardly glanced at him. I kept my eyes on the honeycomb Jack had served for dessert, but I could feel Bernie's gaze often upon me. I was tan, too, and my braces had just been taken off. I smiled whenever I could, though not directly at Bernie.

Jack was talking about the bee dances; beside his plate was his text, Karl von Frisch's *The Dancing Bees.* "Would you believe," he said, looking around the table, "a bee is able to say quite plainly, 'Well, girls, the best nectar bargain today is Osage orange, sixty degrees northwest and two hundred yards distance from our hive?' "

"I'll bite," Bernie said. "No, I don't believe it."

"Next spring I'll prove it to you. I'm thinking of ordering an observation hive for the kids. We might even try to reproduce these experiments," he said, pointing his fork at the von Frisch book.

"Don't forget what happened during your last famous experiment," Mama said.

"I could hardly forget." Jack gave Stevie a look. "I was hoping we're more grown up now."

"We're not any less allergic to stings," Mama said.

Bernie looked back and forth. "By the way, I was just telling Beatrice her new chapter is really terrific."

Mama beamed. "He thinks the first part is ready to send off, Jack."

"Oh?" Jack said.

"I do, I do." Bernie held his napkin to his mouth to get rid of the wax he'd been chewing. "Don't you, Fonteyn?"

Jack shrugged. "You're the expert." Then, looking at me, he

said, "I think we're going to make a writer out of Beryl. You ought to show Bernie your poems sometime, honey."

"I'd like nothing better," Bernie said, winking at me. I could feel my face turn red to the rims of my ears.

"Excuse me," I said, standing up, "I'm going to go read now."

"Someone's blushing," Mama said in a not very friendly voice.

I managed to get out of the room, but as I rounded the table I felt Bernie's eyes on me. It was a look, I decided as I lay on my bed, my heart pounding, just like Rhett gave Scarlett when she thought, "My goodness, it's as if he knew what I look like without my shimmy on."

————

The dark blue dust jacket of *The Brothers Karamazov* was a perfect fit for my copy of *Gone With the Wind*. Thus concealed, Margaret Mitchell's novel went often with me to the tree house. The next time Bernie came to the house — he was on the tennis court, hitting against the backboard — I lay on the platform with the book against my chest.

"Beryl O'Hara was not beautiful" (I thought this as though I were reading) "but men seldom realized it when caught by her charm as Bernard Hoffman was. In her face were too sharply blended the delicate features of her mother, a Coast aristocrat of French descent, and the heavy ones of her florid Irish father." For the particulars of Scarlett's face I substituted my own: "Titian blond hair bleached by the sun, brilliant white straight teeth, eyes that ranged from hazel to green, depending on her mood, a face that was perhaps a little too long."

Below me I could hear the steady rhythm of the ball against the backboard, and I knew just how Bernie looked as he switched easily from forehand to backhand, as graceful as a dancer. I imagined him in a black suit and ruffled white shirt as he approached me across a ballroom. "May I?" he said, but it wasn't really a question, he wouldn't take no for an answer, even though I was in mourning and everyone was shocked.

"Beryl!" Mama called. "Beryl Fonteyn! I thought I told you to set the table!" Then, in a flutey voice, "Bernie? Want a drink?"

"Yes, *ma'am*," Bernie called back in a pretend Southern way that gave me a little chill; it was almost as though he'd known what I'd been thinking.

I sat up, tucked in my shirt, and smoothed my hair. Then, with my book under my arm, I began the descent, stepping through air to the first branch, circling downward limb by familiar limb until I reached the steps. The top steps were always tricky going down so I hugged the trunk, digging my nails into the bark until I'd gotten down the first rung and could then hold onto it. Today this part was even more awkward than usual, because I could feel him watching me from the tennis court steps.

But I got to the second rung and the third and then my feet were confidently descending. I could see myself as he must, blue Keds, bare ankles, jeans, plaid shirt, hair that looked pretty decent today, thank goodness — I'd slept on rollers the previous night, as I'd known he was coming. On the fourth step I paused, trying to decide whether to turn and jump, as I'd done several times before with considerable grace. I inclined my head slightly in his direction — he *was* watching, and smiling. I pushed off from the tree — too soon, I instantly realized, I hadn't been ready — and as I tried to twist around, my foot caught in the step. I fell heavily, landing on my back.

I screamed, but no sound came out. I could feel my mouth open, trying to cry, and I heard him running toward me. I couldn't breathe, couldn't move; maybe my neck was broken. Then he was bending over me, touching my forehead, my wrist.

"Tell me what hurts," he said.

"Everything," I finally managed to say. "I couldn't breathe."

"You had the wind knocked out of you, poor baby. Your back hurt?"

I nodded.

"Can you move this?" He put a hand on one leg; I lifted it for him, and then, when he touched the other leg and said, "How about this?" I raised and lowered that one. We did the same with each arm. Then he knelt there awhile, looking at me with those beautiful worried brown eyes. He bent closer. Good night, was he going to kiss me? I closed my eyes and waited. He put his hands on me gently, covering both ears — my heart beat faster, this was better than anything I'd ever imagined — and turned my head slightly toward him. I opened my eyes to give him a dreamy look, but then he turned my head in the other direction.

"That hurt?"

"Yes!" I said, and began to cry.

"I don't know if you should be moved. Beatrice!" He stood up. "Don't move, sweetheart, I'll be right back."

Sweetheart. I put my hands on the sides of my head, where his had been, and pressed my arms against my chest.

Then he was there again with Mama, in her long-sleeved Japanese apron. She bent over me, looking worried and also guilty, I thought, for having yelled at me in such a mean way. I eased my hands to my waist and cried on quietly while she and Bernie decided what to do with me.

Mama wanted the two of them to take me in a fireman's carry, but Bernie didn't think I should sit. Mama went ahead to call the doctor, and Bernie bent down to scoop me up. "This yours?" he said, picking up my book.

"Yes," I said, reaching for it. The cover was partly off but he didn't seem to notice; I held the book against my chest as Bernie lifted me and carried me toward the house. He walked slowly, careful not to jounce. "You doing OK?" he asked. "Yes," I whispered, and leaned my head against his chest.

Going inside he had to shift me, so I helped by putting one arm around his neck. After we'd gone across the threshold I left my arm where it was; I could tell he didn't mind. He carried me through the kitchen — Mama, holding the telephone receiver, followed us with her eyes — and through the dining room to the living room, where he eased me onto the couch.

"Can I get you anything?" His gaze warmed me like a blanket.

"No," I said in a voice that was new to me, low and husky. "Thank you, though. Thank you so much."

I looked at his knees that were marked with crisscross lines from kneeling in the grass and at his strong, hairy calves. I noticed that the skin between the hairs was scaly. "You should use skin lotion," I said, and touched to show him where.

He jumped. "Your mother should be here in a minute."

I jerked back my hand and put it over my face. God, what must he think of me? "I thought I was dead," I whispered.

"Well, you're as alive as ever." He took my hand and moved it to one side, then made a funny face. "Lovely as ever, too," he said, giving my hand a little squeeze before he let it go.

"I'm *not* lovely. My face is too long."

He straightened. "Oh, no," he said, very decidedly, as though he'd already given this some thought — in days to come I replayed this sentence over and over in my mind — "you have a little Botticelli face."

"Huh? What's that?"

"Botticelli was a painter of the Italian Renaissance, famous for his lovely, long-faced girls. They all had long legs too, and graceful bodies. There's one painting in particular, *Primavera* — you're like a younger version of one of the three dancing Graces." Then he turned and left quickly, as though he'd said too much, and went to the dining room.

I lay there bathed in his words. Lovely, he had said, graceful.

Suddenly Mama was there, her face floating above me. I sat up, then stood.

"Well, Lady Lazarus, I gather we don't need to take you in?"

"No, I'm OK, I guess."

"I'll say. You look like the cat that swallowed the canary. Come on to dinner, then."

"I don't want any dinner," I said, giving her my coldest look. "I still don't feel all that well." Carrying my book, I stalked from the living room and through the dining room to the stairs.

The others were already at the table.

"Feeling better, honey?" Jack asked.

"A little better, thank you," I said. Though Bernie didn't speak, I could feel his gaze defining my profile.

Upstairs, I lay on my bed in a delicious haze until I heard Bernie leave.

It was dark by then. I turned off my light, got under the covers with my clothes on, and turned on the radio. As Fats Domino sang "I'm in Love Again," I imagined myself dancing at a school sock hop with Robert while Bernie, who had come as a chaperone, watched from the bleachers. I had on tight jeans, a shirt tied above my midriff, and bobby socks. The beat was fast, and our feet were quick and graceful. Robert spun me around and did all kinds of tricks — the quick arm slide, the slide under his legs, and then a high lift. By the end there was a circle of people around us; everyone, including Bernie, applauded.

The next song was the Platters' "Only You." This time I was in a blue organdy prom dress as I danced cheek to cheek with Robert. Bernie was watching from the bleachers again; he couldn't take his eyes off me. Finally he came over, tapped Robert's shoulder, and said to me, "May I?" When Robert had gone, Bernie whispered, "I just couldn't help it. . . . Do you mind?" "No," I whispered, putting my head on his chest. I could feel that his heart was beating as fast as mine.

I turned off the radio and pulled my clothes off under the covers. As I lay there with the sheets touching my skin all over, I went back to the afternoon, me on the grass and Bernie bending over me, his brown eyes so worried. "Beryl, sweetheart, are you all right?" His hands touched my face, smoothed my hair. I shut my eyes. I could feel his breath; then his lips touched mine, gently at first. I made a pair of lips out of two fingers and pressed them against my own. I ran my other hand down my neck, across my breast and stomach, to the top of one leg, then back up again, pausing at the nipple. Oh, Beryl. Bernie. The hand traveled slowly down again to the place between my legs. "Let's move this leg out a little, sweetheart," I heard him say. "Now the other." And then his hand was touching me, loving me, his lovely little Botticelli dancing girl.

––––

The day after Bernie's compliment I asked Jack if he had in his library any books about Botticelli.

In case he inquired about my interest, I was prepared. One day when I had been downtown with Mama in Belk's, I would tell him, and she was in the dressing room trying on girdles, I had seen Miss Cornette, my art teacher from last year. (Up to this point the story was mostly true, except it was a history teacher I had seen, at a distance.) Miss Cornette had oohed and aahed about how I'd blossomed over the summer and said I looked just like a Botticelli painting; naturally I wanted to know what she had been referring to.

If Jack should say that Bernie had mentioned the Botticelli resemblance to him, I would respond with, "Oh, yes, he said that to me, too. I had forgotten." Or should I say, "had almost forgotten"? Up to the last minute I hadn't worked out this detail, and I felt, after I'd put my question and Jack looked up from his newspaper, a moment of panic.

But he merely said, "Yes, I probably have something," and led me upstairs to his study, eager, as always, to respond to my intellectual curiosity.

While Jack jingled change in the pocket of his tennis shorts and scanned the shelves of art books, I sat in the chair at his desk.

"Here we go," he said, and brought over a large blue book with the title *Treasures of the Uffizi* printed on the cover in gold letters. He laid the book before me and opened it, beginning to turn pages with a moistened middle finger. Each color plate had a page of tissue covering it; his wet fingertip made a little mark on each one.

I remember liking the odor of the paper and the bright colors of the pictures, but the subjects at first disappointed me: nothing but madonnas and angels and a man in a red hat that Jack said was famous but I thought was the ugliest thing I'd ever seen.

Then Jack said, as he lifted and smoothed back a tissue, "Here's your man, Mr. Botticelli." It was just another madonna, but at least she was prettier than the others.

"Didn't he paint any dancers?" I asked.

"Dancers? Maybe you're thinking of someone else — Degas?" He turned to another Botticelli, this one of a woman carrying a man's head on a platter. *"Salome with the Baptist,"* Jack read.

I bent closer to get a look at the bearded head on the tray and at the woman. She was crazy-looking and not the least bit pretty.

"OK, here's *Primavera*," Jack said, turning the book sideways, "probably his best-known painting."

Primavera, that was it, the one with the dancing Graces, who looked like me. I remember my excitement as I tried to make out the picture through the tissue and then, when Jack unveiled it, the surprise I felt. It was obvious who the dancing Graces were — three women holding hands in a ring-around-the-rosy circle — but they were practically naked, wearing only see-through dresses. I looked more closely: at least you couldn't see everything.

Jack began to read the caption about where the painting had been done.

"Are these the dancing Graces?" I pointed to the middle one, who had reddish hair like mine.

"Yes, how did you know?"

"Does this one look like me?"

"Well, I guess maybe so, now that you mention it." I sensed Jack's eyes on me. I knew he was wondering.

"Miss Cornette, my art teacher, said I looked like a dancing Grace." I could feel myself blushing.

"Ah, Miss Cornette." I looked up at him, at his amused, disbelieving smile.

"I don't know, other people may have mentioned it, too."

"Uh-*huh*, I *see.*" Still smiling, he looked back at the picture.

I looked again, too, and realized that the middle dancer was looking right at a man in a red toga who had dark curly hair that was like Bernie's, only longer, and that a flying Cupid was aiming a dart right at that Grace's head. I held my breath, waiting for Jack to guess my secret.

"You *are* a pretty girl, Beryl, frizz and all." When he touched my hair, maimed by being chopped off and permanented, the warmth of his hand seemed to be healing it. "And you're really growing up, aren't you?"

He took away his hand, turned one more page, lifted one more veil.

"*The Birth of Venus,*" he announced. I was shocked: this girl standing on a seashell didn't have a stitch of clothes on. Except for the long hair she held between her legs and the hand that covered most of one breast, she was completely exposed.

"Now, this is who *I'd* say you look like — or are going to look like, in three or four years. She's even got your wistful expression, and the same color hair — but you'll have to let yours grow."

It suddenly seemed to me that this was a naked picture of me we were looking at. I felt my face growing red, and I wanted

Jack to shut the book, but he kept on looking. I was aware of his arm next to mine, the red hairs all going in the same direction, as though they'd been combed that way. "So graceful," he was saying. "She looks more like she's floating than standing." When I looked at her feet I saw that even they were like mine, with the second toes longer than the big ones: this embarrassed me more than anything else.

Jack closed the book gently and took it back to the shelf.

I stood up and we walked down the steps; there was an uneasy silence between us.

Jack got his tennis racket from the closet in the foyer. "Is Bernie coming over?" I said, then could have shot myself.

Jack gave me a quick glance. "Why do you ask?"

I was blushing again. What a dunce I was.

"A little old for you, isn't he, Beryl?"

"Who?" As if I didn't know what on earth.

"Of course he's not exactly a ladies' man."

"What do you mean?"

He bounced the racket against one hand, testing the strings. "Well, honey," he said, his mouth pulling to the side in something like a smile, "to put it bluntly, he's as queer as a two-dollar bill."

Fifteen

THAT AFTERNOON I called Eunice, planning at first to ask her what she knew about queers. By the time she came to the phone I had decided against it. She would only ask nosy questions, and besides Bernie wasn't queer anyway. He couldn't be; he was too interested in me.

For months Eunice had been saying she wanted to fix me up with Wayne's friend Zeke. So what I blurted out when she said hello was, "OK, if you're dying for me to meet Zeke, I will."

"It's about time you had a date," she said. When I said I wouldn't be allowed to go on an actual *date,* she said I should come to her house the following Saturday afternoon; Wayne and Zeke could just happen by.

As I left for her house on the appointed day, I told Mama and Jack that I was going to help Eunice with algebra, so not to expect me before dinnertime.

I had changed clothes a dozen times but finally ended up in the same jeans and shirt I'd worn the day Bernie called me a Botticelli girl. Eunice, however, who had on a yellow playsuit (in spite of the cool day), a matching ribbon on her ponytail, and bright red lipstick with nails to match, said I looked like something the cat dragged in. She had some shorts and a top that were too big for her, she said, but would probably fit me perfectly. We went upstairs to her room for the transformation. I was already nervous, and Eunice's criticism had made me more so. While she rummaged through her drawers, I stood in the middle of her room and thought about going home. But once I'd put on the white shorts, sleeveless red top, and white cinch belt I changed my mind. As I stood looking at myself in the mirror I arranged my legs with one leaning against the other, like Venus on her shell.

"Not bad," said Eunice, giving me a brief glance. She elbowed me aside, turning this way and that, smiling at herself over one shoulder.

We carried Eunice's record player down to what her family called the parlor and took the sheets off the red velvet love seat and matching chairs. While Eunice put on a record, I looked at myself in the mirror over the love seat. I didn't look nearly so good as I had in Eunice's mirror: my pimples showed up more, and my face was long and sallow. I surreptitiously wiped my damp underarms.

When Frogman Henry's "Ain't Got No Home" began to play, Eunice grabbed my hand and started dancing. We did the beach step that she had taught me, but my feet were always just a little behind and I couldn't seem to catch up. Frogman sang, first in his normal voice, then like a girl, about being lonely and without a home. He was singing like a frog when we heard the car in the driveway. I stopped dancing, but Eunice hissed, "Keep on," and dug her nails into my palm. The record started over.

There were footsteps on the porch, then a loud knock. My hand had grown so slippery in Eunice's it was hard to hold on. I heard the front door open. More footsteps. I didn't dare look up, but watched my feet and wished I had a ponytail that swung back and forth like Eunice's.

The song ended and Eunice looked sideways, as if by chance. "Oh, *hi*," she said.

They leaned against the doorframe, one on each side, Wayne

— I knew him from the pictures in Eunice's wallet — grinning, and Zeke, scrunched down and looking across the room through the side window, as if something of great interest was taking place outside. He was thin and not very tall, with a face pockmarked by acne scars; his black hair was combed back in a scraggly d.a.

Eunice sashayed across the room. "Hey, y'all." When Zeke turned to look at her, his glance swept the room, taking me in as if by chance.

"Hi, princess." Wayne pulled Eunice's ponytail, then hugged her neck with one arm, so that her face was against his chest.

She giggled and ducked back. "This is Beryl," she said, turning and waving me forward.

I edged a little closer as the two boys looked at me, then at each other.

"Well?" Eunice said.

"Deep subject," Wayne said. He and Zeke both snickered. I felt ugly and miserable.

As we walked outside I tried to think of something to talk about, but I couldn't even remember what sports season it was.

Wayne's car was large, black, and low-slung, with woven straw seat covers that prickled my legs when I slid in the back. I sat next to my window, and Zeke by his.

Wayne backed the car out of the drive and turned down the road in the direction away from my house.

"Where are we going?" I said. "I have to get home soon."

Wayne looked at me in the mirror. "Oh, just this little place I know. Don't worry, Zeke won't bite." He turned the radio up loud: Buddy Holly singing "Peggy Sue."

I glanced at Zeke. He was staring straight ahead with his hands on his knees.

"You go to high school?" I asked.

"Did last year," he said, turning. "Waste of time."

"Really?" I was shocked, but also slightly thrilled.

"Yeah, I got a job laying brick. Saving up to buy me a car. How old are you, anyway?" he asked, glancing at my legs.

"Going on fifteen," I said, adding a year.

"Yeah? I woulda said sixteen, maybe seventeen." He put one arm on the back of the seat and began drumming his fingers in time with the music. I took this as a sign that he liked me since his arm was reaching in my direction, but then he took it back and replaced the hand on his knee. I noticed he wore an identification bracelet on that wrist; I could not make out the initials.

When we turned onto a gravel road winding through thick woods, I realized this must be the lovers' lane Eunice had told me about. My heart started to beat faster, whether from excitement or fear I would not have been able to say.

The car slowed, then stopped. "Where are we?" I asked. No one answered.

We sat a few moments in silence. Wayne and Eunice started kissing, right there in broad daylight. Wayne glanced at me again in the mirror; then he and Eunice began whispering. Zeke looked out my window, but every once in a while I saw his gaze drop to my legs. I looked down at my legs, too, my shiny tan knees.

"Nice day for a walk," Wayne said. He turned to wink at Zeke. "Me and Eunice'll be back in a few minutes."

Eunice didn't look at me as she slid out. She and Wayne walked down the road and soon were out of sight behind trees.

Zeke edged a little closer. I wiped my damp hands on the car seat.

"Do you have any hobbies?" I said.

"I like to work on cars." He studied his hand, the one closest to me, as if he didn't know what it might do. "What kind of car do you like?"

"Convertibles."

"Convertibles!" He grinned, showing me his upper gums. "What are you, a daddy's girl?"

"No."

"I bet you are. I bet you're a daddy's girl."

"I am not. My daddy was killed."

"Whoops!" He grabbed one of his feet and lifted it toward his open mouth. "Open mouth, insert foot."

"That's all right," I said. "I do it all the time."

He took a cigarette from his shirt pocket, lit it, and offered it to me. I shook my head. While he smoked I began to babble on about all the stupid things I'd said in my life. "Once I sat next to a boy at a swimming pool who looked like he had six toes on his foot, and I asked him how he *did* that. It turned out he was just born that way."

He put his cigarette out in the ashtray and studied his right hand some more, turning it back and forth so that the silver bracelet winked in the light.

"What are your initials?" I said.

He held his hand toward me in a fist so I could read the bracelet: ZMS.

"Zeke what?"

"Settlemyre's the last name. You'll never guess the middle one."

"Michael?"

"No." He put his arm on the back of the seat and slid closer.

"Mark?" He didn't look so bad close up; he had really nice brown eyes.

"Noooo. One more try."

"What if I don't get it?" The flirtatiousness of my voice surprised me.

"You'll have to pay." His eyes were on my mouth, and his tongue darted out to moisten his lips.

"Methuselah."

"Wrong," he whispered, and bent toward me. I shut my eyes, thinking, This is *it*, this is *it*, and then was shocked by his tongue against my mouth. I drew back, but he put both arms around me and kissed me again, his lips closed this time. At first I was mainly aware of his startling closeness — the large pores of his skin, his fluttering eyelids — but then I closed my eyes. His lips were soft at first, then pressed harder; he ran his fingers up and down my arm in a way that made me tingle all over. "You're nice," he whispered, kissing my face, then my ear. I inhaled the smells of him: hair oil, deodorant, the faint margarine odor of his skin. When he put his tongue in my ear, I felt embarrassed — probably it was waxy, I never washed my ears — but then I forgot when he hugged me tighter and I could feel my breasts against him and his heart going fast. He was kissing me again when the car door opened. We both jumped.

"Well, hot dog!" Eunice shouted. "Beryl's finally been kissed!"

We took the long way home, Eunice snuggled next to Wayne in front, me with my head on Zeke's shoulder. I was shivering with cold now that the sun was going down, but Zeke rubbed my right arm and leg to keep me warm. He also kissed me a few more times, and I kissed back, beginning to feel like an expert.

It was dark by the time we got to my house. I didn't know Jack was in the driveway until he shone his flashlight in at us.

Zeke and I sprang apart. My heart thudded as Jack opened the door and pulled me out. The door slammed and the car sped away, throwing gravel.

Jack trained the flashlight on my face. His hand was tight on my upper arm. "Where have you been?" he hissed. "Who were those hoodlums?"

"I was at Eunice's," I said, "and those weren't hoodlums!"

"We called Eunice's," he said. "You'd been gone an hour." The light traveled down to the red shirt, the shorts, my bare legs. "What is this getup?"

He jerked me forward and began to walk me across the yard. "You have some explaining to do, young lady." I was crying by the time we went into the house. He pushed me through the kitchen and into his and Mama's bedroom.

Mama was at her desk typing. She looked up through a cloud of cigarette smoke as we came in.

"Here she is," Jack said. "That Whitaker girl and a couple of thugs brought her home, lying about where they've been. And just look at her, flaunting around in tight shorts when it's fifty degrees outside."

"I wasn't lying," I shouted. "We were at Eunice's — then we went to the dairy bar."

"Dairy bar, my eye. *You* talk to her, Beatrice, or by God, I will." Jack went out and slammed the door.

Mama lit a new cigarette off her old one. "Well, miss, what *have* you been up to?"

"I was just at Eunice's doing algebra like I said and Wayne happened to come over with this other boy and we went to the dairy bar. That's all, honest." Tears came to my eyes.

Mama sighed. She looked like she might believe me.

"Jack has no right to call me a liar. He's not even my father."

Mama's face hardened. "He's the only real father you've ever had. He's upset because he cares about you. I promise you, Jack would never write you off the way your 'dear daddy' wrote you off."

The tears froze on my face. "What do you mean, wrote me off?"

"What do you mean, what do I mean? You know very well what I mean."

We stared at each other a few moments, then I turned and walked to my room. I wasn't going to think about it. I got into bed in the dark with my clothes on and willed myself to sleep.

Sixteen

"IT HAPPENED!" I wrote in my journal. "My first kiss.
Kisses, I should say. His initials are Z.M.S. and he's incredibly
handsome, not to mention crazy about me."

I shut the journal and looked out through the yellowing
leaves of the Osage orange. The light had changed in a way that
felt like fall. I thought that must be why I was melancholy in
spite of having a boyfriend and in spite of Bernie (who had
whistled at me in my tennis dress) playing on the court below.

It was a Sunday morning. Mama had taken Stevie to the
Catholic church in town, a whim she'd decided to indulge, she
told Jack, since Stevie asked so little for himself.

Jack had hardly spoken to me this morning, even though I'd
put on the tennis dress and hit some balls against the backboard,
as if I might want a lesson. But when he and Bernie came onto
the court, all Jack had said to me was "Fore!" — meaning I
should move out of the way when he served.

I lay on the platform and, shutting my eyes, thought about
having a heart-to-heart talk with Bernie. Even if he was queer
(and I wasn't altogether sure what that meant) he obviously
cared about me. I could tell him how mean Jack was — I had
a feeling he'd understand. Probably he'd understand about
other things too. I imagined talking to him about Daddy, how

he'd written me off because he had a new family. "You poor baby," Bernie would say, looking at me with those worried brown eyes. When I began to cry, he'd put his arm around me and tell me to go ahead, cry it all out.

Tears were running down my face when I heard below me, "Beryl! Hey, Beryl!"

I blotted my face on my sleeve, sat up, and looked over the edge of the platform.

There was Eunice dressed in church clothes and grinning up in my direction. "Guess what?" she said, drawing out the *what.*

"Wait a minute," I said. Putting my journal under my arm, I hurried down so she wouldn't say anything in front of Jack.

"Oh, I know what you've been writing," she said in a too loud voice, trying to snatch the book from beneath my arm.

"Let's go up to my room," I said. I could tell by the silence on the court that Jack and Bernie were between points and looking our way.

I turned and walked quickly toward the house. Eunice hobbled after me in her straight skirt and high heels. "Hey, wait up!" she yelled. "What's eating you, anyway?"

In the house, Eunice wanted to make a detour to look at the naked statue in the living room, but I steered her upstairs. "This is the *weirdest* house," she had to say as we went up the winding metal steps.

In my room, Eunice and I lay crossways on the bed, our heads hung over the edge to help our complexions, while Eunice reported on last night's phone conversation with Wayne (the mushiest ever, she said, he'd almost asked her to wear his ring); then she said Wayne said Zeke liked me and he wondered if I liked him, too. He wanted to date me, in fact.

For a fraction of a second I let myself feel excited. I think I even screamed. Then I imagined Jack's reaction, and what Mama would say when she actually saw Zeke. If they found out he was a dropout, they'd have a fit. "I don't know," I said, "my stepfather's pretty strict. He was furious about last night."

Eunice was prepared for this: she already had a plan. Her mother could take us to the movies next Saturday night, just drop us off and come back later, and we could meet the boys in the balcony.

Privately I thought Jack would see through this scheme, even if Eunice's mother could not. I said maybe I could spend the weekend with my grandparents in town and meet Eunice and the boys at the show Saturday afternoon. I wasn't sure how I could arrange this visit without arousing suspicions. Maybe I could say I wanted to go to church with Grandpa and Grandmuddy. Mama couldn't say no to that now. I figured I could work out the details later.

Eunice agreed to the general plan and then started talking about Wayne again — when he might give her his ring, why he hadn't up to now, blah blah blah.

As we went downstairs I heard Jack in the kitchen fixing lunch; when we went outside I saw Bernie still on the court practicing his serve.

"Hey," I said to Eunice, "want me to tell your fortune? I can predict anything from an Osage orange, including whether or not a boy is going to ask you to go steady."

Eunice said sure and followed me across the grass to the court. I walked more slowly this time, out of consideration for Eunice's high heels and also — in case Bernie looked up and saw us — so I wouldn't look like I was in any kind of hurry.

Eunice and I sat down on the tennis court steps. I picked up an Osage orange from the grass and broke it open on the step, then studied the stringy pulp with its flat brown seeds.

"Well, come on," Eunice said. "Is he going to?"

"It depends on how many seeds fall out, and whether it's an odd or even number." I hit the Osage orange again, split side down, and whispered a chant, *"Mene mene tekel upharsin.* Eight seeds," I told her, "The answer is very probably yes."

When Eunice cheered, Bernie looked toward us and waved.

Eunice waved back and giggled. "He's cute," she said.

"I hate to tell you, Eunice, but he's kind of got a crush on me."

"Oh yeah?" Eunice did her hands like binoculars to get a better look at him. "Here, let me have that thing, we'll see if he does really." She hit the Osage orange on the step and three seeds fell out. "Nope — sorry." Then she held it to her nose. "Oooh, gross. You know what my cousin calls these things?" she whispered. "Cum balls."

"Huh?"

"Cum," she giggled in my ear, "the stuff that comes out of a boy's whangdoodle."

We were giggling and smelling the Osage orange when Bernie came over. He grinned down at us as if he wanted to be let in on the joke.

"Here," Eunice said, holding up the split Osage orange. "What do you think this smells like?"

Bernie took the Osage orange, held it to his nose, and inhaled. "Hmm," I don't know. It's a strange odor — strange, but familiar."

Eunice began to splutter; I did, too. We laughed so hard that tears ran down our faces. Then, as Eunice and I staggered to our feet, Bernie's gaze sobered me. His eyes were cold, not at all amused. Oh God — the realization went right through me — he thinks I'm a *child*. It also occurred to me as I followed Eunice across the yard that he thought I'd been laughing at him; he would hate me now.

"See ya," I told Eunice at the top of the drive; I wanted her to hurry so I could go apologize.

But Eunice wasn't ready to leave. "Strange but familiar!" she gurgled, bending over and holding her stomach like she was going to be sick.

"Shut up," I said.

She straightened, wiping her face. "What's the matter with *you*?"

"There's such a thing as hurting people's feelings."

"What are you talking about? You're just a sour grape, Beryl, no fun at all. This is what I mean about why you're not popular." And she flounced recklessly down the drive in her high heels.

"You're wrong," I yelled after her. "That's not what sour grape means. And it's grapes, not grape, you stupid idiot."

She whirled around. "Go to the hot place!"

I laughed, loud and mean. "The hot place? You mean Florida?"

"*The hot place,*" she screamed.

"You mean hell? Say what you mean!"

"We don't talk like that in our family. We don't talk like a bunch of filthy atheist commies."

"Oh, yeah? What about cum and whangdoodle? But you won't say a normal little word like *hell?* That's ignorant, Eunice, that's why people like you are called ignorant hicks."

Eunice picked up a rock and flung it, then turned and ran down the drive. She hadn't even bothered to see if the rock had hurt me; she didn't even care.

I ran to the house, trying to keep back tears until I got to my room. As I went through the dining room where Bernie and Jack were sitting at the table I turned my face from them, but Jack said in a sarcastic voice, "What's the matter, trouble in loveland?" Running up the steps, I heard Jack say something about hoodlums.

I flung myself on my bed and sobbed. No one understood, no one cared, I didn't have anyone in the world to talk to. It wasn't my fault I had to live in this place with no one but hicks for friends, it wasn't my fault I had a stepfather instead of a real father.

I sat up, suddenly so furious the room went dark. I ran to my jewelry box and snatched out Daddy's Christmas card and the three postcards. A growling noise rose from my throat as I tore the cards to bits. I reached under my bed, snatched out my knapsack and stuffed the ripped cards in it, then pulled out the box that had Daddy's records inside. I tried to break a record over my knee, but it wouldn't crack; I shoved the records in the knapsack and zipped it up.

With the knapsack on my back, I ran down the steps and through the dining room past Jack and Bernie. "Beryl?" Jack called. I slammed the door, ran to the shed by the driveway, and got out Stevie's bike.

I was down the drive before anyone could come out and stop me. My legs were too long for Stevie's bike and they stuck out to the sides but it didn't matter, I pedaled so hard the wind blurred my eyes and the trees flashed by. On the hills I stood up and pumped until I had a stitch in my side, but I didn't stop to rest, didn't slow down, until I got to the dump.

There was a family at the dump throwing in their week's garbage. I hid behind a tree and watched them: a fat mother and father and three fat, stupid-looking little brats, all in church clothes. They were probably so dumb they'd gone all the way to church with their smelly trash right inside the car. The father looked especially stupid, with his big fat bald head and big belly that he thought was hidden under the shiny suit jacket.

When they rattled away in their old green car, I jumped back on the bike and wheeled toward the dump. As I went past, I pulled off the knapsack and flung it in, not even bothering to see where it landed.

Seventeen

THE DATE with Zeke was almost frighteningly easy to arrange.

I wanted to go to church, too, I told Mama. Why couldn't Stevie and I just spend the whole weekend with Grandpa and Grandmuddy? We hardly ever got to see them anymore. Mama readily agreed; she and Jack could use the time alone, she confided.

The plan was to meet Eunice in the Carolina Theatre on Saturday afternoon; then she and I would go to the balcony, where the boys would be waiting.

Stevie was the only fly in the ointment. He wanted to go to the movies with me, and Grandmuddy insisted it was only fair. So I had to let him in on the secret and pay him five dollars (plus comic book and milkshake money) to leave the theater as soon as Grandpa's car pulled away and go to the drugstore on the corner for the next two hours.

Eunice rarely stayed mad for long, and we had too much in common just now for our friendship to be over. But I was relieved when I saw her in the lobby and she said, "Want to use my lipstick?" It felt like a truce. After we went to the ladies' room we went upstairs to find Zeke and Wayne.

The balcony was so dark that Eunice and I had to stand a

moment to let our eyes adjust. Then we saw them, up near the top behind a railing. Wayne was waving, but Zeke stared at the newsreel as if he hadn't even noticed we'd come in. Eunice and I climbed the steps and slipped easily, like missing pegs, into the seats the boys had left between them.

Zeke was on my left, which I was glad of because it was my best side. "Hiya," he said, hardly glancing at me. He smelled strongly of after-shave and was wearing a long-sleeved white shirt. I liked the way his neck looked above the collar.

"Here," he said, pulling a package of candy from his shirt pocket without looking at me. "I hope you like Junior Mints." The package was warm from having been against him; I opened it and put a mint on my tongue, letting the chocolate melt slowly.

First there was a Woody Woodpecker cartoon (Zeke and Wayne made woodpecker noises throughout), then the main feature, *The Eddy Duchin Story,* which I later gave four stars in my journal in spite of having seen almost none of it.

Eunice and Wayne began kissing the moment the movie started. I could see them from the corner of my eye. Zeke put his arm on our shared armrest and leaned toward me. At first our arms were barely touching, then he leaned some more and we were joined, shoulder to elbow. I stared unseeing at the screen, paralyzed by the delicious sensations in my arm and entire left side. I was having trouble deciding what to do with my hands. Keeping them loose in my lap felt too obvious, but when I folded my arms across my middle he couldn't very easily get hold of one. Finally he put his right hand on his knee and edged the knee close to mine, so I slid my hand into position on my knee where he could reach it.

And then, he did.

My whole body warmed as his hand kneaded mine. I looked blindly ahead, mesmerized by the electric messages up my arm, and by the suspense of what next.

Abruptly he coughed and jerked away his hand to cover his

mouth. My hand felt abandoned for a moment, but then his arm went around my shoulder and he pulled me toward him. I put my head on his shoulder, on an uncomfortable bone, then moved down to the edge of his chest. I could hear his heart going, almost a familiar sound to me now, and I raised my head a little, to help out. Popcorn crunched beneath his feet as he shifted, and then we were kissing.

Throughout the movie we kissed, and I was in a trance. His lips were closed at first, but then his tongue dabbed gently — almost politely, it seemed — at my mouth. When I let my lips open, his tongue pushed in and explored everywhere, even my teeth — I was glad they were clean. Then with the tip of his tongue he outlined my lips in a way that made me go limp. "Oh, Zeke," I whispered. I wanted to say I loved him, but knew better: he should say it first. I saw him glance quickly around us. Then his hand settled on my breast, shakily, as if he thought I'd say no, but I didn't. It felt wonderful. I began to do what he'd taught me with my tongue and after a while his fingers inched toward an opening in my dress. One trembling finger went in, touched bare skin, drew back as if it had been burned, but I let him know it was all right by undoing one button.

When the lights came on, I sat stunned, staring at the empty screen. Only when we got up did I glance at Zeke. His shirt collar, I noticed, had lipstick on it, and the skin around his mouth was red; probably mine looked the same. I was wet between the legs, and ashamed. What must he think of me? Following Eunice and Wayne and holding Zeke's hand, I stumbled down the steep steps of the balcony, then down the carpeted steps and into the lobby, past the popcorn machine and velvet ropes.

At the door, Zeke squeezed my hand and let go. "See ya, babe," he said, and without looking at me, went out by himself. Though this was just as we'd planned, I felt like crying.

I stepped outside into the shocking light of Saturday afternoon. I stood a moment staring at the posters of coming attractions, the grimy ticket booth, the crowd of people, the traffic in the street. Then I saw Grandpa's car at the curb and Stevie's scared face looking out at me through the back window. The stupid little rat. Why hadn't he had the sense to come inside to wait?

I walked toward the car, beginning to work up an excuse — Stevie had decided he didn't like the movie after all, so I'd let him go out early — when Eunice, standing at the edge of the crowd with Wayne and Zeke, yelled, "Bye, Beryl!" I saw Grandpa hunch down to see who had called my name; then he kept on looking.

My hands were shaking when I opened the car door. "Those are just some neighbors," I said. "I just happened to run into them."

Grandpa turned to stare at me, but he said nothing.

All the way back to Grandpa and Grandmuddy's house, I watched the back of Grandpa's neck and what I could see of his profile — the clenched jaw, the ragged eyebrow. I had heard stories from Mama about canings in her youth; I expected no less.

When we got to the house, Grandpa went into his study with his Bible and slammed the door. I quizzed Stevie: Grandpa had found him in the drugstore, and Stevie had told him about everything except Zeke and Wayne. I tried to get my five dollars back, but he had spent most of it and lost the rest in the street. "You'll pay for this," I promised him.

For supper there was crackling cornbread, turnip greens, and turnips: punishment enough, I thought, staring down at my plate while I waited for the blessing.

"Heavenly Father," Grandpa began in a wavery voice. His head was more deeply bowed than usual, and he clutched, on the table, his knife and fork. "Almighty God . . ." I glanced at Grandmuddy. Her closed eyes were fluttering a little, as they always did, and her face was peaceful; he hadn't told her yet. "I beseech Thee, cast Your all-seeing eyes upon this wicked, wayward girl . . ." Grandmuddy's eyes flew open; I quickly shut mine. ". . . and give her Your help, Lord. Remind her of the terrible dangers of prevarication and lust," he went on, his voice rising, "let her know how slippery is the slope into the pit of carnality, that hole that has no bottom, that hellfire, that brimstone — "

"Good heavens, Beau," Grandmuddy said, glancing at me, "what has she done?"

"She lied. She went to that picture show with . . . *boys*." Droplets of spit fanned out from Grandpa's mouth. "The trashiest-looking white boys I have ever seen. And she hooked her brother in on her scheme. I found him down at Johnson's Pharmacy gorging his eyes on funnies."

"Is this true, Beryl?" Grandmuddy's eyes were level on me.

"They are *not* trash. They're nice boys, friends of Eunice's, and we just happened to run into them. Cross my heart and hope to die."

"I've a good mind to give her a switching," Grandpa said.

"You'll do no such thing," Grandmuddy said. "This is for her mother to handle."

"Her mother can't handle doodly squat, that's the whole problem. I'll tell you one thing, girl — look at me!" I fixed my eyes on the wall above Grandpa's head. "There better not be any such carryings-on again. And meantime, your stepfather is going to hear about this."

———

When Jack and Mama came to pick us up the next afternoon they already knew; I could tell by the way they held their faces away from me. On the drive home, Stevie and I stared out our windows. No one spoke.

When we went in the house, Jack said, "You get upstairs. You and I have some talking to do."

I sat on the edge of my bed and waited, my heart thumping hard.

Jack came in and shut the door.

"I want to talk to my mother," I said.

"Let's get one thing straight." He pulled the dressing table chair close to me and sat down. "This is my house, I am your father. Now tell me the truth, or there'll be trouble. How many times have you seen this boy?"

"Just twice."

"What did he do to you?"

"What do you mean?"

"You know what I mean. I mean this." He reached out and rubbed his thumb hard against my mouth. "And this," he said. He flicked his hand across my breast.

"Stop it!" I said, hitting out at him. He caught my wrist and held it.

"You can't go with boys like that, Beryl. They've got one thing on their minds." He tapped a finger on my wrist. "You may not see him again."

"NO!" I yelled. I tried to jerk back my hand but he held tight. "I hate you!"

"Oh, that's a fine thing." He dropped my hand as he stood. "After I take you in, after I pick up the pieces. Maybe I shouldn't even bother." He walked out of the room and slammed the door, then opened it again. "I'll be in my study," he said, "if you see fit to apologize."

I remember how I sat looking into my room, remember how thin the air seemed. I remember how I stood already feeling nothing and walked down the hall to his study: because I thought I had no choice.

I knocked and went in. He was sitting at his desk, his back toward me, gazing out the window. From the angle of his head I thought he was looking into the Osage orange tree. I had a sudden vision of myself there on the platform, my sad face among the leaves.

"I'm sorry," I said.

He turned and looked at me. "I accept your apology," he

said. He stood and walked toward me, his face changing as he came closer. "I'm just trying to help you, honey. You know that, don't you?"

I nodded.

"Tell me why," he said.

"Because you're my father."

"That's right. Why else?"

"I don't know."

"Because I love you, silly goose." He put his hands on my shoulders and shook me. His eyes were shiny with tears. "You love your Jack?"

I nodded.

"That's my girl." He pulled me toward him and hugged me against his chest. I could feel the warmth of his skin beneath the tennis shirt. "Everything's going to be all right, Beryl," he whispered, kissing the top of my head. "You'll see."

———

That night during dinner the phone rang. Jack went to answer it in the kitchen. "Beryl!" he called.

I went into the kitchen. Jack held out the phone. "Tell him," he mouthed.

I took the phone and said, "Hello, Zeke. I can't go out with you anymore. My father won't let me."

"Good girl," Jack said when I hung up. "I know that was hard."

I walked back through the dining room toward the stairs.

"I'm sorry, Beryl," Mama said, trying to catch my arm as I went past.

"It doesn't matter," I said, and it didn't. I walked up the stairs; nothing mattered at all.

Eighteen

THAT WINTER Jack went into the honey business, and he made me his partner. Since the bees made more honey than we could eat or he could give away, I might as well profit from the excess, he said. I could do anything I liked with the money — save it for college, even blow it all on clothes if I wanted to. I knew without his telling me that this was my consolation for giving up Zeke.

Mama said it was unfair that I should get all the money and Stevie none. Jack scoffed at that: how could she think of Stevie going near the bees, after all that hullaballoo over stings? And this enterprise was to be based on the Little Red Hen principle; only she who worked would profit.

Though I liked the idea of getting the money — I had visions of a sumptuous wardrobe — I wasn't altogether enthusiastic about the honey business at first. I didn't like doing something that made Mama mad, and I didn't want to get too near the bees either because I had my own fears about getting stung. But Jack said I could start out by helping strain and bottle the honey and doing the bookkeeping. And — this would be the most fun, he promised — I could write up some interesting facts about bees to give our customers; not only would I learn a lot from doing these flyers, but it would be the best kind of advertisement we could have.

Our first task was to choose a name. I proposed Minding Our Beeswax. Mama in a sarcastic voice suggested King Bee, to which Jack's only response was that I could do a flyer called "Feminism in the Hive." The early writers had actually thought the colonies were run by kings, and the discovery of queen bees was truly a fascinating subject, he said, with an angry look at Mama. Jack's idea was The Sweet Bee Apiary, especially appropriate for us, he said, since writers in ancient Greece and Rome were called sweet bees. I agreed that would be the best name; Jack said Minding Our Beeswax would be perfect for a newsletter, if we decided to do one later on.

Jack and I went to the printer to pick up the labels he had ordered. They said "Sweet Bee Apiary" in fancy type, with the address and phone number underneath. That same day we went to Raleigh to buy mason jars at a wholesale place he knew about.

After we left Blacksboro we rode awhile in silence. I looked out my window at the passing scenery but occasionally I felt his glance upon me. I knew he had something to say.

"I'm sorry I had to do that about that boy," he finally began. "I imagine you must still be feeling blue."

I shrugged. I had actually mourned Zeke very little.

"You'll thank me some day," he said. "He was just all wrong for you. You can't get started out on the wrong foot like that. This may sound snobbish to you now, but you need to go out with boys from good families — well-educated, smart boys."

When I didn't respond he said, "I guess you're still pretty mad at me."

"I don't know."

"Well, if you are, that's normal. I remember how mad I used to get at my parents — my father, especially."

I fixed my eyes on a tobacco barn and kept it in my vision as long as I could without moving my head.

"I used to think I hated his guts. I even wished he would die. And then he did die, quite suddenly. I wasn't much older than you."

I looked at him. "What did he die of?"

"Influenza," he said, turning as he felt my stare.

"I'm sorry."

"Thank you, honey." He reached across the seat for my hand. "So, you see, I know what it's like to lose a father. I truly feel for you, sweetie," he said with a sad smile. "And I want you to know, whatever kind of scrape you get in, I'm always here. You can talk to me about anything, OK?" He gave my fingers a squeeze.

"OK," I said. I took his hand and squeezed back. It was true, I thought, he really does understand.

———

Jack and I bottled the honey using Mama's pots and sieves and made such a mess of the kitchen that she complained for days. Though he didn't actually build it until the next year, that's when Jack got the idea of the honey house, a shed where we could bottle and store honey as well as keep supplies. And we were going to need a lot more supplies, he said, a honey extractor for one thing, for those sissies who didn't like their honey in the comb, and thermometers, pollen traps, mouse and skunk guards, a swarm catcher, a filing cabinet, a cashbox, maybe even a safe.

My first flyer was "Bees in History." It included, from Jack's lectures, facts such as Assyrians burying their dead in honey, and Aristophanes using beeswax to seal his love letters, and, from a book Jack gave me to read, a description of how, in 1670, Swammerdam of Holland determined the sex of the queen bee by dissection. "Though that was a great advance," I wrote, "Swammerdam did not figure everything out. He thought the queens were fertilized by the 'odoriferous effluvia' of the drones; it was many more years before the nuptial flight of the queen was discovered."

Jack thought this was so well written that he had several hundred printed for our customers, and he also encouraged me to submit it to my school newspaper as a feature article. I was surprised and proud when it was published.

Mama worked hard on her novel that winter. Often when I got home from school she was still typing; sometimes she didn't come out of her room until Jack or I called her to dinner. I remember how her eyes looked after writing — calm and mysterious, as though she'd been asleep and dreamed something beautiful. I didn't mind Mama working late, not even when I had to start supper, not even when she was grouchy. I could tell that underneath the grouchiness Mama was happy; for a time, I thought she was happy in a way that would last.

In March, Mama sent the first part of her manuscript to Bernie's editor. Jack took her to the post office; Stevie and I went along to help celebrate. During the drive Mama read us, to my surprise, her summary of the novel: "*The Book of Night* tells the story of Ruth Haighherra, a young American girl born to missionary parents, as she grows up in prewar Japan. The title has reference to the hellfire and brimstone sermons of the father, Job Haighherra, as well as to the shadows of the coming conflict."

"Is Job Grandpa?" I asked.

"Of course not. This is fiction. Besides, it doesn't matter. Grandpa doesn't read."

"What about Grandmuddy?"

She shrugged. "Probably she won't read it either. But maybe she'll finally be proud of me, if I get my name in the paper."

Two weeks later the manuscript came back.

When I got home from school that day Jack was in the kitchen chopping vegetables for soup.

"Where's Mama?" I said. Jack almost never cooked.

"In her room," he said in a low voice. He looked worried. "Is she sick?"

Jack nodded toward the letter lying on the counter. I picked it up and read it. "This is well written, indeed, but it is not, alas, for us. Please try us with your next book."

"Oh, no," I said. I strained my ears to hear Mama crying in her room: nothing but silence.

Jack's eyes met mine. "It's too bad, but I must say I was expecting something like this. I told her it wasn't ready." He shook his head and went on chopping. "She doesn't seem to know the meaning of revise."

Bernie thought Mama should send the book to another editor he knew, or to his agent, but she put the book away in her desk drawer. For weeks afterward, when I came home from school she would be sitting on the sofa in the living room or at the dining room table staring into space. One afternoon I heard her sobbing in her room; she did not come out for supper.

That night I had trouble sleeping, thinking of Mama's bad time at Grandpa and Grandmuddy's house. The next day, riding home from the grocery store, I said, "Mama, I wish you'd work on your book some more."

"Why?" she snapped.

"You're so sad all the time. If you worked on it some more, I bet you could get it published."

"How the hell do you know what I'm sad about?"

"Well, I just thought — "

"If you must know, it's Jack. He's having a flaming affair with that bitch."

"What bitch?"

"Mackey Tull." Mama screeched the car to a stop at a red light and looked at me angrily, as though I'd just been pretending not to know.

"He is not," I said, my heart beating faster; I feared it might be true. He will leave us, too, I remember thinking.

"There's a lot you don't know, Miss Priss — like all the times he claims to be at his office but doesn't answer the phone — "

"Maybe he goes out to eat."

"Not by himself." Mama glared at me. "He never goes out to eat by himself."

The car behind us honked. As our car lurched forward, Mama said, "I found a letter, a billet-doux."

"That he wrote?"

"That *she* wrote — but it makes it all very clear. I'll show you if you don't believe me."

"No."

"No what?"

I turned to look out the window.

"No what?" she shouted.

"I don't want to see the goddamned letter."

"You watch your mouth, young lady." She reached to slap me and missed. The car veered onto the shoulder and shimmied. A mailbox careened toward us; I screamed and covered my eyes. But then the car jolted back onto the road, and with all four tires humming levelly on the pavement, we drove the rest of the way home in silence.

————

Not long afterward Mama came down with a virus — the same one Jack and Stevie had had, but hers lingered on. She began to think she had mononucleosis or something worse, but the doctors that Jack took her to could not diagnose what was wrong. Jack decided Mama's illness was in her head, but Mama swore that wasn't so: no one could *make* their body have a fever, she said, or cause their bones to hurt so much they felt like they were breaking, or give themselves such an awful thirst that their spit tasted salty. She spent a lot of time on a heating pad in bed, usually reading or staring up at the ceiling, though sometimes I found her frowning into a small magnifying mirror as she peeled away bits of skin from the edges of her chapped mouth or tweezed her eyebrows until the skin between them was red and swollen. I hated the way she looked, with her hair so greasy and limp that the back of her head seemed flat, and the way she smelled, in the nightgown and dirty pink bed jacket she wore day after day. I also hated her heating pad with its hot rubbery odor and — when she raised up and asked me to move it to a different spot — the wires I could feel beneath its cover like veins.

Stevie camped outside Mama's door. When Jack drove him outside, he sat beneath her window, drawing in the dirt with a stick. One night he woke me up, crawling into my bed. "Mama's going to die," he whispered.

"No she's not," I said, even though my stomach gave a little lurch. "Don't be ridiculous. Now get out of here and don't wake me up again."

In the morning I found Stevie asleep on my floor and for days after that when I awoke, there he was curled up on my rug. I learned to be careful when I stepped out of bed.

One day in the car Jack told me he was worried that Mama was becoming seriously depressed, as she had been when they met. He was thinking of trying to persuade her to see a psychiatrist again.

"What about Mackey Tull?" I dared to ask.

"What about her?"

"Mama said you were having an affair."

Jack stared straight ahead. "She shouldn't be talking to you like that."

"You're not going to leave us, are you?"

He was silent a moment. When he finally looked at me, he said, "I wouldn't leave you for a million bucks."

The next day Mama called me into her room.

"Sit down, Beryl," she said, patting a spot beside her on the bed. I sat. "Jack said he'd never see Mackey Tull again, isn't that wonderful?" Tears welled up in her eyes. "He said there wasn't anything between them anyway — that letter was just a joke —

but he told me he wouldn't see her at all anymore if it would make me feel better."

"That's great, Mama."

"He said you'd talked to him."

I nodded.

"Thank you, darling," she said. "Come here." As she reached to hug me I could see the long hair beneath her arms and the nipples under her flimsy blue gown, and for a moment I felt sick. But I shut my eyes and held my breath and let myself be hugged.

———

That summer Jack built a honey stand by the side of the road. Until then, most of our honey sales had been to stores. Though there was a HONEY FOR SALE sign by the driveway, not many people ventured up the drive. But a stand would attract a lot of Sunday pleasure drivers, Jack said, especially a stand with such a charming proprietress as myself.

The stand was like a little house; it had walls, a plywood floor, and a tar-papered, flat roof. There was a hinged door at one end and, at the front, a wide shelf for the honey. Above the shelf was a wooden awning to keep me from getting too hot. On the awning, Jack painted, in big red letters, SWEET BEE HONEY. Inside the stand were a kitchen stool, a rocking chair, and a cashbox on a secret shelf.

From the first I disliked being in the honey stand, but I never said so. I didn't like the raw wood smell, and I hated not being able to see in any direction but straight ahead. I was frightened each time I heard a car in the distance; as it came closer, my heart beat faster and I prayed the car would pass. If it slowed, my heart knocked against my ribs and I could hardly breathe until the car stopped and I saw the faces, always harmless, of the people who got out and came to buy my honey.

By promising Stevie half of the profits, I was able to persuade him to come be with me in the honey stand sometimes. And occasionally Eunice came, too, and pretended to help, though really she was there to wave at cars and to flirt when any boys stopped. She practiced cheers by the side of the road — getting ready, she said, for the high school tryouts in the fall, but I knew she was showing off for whomever might drive past.

A couple of times Wayne came by, and once — I felt sure this was planned, though Eunice denied it — Zeke came with him. They stopped right in the middle of the road, the black car vibrating, the radio blaring.

I was glad to be inside the stand; I started straightening the bottles of honey as Eunice ran around the car to see Wayne. Zeke was drumming his fingers on the side of the car, keeping time to the music. He did not turn my way at first. I could see his ID bracelet glittering in the sun, and, in the shade of the car, his familiar profile. When the car screeched off, he ducked his head and gave me a sideways smile. I felt a catch in my chest, but I didn't smile back; I could tell my face had turned to stone.

One Sunday I was at the honey stand by myself. Jack had helped me set out the jars of honey and then gone back to the house; he would stay, he said, but he had metamorphosis work to do.

I sat on the stool and looked at the pines across the road. I could smell the pine needles, hot in the sun. The trunks of the trees were straight and long, like giant legs. All around me was silence. I sat for what seemed a long time, the silence throbbing in my ears as I waited. I heard the faint whine of a car in the distance. I leapt up, my heart thudding, pushed out of the door, and ran up the driveway as fast as I could go. All the way up the drive, even though I heard the car whiz past, I felt something right behind me. Even as I ran across the yard to my tree house it pursued me, a shadow without form.

Later I told Jack that boys were always flirting with me at the honey stand, that Zeke had even been coming by; he didn't make me work there again.

I retreated to the Osage orange. It was to be my last summer there.

I remember that I could not write in my journal. I escaped into books instead, reading until I was groggy. Most of the books were from the tenth grade reading list Jack had gotten for me. In the fall I was going to a new high school, Blacksboro Senior High, in town; it was to this that I attributed my stomachaches and vague jitters. The previous spring Jack had driven me past the school: a large brick building flanked by two smaller ones outstretched like arms. Out front was a walkway filled with talking, laughing strangers. Just to think of it made my stomach tighten, but Jack promised I was going to knock 'em dead there. Blacksboro Senior High had never seen the likes of me, he said. Wait until a real English teacher — and the one he'd talked to seemed to know her onions — saw what I could do.

———

In August Mama still wasn't feeling well — her joints ached and her temperature rose above normal every afternoon — so it was Jack who took me shopping for new school clothes.

First we went to the bank, where Jack let me draw out all my money — honey money, he called it — and then added some of his own to "sweeten the pot."

As we walked toward Belk's I thought of the day I'd met Jack. "Remember when you said, 'Buy that girl a poodle skirt'?" I said.

He looked at me and laughed, then caught my hand. We went on down the street holding hands.

In the store we rode up the escalator and then walked past the perfume counter, where Mama had worked, to the dress department.

Jack helped me look through the racks of clothes, then sat down and waited for me to show him each outfit. Each time before I emerged from the dressing room I seemed to know whether he was going to whistle or shake his head solemnly side to side.

My favorite new dress was emerald green, with buttons down the front and a full skirt. Scarlett would have loved it, I thought. As I stood before the three-way mirror I could see several views of myself — small-waisted, radiant, perfect from every angle — and, reflected behind me, Jack, with the dumpy saleslady off to one side. "Turn around," Jack said, and I spun, looking at my pretty tanned legs and at Jack's smile; that's when I decided maybe high school wasn't going to be so bad after all.

After the saleslady wrapped up the new clothes — there were several large boxes, more than I could carry myself — Jack said, "Don't you need some underthings?"

In the lingerie department Jack laughed when he saw some day-of-the-week underpants. "You'd never get confused in these," he said, holding up the black Saturday pair and the red Monday ones.

"Oh, they're just like Eunice's," I said. "Can I get them?"

"Get a fortnight's worth if you want to," he said, but they just had one set in my size. Each pair, I remember, was a different color nylon with a flower worked into the script at the top of the right leg.

When these panties later turned up in the wash at home, the red ones had streaked a tablecloth, the light blue Wednesday pair had come loose from the waistband in one place, and Mama pronounced them all ridiculous and a waste of money; she had always ordered my underpants, along with Stevie's, from Sears, plain white cotton for us both.

Nineteen

THERE WAS A BUS to my new school, but the ride was over an hour, so Jack drove me. Mama was mad that he didn't take Stevie too, though his school was in the opposite direction and not such a long bus ride.

Mama said if we had another car she would take Stevie herself, but I didn't see how she could. Her arms and legs hurt so that it was hard for her to get up in the morning and often when I came home from school she was still in bed.

The first several weeks of high school were terrible. Not only was I worried about Mama, but Eunice deserted me for two popular girls — Brenda Dale and Patti Lou Apple — and I felt painfully conspicuous, walking down the crowded halls alone, eating lunch at the edges of groups. Though we didn't talk about it, Jack seemed to understand I was having trouble making friends. During the drives to school I could often feel him glance at me and when he let me out at the crosswalk he said, "Knock 'em dead, now" or "Don't forget, everybody puts on their pants one leg at a time."

I did do well in classes, especially English and Latin. Jack kept telling Stevie he needed to follow my example and study hard; Stevie had already brought home two D's in arithmetic, in spite of Jack's having drilled him with flash cards.

One day Jack came to talk to my Latin class; this was, to my surprise, a great success. He started out his talk about the influence of ancient Rome on modern America by pulling a can of Ajax out of his briefcase and singing, off-key and funny, the commercial; he then went on to tell Homer's story of Ajax, the great warrior. Not only did the class think he was a riot, Brenda Dale asked me to sit with her the next day at lunch to help her with her Latin translation.

On the way home that day, Jack poured compliments on me: from my Latin teacher (one of the brightest students she'd ever had); from my English teacher (quite a writer, and such a lovely girl); and from the principal (already quite a reputation, she's going to shine at Senior).

"I'm glad I have *you* to be proud of," Jack said.

———

There was a long Indian summer that year; it stretched from late September all through October — except for a few warning days of hard frost around Halloween — and well into November.

In October, Mama began to revive.

One Sunday Bernie came, bringing chicken salad he had made himself and flowers for Mama; after supper he talked to Mama in the living room while Jack and I washed the dishes. After Bernie left, Mama told me — her face flushed with excitement — that he had convinced her to start writing again. Her book was too good to let go, he'd said, in fact it was wonderful. Flannery O'Connor was still writing up a storm, in spite of having lupus; there was no reason, Bernie said — and Mama agreed — why she shouldn't do the same.

After that when I came home from school, I would find Mama propped up in bed writing in a black-and-white-speckled notebook. She did look better, with her hair washed and tied back with a ribbon, and high color in her face. "I'm in bed with my book!" I heard her tell people on the phone. She was nicer to me, with compliments on my cooking, thanking me (it was about time) for all I'd been doing around the house, and a few times she even came out into the kitchen to help, grating cheese or peeling vegetables until her arms gave out. She was so weak that she began to think maybe she had lupus herself, but Jack scoffed: two months lying around would make anybody weak, he said.

Jack told me privately that the hard work of writing was the best possible cure for whatever ailed Mama, and if she would actually finish this novel — Mama's problem, he said, was that she never finished anything — it would give her a confidence she'd never known she had. That would be true, he said, even if this particular book didn't get published.

Mama didn't know Jack had any doubts. She reported to me compliments he'd given her after reading her new work: "real talent with flashes of brilliance"; "better than the Brontë sisters rolled into one"; and — this a note on her breakfast tray one morning — "You could whip Virginia Woolf with one arm tied behind your back."

———

In November, we learned that Stevie was in trouble.

The day report cards came out I had stayed late at school for a Latin Club meeting. It was almost dusk when I ran down the front walk to Jack's car and showed him my report. Five A's, one B (in algebra), and a note from my homeroom teacher: "Special Honor Roll, Bravo!" Jack whistled, said I needed to dig a little harder in algebra, and then, turning solemn-faced as we pulled away from the curb, told me about Stevie.

The principal of Stevie's school had called about his report card that morning — probably to make sure it got home, Jack said. It turned out that Stevie was failing every subject but one, spelling, and since he seemed "a bright enough boy, though a little backward in sports," Jack reported Mr. Sawyer as saying, his poor showing must have to do with his unusual number of absences — twenty since school began.

" 'Is your son having a health problem?' " Jack said, mimicking the principal's gruff voice.

"I said he would when I got through with him," Jack went on, "because these absences were news to me. Then Sawyer says, 'Well, this puts a new spin on it. I got right here in front of me a wad of notes supposedly written by his Mama.' "

Jack shook his head and looked at me. "Can you believe it?" he said, but not in a way that sounded surprised.

"I didn't know he could write that well," I said, giggling, then added, "Poor Stevie."

"Poor Stevie, my eye. Your mother didn't want me to, but I went right over to fetch him from school so we could get to the bottom of this. When I got him in the car and confronted him with the facts, he swore he hadn't played hooky — that is until I threatened to march him back to Sawyer's office and tan his hide on the spot if he was lying. Then he allowed as how he'd 'missed the bus' a few days but had been afraid to come tell us — so he hid in the woods until late afternoon when he could see the bus coming back. I stopped the car and said there was going to be a public licking if he didn't come clean.

"And you know what he told me? Some boys on the bus" — Jack was mimicking again, this time Stevie's whine — "called him . . . Kotex."

Jack stared at me silently a moment, to let this sink in, but I looked away, squirming at the mention of Kotex, and watched the houses go by.

"Can you beat that!" Jack said. "To think he'd let a little name-calling — which wouldn't have happened in the first place if those boys hadn't known they could buffalo him — to think a little thing like that would make him play hooky, lie about it, commit forgery, and then when caught red-handed, go howling to his Mama, which as you can imagine is exactly what he did when we got home."

"Was it the Latham boys?" I asked.

"Was what the Latham boys?"

"Who called him that."

"I don't know," Jack was saying. "Any red-blooded boy who sees an easy target is going to take aim. Boys can be mean, but you just have to learn to be tough. I remember one time when I took a licking at school and went home with my tail between my legs, my father called me a milquetoast and a tattletale. Not only did he give me a good scalding, but he made me go over to that boy's house and even the score. My father told me not to show my face at his house again until I'd earned some self-respect. And I did, too. Stevie's problem is, your mother frets over him too much."

"She doesn't fret over me at all," I couldn't help saying; I felt tears start to my eyes.

"Well — " Jack glanced at me several times before he spoke. "That's because you're *tough*. Your mother knows you'll be OK. And Stevie would be, too, if she'd just leave him be."

When we got home, Mama and Stevie were in the kitchen playing chess, and there was spaghetti sauce cooking on the stove, which amazed me: it was the first time Mama had fixed supper in weeks. What's more, she was dressed, her hair was combed and fixed in a neat bun. She looked normal, really, except for being pale and overweight after so much time in bed.

"Well, this is a cozy little scene," Jack said, as we went in. "Steven, go get on those books."

Stevie gave Mama a look. She nodded and he left, not glancing at me or Jack.

"Your daughter, meanwhile, has made special honor roll."

"That's nice," Mama said. She went to stir the spaghetti sauce.

"I've always hated the word *nice*," I said. "It doesn't mean anything." No one changed. Mama continued to stir sauce; Jack remained silent by the door.

I looked at Mama's pants pulled tight over her bottom. "Boy, Mama," I said, "you need to go on a diet."

Jack snorted. Mama turned, her eyes filled with tears, and glared furiously at us both.

"Run along, honey," Jack said, giving my elbow a little squeeze. As I left and went up the stairs, I tried not to hear the low, angry back-and-forth of their voices.

Stevie was crying in his room, but I wasn't going to feel sorry for him. After all, I thought, slamming my door, he had Mama on his side.

But as I stood there listening to Stevie, I began to think of him all alone at the edge of the road as the bus came up the hill, the Latham boys leaning out the back window and calling, "Kotex! Hey, Kotex!"

I walked slowly across the room and knocked on his door. His crying had slowed into sobs. "Stevie?" When he did not answer, I turned the knob: locked.

"Stevie, please let me in."

I heard him get out of bed and walk sniffling toward me. He opened the door and stood there in the dark with his arms drooping at his sides. I reached inside to turn on the light switch, and he stepped back, blinking, not bothering to hide the fact that he was wearing nothing but underpants and a T-shirt. His face was puffy and his eyes swollen, one of them especially so: had they beat him up, too? He looked pathetic, a long-legged boy with the eyes of a baby. It was easy to see why he was picked on.

"Was it the Lathams?" I asked. When he didn't say anything I added, "You can't let them get your goat, Stevie. Remember, *illigitimis non corroborundum.*"

"Jack," Stevie said. He looked in the direction of the window, trying to keep his face still, but I saw his nose pull down in that way it did right before he was going to cry.

"Jack?"

"He beat me with a great big board." He ran and dove onto his bed, put a pillow over his head and lay there sobbing. "You can look if you don't believe me," he said in a muffled voice, and pulled his underpants partway down.

I saw the edge of the bruise — purple, swollen — then quickly looked away. "Oh, Stevie . . ." I said. My head spun and the air felt thin and empty around me. I walked out of the room and halfway down the steps, then stood there listening. Jack's and Mama's voices had stopped, and there was no sound from Stevie's room now. There was only silence, except for the small noise of my breathing.

I went back to my room, got into bed with all my clothes on, and turned out the light. I should get up and change into pajamas, I told myself, but I couldn't move. I kept thinking of myself in the three-way mirror, and Jack behind me, his reflection looming there. Finally I put the pillow over my head and pushed myself down into sleep.

Jack was not at breakfast the next morning — out working in the yard, Mama said. She was dressed but looked awful — baggy-eyed and yellowish. Stevie looked bad, too, his face still puffy, and I noticed that he shifted from one side of his bottom to the other as he perched on the edge of his chair. Mama kept her eye on him; he didn't look at her or me but kept stirring his oatmeal in long, slow circles.

"I'm going to call Grandpa, sweetie," Mama said to Stevie, "and ask him to come. He and I can take you to school."

Stevie looked up, his eyes flooded with tears. "No, Mama!"

"Well, what if I drive you in Grandpa's car?"

"I'm never going back there!" Stevie got up and ran up the steps; Mama followed.

Jack came in the door just then. I did not look at him. I jumped up and shouted after Mama, "You can drive Stevie in our car. I'm taking the bus from now on." Then I ran upstairs to get my books, leaving Jack speechless behind me.

Mama and Stevie were in Stevie's room with the door shut. "I'm leaving now," I said, going down the stairs. "Getting the hell out of here," I added, loud enough for anyone to hear if they cared to.

Jack did not mention my riding the bus. When I got home in the afternoons he would still be at his office — working on the final draft of *Metamorphoses,* he mumbled one night at supper. He had brought food home from the delicatessen — a hot dog for Stevie, corned beef sandwiches for the rest of us (mine with mustard and a pickle on the side, just the way I liked it) and big slabs of cheesecake. Mama was in her room with a migraine headache. Jack and Stevie and I ate in silence, avoiding one another's eyes.

For several nights after that Jack brought supper to me and Stevie upstairs. *"Le dîner, mademoiselle, monsieur!"* he'd call, and when we opened our doors there would be on the floor two trays of delicatessen food arranged on china plates, along with cloth napkins, the best silver, and little vases of flowers.

Stevie never went back to the county school. He stayed at home in his room for days. I'd get off the bus and walk up the drive, hoping to find Mama and Stevie playing chess in the kitchen. But the kitchen would be empty and the house silent. I'd listen at Mama's door; a couple of times she was talking on the phone (once I thought I heard her say Stevie's name), but usually there was no sound at all. "Hello," I'd yell, "I'm home," and then without waiting to listen for the faint echo back, would go upstairs to see Stevie.

The hall door to Stevie's room was always locked, but not the one between our rooms. I'd open it and say hi; he'd say a muffled hi back from where he lay on his bed reading comics and eating Jawbreakers. He would not look at me. His hair was uncombed and he'd stopped changing clothes; his room was a terrible mess and stunk of dirty socks. I thought of going in to help him straighten up, but I always shut the door instead and went to sit at the dressing table, watching my face grow blurry in the mirror.

One afternoon when I got home, Mama's door was open; I could hear the loud clatter of her typewriter.

"Beryl!" she yelled. "Come in here a minute."

I went in and stood by her desk.

"Just one second," she mumbled, and kept on typing. She had on a tweed suit and alligator shoes. With a lit cigarette in one corner of her mouth, one eye squinting against the smoke, and her fingers flying, she looked like the newspaper reporter she once told me she'd wanted to be. The typewriter, which used to be in Grandpa's office before he retired, was an old black Royal with the letters worn off the keys. When she started her novel, Jack had offered to get her a new typewriter but she said she liked this one. What I thought she liked about it was showing off how well she could type without letters on the keys; I knew she always typed faster when someone was watching, like now.

"Well," she finally said, cranking the page out of the typewriter. It was a letter, I couldn't see to whom. "It turns out the only thing wrong with Stevie is, he's a genius." Then she glared at me, as if I'd been the one to say something was wrong with him. "His IQ is either a hundred and seventy-five or off the chart, depending on how you look at it, Dr. Becker said. So of *course* he was bored at that county school. In fact," she went on, "geniuses rarely do well at any school."

"So what's he going to do, stay home like the crown prince?" Mama had recently been reading *Windows for the Crown Prince,* by Elizabeth Gray Vining, tutor to the Japanese emperor's son. Mama claimed that this woman had once visited her elementary school classroom in Tokyo and singled her out as being especially bright.

"He's going to private school, but I don't know where yet." Mama laid the letter on her desk; it was addressed to the headmaster of some school in Virginia. "Jack has promised to foot the bill," she added, "wherever he goes."

"Woo woo," I said. "Maybe you could send him to Tokyo."

I stamped out and marched straight up the steps and into Stevie's room, where he lay, all 175 points of him, reading Spiderman.

"Hello, genius," I said.

He craned his neck backward to look at me. Upside down, he looked like a comic book monster. His open mouth with the Jawbreaker in the middle looked like a single red eye in his forehead, and there were lines of wrinkles where his chin should be.

"Did you know you're being sent off to school?" I said.

"Huh?" He sat up, spitting out the Jawbreaker, and stared at me.

"Away from home," I added, enjoying for a moment his stricken look.

His eyes filled. "No, Beryl, not without you! I'd die!"

I stood staring at him. "Maybe it would be better away from here," I said, thinking of Jack.

"You come with me — we can run away."

"To where?"

"Florida. We could sleep in the orange groves and pick fruit to eat. And we could go swimming a lot."

It sounded like he had it all worked out. "How would we get there?"

"On the train. You jump onto the freight car when they slow down at the crossings. The hoboes help you get on and give you food and stuff. I read a book about it once."

I walked to Stevie's bed and sat down beside him. I looked at the dirty underwear on the floor, the empty ice cream cup under his desk chair, the rickety orange desk, and on his desk the lamp with a burned place in the shade, and a half-braided lariat draped over it; I felt for a moment what it was like to be Stevie.

"Don't worry," I said, putting my arms around him, "I won't let them do it." As I rocked him I could feel his tears seeping into my blouse, but I didn't move. I sat there holding him a long time, until Mama called us to dinner.

Twenty

IN ALGEBRA CLASS one morning, I got a note from the principal that said, "Come to my office — your father is here to pick you up."

I ran down the steps, my heart drumming; something must have happened to Stevie, or Mama, or maybe both.

Jack was in the front hall. When he saw me coming, he grinned and started walking toward me, jingling the change in his pockets.

"What's wrong?" I said.

"Nothing, except it's too beautiful a day to be in school. Let's blow this joint."

When I didn't move, he said, "Your mother and Stevie are in the car — and I have a surprise for you all."

"OK — but I need to get my books."

"Just leave 'em — they'll wait."

"And my pocketbook — my comb and lipstick — "

"I'll buy you new ones," he said, taking my arm and steering me out the door. "Plus, you get a special prize if you can guess what's on top of the car. Steven and your mother have tried and struck out, but I bet you can get it."

Outside I could see at the bottom of the hill Jack's car with a dark green mound on the top. When we got closer I saw it was canvas that bulged on either side of the straps like a fat stomach.

"Feather beds," I guessed.

"Close." Jack laughed. "Try again."

Mama, in the front seat, smiled and waved; Stevie, in the back, looked at me straight-faced. They both had on new hats — Mama a white wool one that looked like a flapper's; Stevie a straw cowboy hat.

"What is this?" I said when we got to the car.

"An Indian summer picnic is all I know," Mama said. She looked pretty again: her eyes shining, the hat covering up how thin her hair had gotten.

I gave the canvas a poke. "Something hard and rattly," I reported, getting in.

"No fair touching," Stevie said. "But I know what it is, anyway."

"You also have to guess where we're going," Jack said, walking to his side of the car.

In my seat was a straw hat like Stevie's except it had fringe around the edges. I put it on and looked at him. "The Bobbsey Twins," I said.

"Yeah," he said, with a snort.

We drove in silence through town and to the highway. When Jack turned onto the big road, Mama announced, "Well, we're headed west."

"This is too easy," Jack said. "I should have you all blind-folded."

"We're going to the mountains," Stevie said. "I knew it was either the mountains or the beach. And that's camping stuff on the top."

"You peeked!" Jack said, but added, when Mama gave him a look, "OK, you win a prize. Now Beryl gets a chance to guess where in the mountains. Here's a hint: heavy, heavy, hangs over your head."

"Hanging Rock," I said. He'd talked about taking us there.

"Bingo!"

"Where are the prizes?" Stevie asked.

"I don't know. I'll have to consult with the prize committee. There's also a consolation prize," he said, smiling at Mama.

"I can hardly wait," she said in a sarcastic voice, but she smiled back at him, and he reached across the seat and took her hand.

Two hours later we were in a rowboat on the small lake at Hanging Rock State Park. Even here the air was warm, and the water was as smooth as dark glass, except where we disturbed it and where patches of yellow leaves had collected on its surface. Jack rowed; Stevie and I sat on the middle seat and unpacked the picnic basket. Mama leaned against the bow — like Cleopatra, Jack said — and trailed her fingers in the water.

"I feel like I'm in a painting," Mama said.

"You should be," Jack said, then added, in a soft voice, "We all should be. This is a happy moment."

We ate in silence. I was aware of the noises we each made, chewing and swallowing: lobster salad, and some kind of meat sandwiches Jack wouldn't identify until Stevie and I had almost finished ours (when he learned it was tongue, Stevie spat what was left of his into the lake). For dessert there were chocolate éclairs. After I ate mine, I slipped to the floor of the boat and put my hand in the water: there was a warm layer, then it was icy cold. Leaning over, I lowered my arm to see if the water got even colder farther down and was startled to see the reflection of my fringed hat — I'd forgotten I had it on. I hung there, feeling my arm go numb to the elbow, staring at my fringed head and at my fingers — white and swollen-looking in the tea-colored water, like something that might have risen from the lake bottom — while Jack rowed us back to shore.

After lunch, we went to the campground. While Jack and Mama set up the tent, Stevie and I hiked up the trail to the top of Hanging Rock.

The climb was so easy at first that we ran, Stevie hitting his snake stick against trees along the path. We passed a family with small children and a gray-haired couple who looked as old as Grandpa and Grandmuddy; the man even scowled like Grandpa when Stevie brushed past, nearly knocking him down. I told him to be more careful, but after that we saw no more people. As the path got steeper we slowed down, stopping a few times to rest. When we came to the rock cliff I went first, showing him the footholds and pulling him by the hand over the rough spots.

Soon we were on a high ledge, looking out over miles and miles of woods and farmland. In the far distance we could see the soft blue line of what I knew were the high mountains, but that made me think of the ocean.

There was a strong breeze here; I shivered and buttoned my sweater and we sat down against a boulder, out of the wind.

I looked far below us at the miniature trees, most of them leafless now, except for a few spots of yellow here and there and large clumps of evergreens. Through the trees I could see the dark, twisting line of the park road and the occasional flash of a car.

We were quiet for a long time, watching a large bird — hawk or buzzard, I couldn't tell which — glide back and forth, tilting with the wind, in the big empty space before us.

"What did you do in the woods all those days you didn't go to school?" I asked.

He hesitated a moment, then said: "Prayed."

I looked at his profile. I could see the scar in his eyebrow where he'd been cut by the Osage orange thorn. "Prayed what?"

"That I would die."

"Stevie!"

"I'd go to heaven," he said quickly, looking at me, "and be with Daddy."

"You think Daddy is dead, too?" I felt a peculiar sensation in my stomach, something like fear.

"He's in heaven. I know he is." He paused, then picked up a rock and threw it, overhand, like a baseball pitch, into the space before us. We heard it hit far below and then bounce, fainter and fainter, going down.

When we got back, the tents were set up and a campfire was roaring. As it turned dark we cooked beef stew over the fire and then toasted marshmallows while Jack told stories of metamorphosis.

————

The sky was gray the next morning; during breakfast it began to thunder. Mama wanted to go home, but Jack said there was another chapter to this adventure. He took down the tents, packed the car, and drove us several hours through the rain. He would not tell us where we were going until we were there — a huge hotel made of rock, and out front, a mint-colored lawn glistening in the rain.

"All out for the Grove Park Inn," Jack said. "This is where Zelda and Scott stayed." Then he hopped out and carried in the bags.

That night we ate in a fancy dining room that had a live band, Lucky Clover and His Shamrocks. Our waiter said they'd played all over the world. All the musicians but two were black; I studied the faces of the white men closely, even though they played the wrong instruments — piano and drums. Neither bore a resemblance to Daddy, but maybe one of them knew him, or had known him. It was possible that he went by a different name now.

After dinner Mama and Jack danced, looking so silly as they tried to jitterbug that I wanted to crawl under the table. Jack bounced up and down without moving his feet, and Mama did something that looked like the Charleston. Neither one of them was in time with the music, though that would have been hard for anybody — the song was "Sea Cruise," but sour-sounding and too slow, like a record played at the wrong speed.

"Let's get out of here," I whispered to Stevie. He and I went up to our room and watched TV, the best part of the trip, Stevie said, since we still didn't have a television at home. We saw "The Honeymooners" with Jackie Gleason as Ralph; I remember we laughed until the bed shook when Ralph pulled back his fist and said, "One of these days, Alice, one of these days! Pow! Right in the kisser!"

The next day's drive home was long. At lunch in a place called Frannie's, Mama and Jack got into an argument because she said he was staring at the waitress. When Stevie and I were sent out to the car Stevie deliberately rubbed his muddy feet against the back of Jack's seat, and when I told him to stop it, he said, "Shut up, skunk."

Jack and Mama said nothing when they got in the car. The ride from there on was mostly silent until we were nearly home.

"Remember the prizes you promised?" Stevie said. "I want mine to be a TV."

"If wishes were horses . . ." Mama said.

Jack didn't say anything, but he started doing his amazing whistle — he could whistle in two-part harmony. I noticed that he smiled at Stevie and me in the rearview mirror every once in a while.

Jack went past the turn off to our house, ignoring Mama when she said he'd missed the road, and drove on, still whistling, to downtown Blacksboro. He parked, said, "OK now, hold those horses, I'll be right back."

He returned with a large box, which he put on the back seat beside Stevie. "Magnavox," he said, "twenty-one inch. Will that do?"

"Yeah," Stevie said. He looked like he might faint.

"What about you, miss? What would you like for a prize?" Jack asked, looking at me. I saw the nervousness in his eyes: he was pleading.

"Gum," I said.

"Oh, come on, you can do better than that. Haven't I heard you yearn for a watch?"

"Gum."

"OK." He shrugged and left again. This time he came back with a huge brown paper bag and put it on my lap. "I cleaned 'em out at Rexall," he said.

I looked inside: there was every kind of gum I'd ever seen — Wrigley's, Teaberry, Juicy Fruit, Dentyne, Chiclets — and one, Blackjack, that I hadn't. I unwrapped a stick of the Blackjack — it really was black — and chewed while they all watched.

"If you put it on a tooth," Jack said, "everyone will think it's missing. We used to do that when we were kids."

I smoothed out the gum with my tongue, arranged it over a front tooth, and grinned at Stevie.

"You are both completely mad," Mama said, meaning me and Jack, but it was Jack she smiled at.

He leaned through her window and kissed her hair. "And you, beautiful lady, what's your heart's desire?"

"Ha!" she said.

He kissed her again, on the mouth this time, then walked to his side of the car and got in. Adjusting the rearview mirror to look at me, he said, "You might want to search around in that bag — never know what you might find."

I scrabbled through the packs of gum until I touched a small velvet box. I pulled it out, spilling gum all over the seat, and opened it. Inside was a beautiful small gold watch. I felt, in spite of myself, tears come to my eyes: it was the nicest present anyone had ever given me.

"Thank you," I said, looking at him.

"You're highly welcome," he said, winking at me in the old way. "It's no less than you deserve."

The watch had a black elastic band and the kind of metal catch I didn't know how to work, so Mama leaned over the back seat and fixed it for me. "Longines," she read from the box, "the world's most honored watch. It must have cost an arm and a leg. You be sure to take good care of this, young lady."

"I will, Mama, good grief." When she turned around I stuck out a black tongue at her.

We drove home, Stevie with his arm across the TV box, me with the watch to my ear, listening to its small frightened tick.

"I wish I had a dog," Stevie said, as we went up the drive.

"What!" Jack pretended to be horrified, and reminded him what happened to the man who'd asked the fish in the sea for too many things.

But the next day, a Monday, when I got home from school, Stevie was out in the yard with a black-and-white splotched puppy on a leash, trying to make it heel. It had one broken-looking ear and a tail so thin it reminded me of a rat's.

Jack and Mama stood by watching.

"Isn't he cute?" Mama said. "Just perfect for Stevie. I've always wanted him to have a dog."

"I've always wanted a dog, too," I said.

"He's just from the SPCA," Mama went on, "but you can tell he has some good blood — mostly Border collie, the SPCA lady thinks."

"Look at the feet on him, though," Jack said. "He's going to eat us out of house and home. Any suggestions for names, Beryl? Sirius, for Dog Star, has been proposed, and rejected. Also Canis Major."

"How about Skunk?" I said.

"His name," Stevie said, "is Ralph."

————

Mama enrolled Stevie at St. Bartholomew's Academy in town. She said he was too young for boarding school, but I knew — I'd always known — she couldn't stand for him to leave. Grandpa hadn't wanted him to go to Catholic school (over my dead body, he had said at first), but Grandmuddy pointed out to him that there was no Baptist school in town, and further-more, the children of St. Bartholomew's were known for having impeccable manners whenever they went on a field trip in their neat, navy blue uniforms. Mama knew Grandpa was resigned when she asked if she could borrow a car to drive Stevie to school in and he gave her, on permanent loan, his second-best one, the white Oldsmobile he'd bought when he worked for the dealership. I loved the car — it had soft red seats and push button windows — but Jack said it was no good, a big white whale of an automobile, too expensive to maintain. There was no reason he couldn't drive Stevie to school, he said. It would save gas, as it was right on his way to work. And Jack warned Mama that chauffeuring would get old, much as she hated getting up in the morning. For several weeks, however, she did drive me and Stevie both, until she started having one of her insomnia spells and had to sleep late. Jack took us on those days, and more and more often — even when Mama hadn't slept poorly — the white car (Jack named it Mopy Dick) stayed behind in the drive.

IV

Twenty-one

AFTER SO LONG A LULL in the weather, winter, when it came, was a shock. One day it was balmy; the next morning the thermometer outside the kitchen window read twenty-seven degrees. It was the sudden drop, Jack claimed later, that killed his bees.

The first sign of trouble was an exodus of crippled bees from the hives. Jack came in to tell us about it one Wednesday morning just before we were to leave for school.

"The poor things are just limping around on the ground in circles," he said, "Thousands of them. Most pathetic thing you ever saw." He sipped at his cold coffee: I had never seen him look so close to tears.

Mama was redoing, for the dozenth time, the tie that was part of Stevie's school uniform.

"Quit squirming, dammit."

"Then quit choking me." Stevie was holding his history book out to one side, trying to memorize a list of English kings he should have learned the night before.

"I'm sorry," I said to Jack, since nobody else did. "What do you think is wrong?"

"I'm afraid it's nosema," he said with a sigh. Then he turned to Mama. "That's a very serious illness, Beatrice."

"What do you want me to do, send flowers?" she snapped, then quickly added as he put down his coffee cup and stood up. "Why don't you call somebody?"

Jack stalked out, slamming the door behind him; I started to follow. "Jack loves those bees, you know," I said.

She turned and glared at me. She hadn't slept well for weeks now, because of Jack's snoring, she said — I was sick of hearing about it — and the bags under her eyes were dark and sore-looking. "There's something wrong with people who care more about insects than their own family." Then her face crumpled; she jumped up and fled into her bedroom, banging the door as she went.

Jack called a professor of apiculture at State College in Raleigh and the local agricultural agent, but it didn't do any good: by Friday morning, all the bees were dead.

The agent, who arrived Friday afternoon after I got home from school, turned out to be a short-haired woman in khaki trousers; I could tell right away that Jack didn't trust her, even before she made her diagnosis.

"You keep bees yourself?" he asked, following her from hive to hive as she lifted the frames to examine the corpses.

"Not personally." She picked up a dead bee with a pair of tweezers and squinted at it in the dim light. She put that bee and several more in a little brown envelope, then said, "I can have these sent off to the lab for you, but I think what we have here is a case of poisoning."

"Poisoning!" Jack said.

"Pesticides." She stuffed the envelope and tweezers into her back pocket. "It's not uncommon. If bees forage a crop that's recently been sprayed, the entire colony can be wiped out."

"That's totally insane," Jack said. "In case you hadn't noticed, this is not exactly a farm. The only 'crop' I ever spray is roses, and as you may or may not be aware, bees aren't partial to roses."

"Drift," the agent said. "What do you have next to your roses?" Frowning, she looked around the yard.

"A few herbs, but — "

"Well, there you have it." The agent crossed her arms over her chest. "You sprayed your roses, it drifted to your herbs, the bees visited the herbs, and bam " — she rocked up on her heels and then down hard again to emphasize the point — "dead bees."

"That's the most harebrained theory I've ever heard in my life," Jack said. "How would you account for the fact that I've sprayed those roses a jillion times and it never 'drifted' before? There are more logical explanations. I talked to Dr. Roane at State College, and he said it sounded like nosema to him."

"Nosema doesn't wipe out entire hives."

"Or the sudden freeze we had Sunday night — "

The agent lifted one of the hive tops and peered in at the top frame. "They had plenty of honey," she said. "They couldn't have starved."

"Bees cluster!" Jack shouted. "When the temperature drops like that they cluster in the bottom of the hive and don't get up to the frames of honey. Don't they teach you people anything?"

With a little smile, the agent reached into her back pocket, retrieved the small brown envelope of dead bees, and handed it to Jack. "Since you knew the answer, you didn't really need to call me, did you, Mr. Fonteyn?"

Jack did not answer. We watched her walk back toward her truck, shining her flashlight in front of her. It was now almost entirely dark.

"That was dumb," I said, to let him know I was on his side.

"That she-male wouldn't know shit from Shinola," was all Jack said. I was a little shocked — I'd never heard him use language like that.

At supper when Mama asked what the agent had said, Jack

replied — his face not giving the least hint that this was untrue: had he forgotten I'd been there? — that though nosema was a contributing factor, the poor things starved to death, basically, because of that night when the temperature fell.

The next day I helped Jack bury the bees. We took the hives apart and, using our hands, scooped the corpses into brown grocery bags. They made a dry, sad sound falling into the bags.

It was already dusk when we went into the woods with our shovels, and by the time we had dug a large hole — not an easy job with the ground frozen — it was dark. I held the flashlight on the hole as Jack lined it with Christmas fern and then, bag by bag, poured the bees into their grave. We stood silently a few minutes, looking down into the dark hole.

"I'm sorry," I said.

"Thank you, honey. You know it's damn hard to try and try and then . . ." He broke off. From the sound of his voice I thought he might be crying. But he took a deep breath and went on, "Especially to be accused of something like that."

It took me a moment to remember about the poisoning. "It wasn't your fault," I said.

"Good Lord, I know that."

Stars had popped out in the dark sky above us. I saw Jack looking up at them. Then he said something in Latin that sounded like a prayer. "That's from Virgil's *Georgics*," he said at the end. "Virgil believed that bees are part of the divine essence, and when they die they become stars. Isn't that lovely?"

"Yes," I said.

Jack picked up his shovel and began to fill the hole with dirt. I tried to keep the light exactly where he needed to see.

By the time he had finished, the sky was full of stars. He came and stood beside me and together we gazed up at them through the dark tangle of bare trees. I was afraid he might ask me to name some constellations, but he didn't.

"There they are," he whispered, putting one arm around me, "our bees."

———

Mama made an effort to console Jack about the bees. When we came in from burying them, she gave him a sad look and offered him a back rub; he thanked her and said he'd take a rain check. But the next day at lunch when he started talking about ordering new bees in time for the spring honey flow, she tried to change his mind.

Why not take up some other less dangerous hobby, she suggested, like wood carving or painting — he was really good with his hands — or if he was set on keeping animals, how about goats? We could use the milk and all learn to make cheese, maybe even sell it.

"Goats eat plants," Jack said angrily.

"At least they don't sting."

"Did you know stings can help cure arthritics? There are some people who even go out of their way to get stung. Maybe you should try it. It might get rid of some of your aches and pains."

"In case you've forgotten, Stevie's deathly allergic."

"I have not forgotten that you *think* that," he said. "I just don't happen to agree. And besides, if you leave bees alone, they'll leave you alone." He left the table and came back with a book he called his bee bible, and standing, read aloud: "The term 'anger' hardly applies to bees, notwithstanding there is a general impression they are always in a towering rage, ready to inflict severe pain on everything and everybody coming near them. Bees, on the contrary, are the pleasantest, most sociable, most genial and best natured little beings that are met in all animated creation" — here Jack paused to give Mama a severe look — "when they are understood."

———

That winter's cold affected us indoors too, as the house was largely glass and poorly insulated. We all put on extra sweaters and I even wore gloves and a wool cap in my room, where I now spent most of my time. I often got into bed, not just to hide the *Mad* magazines that Clyde McAllister in the Latin Club had lent me, but because I was so cold.

Stevie, however, sat night after night, bare-handed and bare-headed at his desk (but with Ralph to warm his feet), reading his catechism book. He was now talking about wanting to be baptized and confirmed a Catholic and was taking special lessons with the priest at his school, Father Gamber, who had given him a rosary of brown beads with a silver cross. On the back of the cross were engraved the initials S.B.T., which stood, Stevie told me, for his real name, his name before Jack, Steven Boyd Thibedeaux. Though I had never seen him actually praying with this rosary, he often had it entwined in his fingers as he sat reading catechism at night. Jack said he looked like a midget monk with his St. Bernard (Ralph had grown quite large), and once at dinner Jack teased him about "having been seduced by the Jesuits."

"Father Gamber says he's not a Jesuit, and that you're mean to talk to me that way," Stevie said the next night. "We said a prayer for you."

"You know who you sound like?" Jack said. "Your grandfather in Catholic clothing. Can't you just see your foot-washing grandpa," he said to me, "in one of those long black skirts? What do they wear under those skirts, anyway?" This last directed at Stevie.

"That's not a skirt!"

"Lay off, Jack," Mama said, "I would think you'd be proud of Stevie, trying as hard as he is. That school has been the best thing in the world for him."

But even Mama didn't seem all that thrilled about Stevie becoming a Catholic. They'd have to see, she kept telling him. First of all, he'd have to show, with his end-of-the-semester grades, that he was putting his studies first; then they'd consider it.

"Your grandfather is going to have a pluperfect fit," Jack said to me one day, after Stevie had gotten out of the car mumbling Latin under his breath and walked toward his school.

"He doesn't have to know," I surprised myself by saying, "if nobody tells him. But I don't guess he'd be any more shocked by Stevie's being a Catholic than by me being an atheist."

"An atheist!" Jack pretended to look shocked himself. "And all this time I thought you were a dyed-in-the-wool pantheist."

After that he called us the Saint and the Sinner. When he brought upstairs at bedtime the towel-wrapped bricks he'd heated in the fireplace to keep us warm while we slept, he'd say, putting them in our beds, "One for the Saint, one for the Sinner. Either one could freeze their little you-know-whats off in this weather."

That made Stevie so mad he threw his brick out every night, or pushed it way down to the foot of the bed, but he didn't need it anyway, with Ralph under the covers with him. I said I didn't see how he could stand Ralph, he smelled so bad; but Stevie said the firebrick stunk worse.

I liked the earthy smell of the hot brick, and the comfort of its damp heat behind my knees. I slept on my side with my legs bent at the knees — like a mermaid, said Jack, who would come to check our bricks during the night to make sure they weren't unwrapped and burning our tender skins. Jack was closer by now, sleeping in his study. Mama said the cold was making Jack snore louder than ever and she couldn't sleep a wink with him in the same room.

Thanksgiving week our furnace broke, so we went to spend the long weekend with Grandpa and Grandmuddy. Jack at first refused to come with us — he said he'd rather camp out in his office, as Grandpa was always trying to save him — but Mama persuaded him and then was sorry. Not only did he snore just as much, but when Grandpa asked him to say grace at Thanksgiving dinner, Jack said it in pig Latin and then there was a scene. Grandpa left the table, shouting that it was just what he might have expected from hogs come to wallow at the trough, and was persuaded to return only after a long talk with Grandmuddy, who had carried to his den (at Mama's insistence) Jack's sincerest apologies.

So Mama was relieved when Jack escaped to his office for the next few days, saying that he would give her manuscript (which she was getting ready to send to Bernie's agent in New York) one final going-over. Trying to get Jack to do *anything* against his will always backfired, she told me.

And when Grandpa made us sit in the living room and listen to readings from *The Upper Room,* Mama whispered to me that it was a good thing Jack wasn't there: he would have made a circus out of it. During these readings (Grandpa's attempt to undo the evil effects of the pig Latin and the Catholic school, Mama said), I sat gazing at the gas log in the fireplace with what I felt to be a reverent (Baptist) expression on my face, but really thinking about the lemon bars Grandmuddy always served afterward and wondering if I should go to the winter formal with Clyde, if he asked me; though he was not all that bad when you got to know him, I knew that going on even one date with him would seal my reputation as a clod. I could feel Stevie squirm occasionally at the other end of the couch, and Mama — afraid he might burst out with some Catholic thought — lay a quieting hand on his knee. But the only interruption in the readings was caused not by Stevie but by Ralph. Grandpa didn't know Stevie had brought Ralph. Neither, for that matter, did Jack.

Jack had taken a great dislike to Ralph; he said he was bumbling, because of his lopsided run, and obsequious, because of the way he wagged so hard when he saw Stevie or his food dish that he bent almost double. It had made Jack furious to see Stevie sneak Ralph bits of food at the table, so the dog had been banned from the dining room.

After saying that the Whitakers had agreed to feed Ralph

while we were gone, Stevie had sneaked him into the trunk of the car as we were leaving home. When Mama had discovered Ralph in the basement, she had expected Grandmuddy to be upset (for she was sure to find out about him — you couldn't hide anything from Grandmuddy) but it turned out that Grandmuddy, for all the noise she'd made about no pets when we lived with her, not only didn't mind, she even carried table scraps down to Ralph herself. When I'd said to Mama I was surprised that Grandmuddy liked dogs, Mama said what Grandmuddy liked was pulling the wool over Grandpa's eyes.

During one of the readings — it had gone on for what seemed like forever, and Ralph hadn't been let out all day — there was a scratching at the basement door and a loud yip.

"What's that?" Grandpa said.

"The Hound of Heaven," Mama said under her breath, like something Jack might have said, if he'd been there.

"It's a mouse," Grandmuddy said. "Steven, would you go see if you could catch it, or at least scare it back downstairs? I declare, that basement has gotten overrun. It must be this weather."

"Mice don't bark," Grandpa said, rising.

Grandmuddy pulled him down by the sleeve. "Turn down your hearing aid, Beau. The doctor told him sounds get distorted when he has it up so high. Bring us some lemon bars when you come back," she called after Stevie, "and take your time. We'll have one more nice story while you're gone." As Grandpa began to read again, she leaned her head against her chair and closed her eyes, a little smile on her face.

We only heard from Jack once the whole time we were at Grandpa and Grandmuddy's, and when Mama tried to call him at his office he didn't answer. She spent hours on the phone talking to Bernie about her book — what to say in the cover letter, how much of an advance she might get. Every night when I went to the kitchen for my bedtime snack (a lemon bar and cold water from an old Log Cabin syrup bottle Grandmuddy kept in the refrigerator), there Mama would be at the Formica table, leaning forward to talk into the old black phone with its too short cord. She looked so young — her face pink, her hair in curlers she had borrowed from me — that I thought what Jack had said was true, writing was a good cure for her.

He came to get us at about four o'clock Sunday afternoon, much later than Mama had expected him. I was in Grandpa's study, trying to concentrate on algebra, but my mind had slipped, first to the Clyde dilemma, then into a new daydream of Robert. In the midst of my trance I heard Jack's car drive up and Mama run outside. Though I went on imagining, I became aware that a lot of time had passed since Mama had gone out. Were they fighting? Kissing? Surely they wouldn't have left, even for a drive, without telling me and Stevie.

I was just about to go out to check when Mama came in, her manuscript held to her chest. "Look what he's done to me!" she said in a shaky voice, and dropped the whole thing in my lap.

She stood by me, breathing hard — I could see her high heels boring into the carpet — as I thumbed through the pages: they were covered with red slashes, question marks, and comments, like his student papers after he'd graded them. "I guess he was just trying to help," was all I could think of to say.

Mama snatched the manuscript off my lap, took it into the bathroom, and dumped it into the trash can.

"Mama!" I said, but she was gone, out of the study and then out the front door without even putting her coat on. I ran to the living room and looked out the window: she was hobbling down the street in those heels and the tight Chinese silk dress she'd put on for Jack's return. I ran to tell Jack. I found him in the driveway in the back, leaning against the car fender and staring into space.

He listened to me silently, then got into the car, gunned it backward out of the drive, and sped off after Mama.

I found Stevie and told him what had happened. He socked one hand into the other. "Pow," he said, "right in the kisser."

"Maybe he didn't mean to hurt her," I told him. "Maybe he was only trying to help." But my stomach had begun to ache.

———

Stevie, Grandmuddy, and I were waiting on the back porch when the car returned. We could see Mama in the front seat, her head down. Jack got out and came to get me and Stevie and the bags. I couldn't read Jack's face: not mad exactly, more like he looked when he had a lot to do and not enough time to do it in. On the way to the car Stevie pulled my arm and whispered "Ralph," so I followed him around to the side basement door and stood guard while he went down the steps. When Jack had gone back inside, I signaled Stevie. We put Ralph in the back seat, but no one noticed. Mama was staring out the side window into the bushes, and when Jack returned with the manuscript under his arm, he didn't give us a glance.

Jack got in the car and put the manuscript on the seat between him and Mama.

"Well, kiddos," he said, adjusting the rearview mirror so he could see us, "glad to see your old pa? Sure did miss you — all of you," he added, looking toward Mama, who continued to stare out the window.

He sighed and started the car.

We drove a few blocks in silence, then Jack said, "Well, I have a nice surprise. Anybody want to know what?"

"I do," I said. "Don't you, Stevie?" But Stevie said nothing. He was staring out his window.

"A nice warm house! While you were all stuffing yourselves silly, I have been crawling around under the house with the heater man. Who gave up his vacation, too, by the way, to get things cozy for you."

Mama whirled to face him. "For three solid days? I suppose you also ate and slept under there with this saint. Did he lend you his red pencil, too?"

Jack wheeled the car over to the curb. "I'm sick of not getting any thanks for what I do. I put a good deal of effort into trying to help you with your manuscript."

Mama made a little strangled sound and turned away to stare out the window again.

"Come on, Beatrice, be reasonable. It's a good book, you know I think that. But if you're going to be a writer, you have to learn to take a little healthy criticism. Your trouble, as I've always said, is that you're too darn sensitive."

"Bernie wouldn't agree with that."

"What Bernie said to me was your style is too lush, but he hasn't been able to tell you that, you're so thin-skinned."

Mama didn't say a word, but I could see the tears sliding down the side of her face into the collar of her dress. Poor Mama, I thought.

"Not that he doesn't think you're talented, of course. He does. He thinks you're terrific. Beatrice? Oh, Christ, I give up!" He stepped hard on the gas, and the car screeched away from the curb.

"Don't use Jesus' name like that," Stevie said. I looked at him, amazed: he'd never spoken up to Jack that way before. He was gripping Ralph, half uncovered now, tightly in his lap.

I could see Jack's neck bend as he located Stevie in the mirror, but he didn't say anything. No one else spoke the rest of the way home.

When we got home Mama opened the door even before the car had completely stopped and ran to the house, pausing halfway to fling off her shoes.

"What are we going to do with your mother?" Jack said with another big sigh.

"Why don't you just leave her alone?" Stevie said.

Jack spun around. "Don't you comprehend all I've done for you — all of you? Who do you think is paying for that fancy Dan school of yours, for one thing, and putting food in your mouth, you ungrateful little — "

"Go to hell," Stevie mumbled as he got out of the car.

"What did you say? What is that animal doing in here? Steven? Steven!" Jack started to get out but then slumped down in the seat and covered his face with one hand: I wondered if he was going to cry.

"I thought I could help your mother, and all of you," he said, his voice tired and sad, "but I guess I was wrong."

"You weren't wrong," I said. "You have helped us. A lot."

I reached to touch his shoulder: he took my hand and held it against his face. I was surprised by how smooth his skin felt. "Thank you, sweetie, you sure are a comfort to your old Jack. Sometimes I don't know what I'd do without you."

We went to the house together. My stomach was hurting so much I could hardly walk upright. Jack put Mama's suitcase and manuscript outside her door. "Why don't you take her things in," he said. "I don't dare go near her right now." Then he went to carry Stevie's and my suitcases upstairs.

When I tiptoed into Mama's room with her suitcase, she was on her bed face down.

I walked closer. She was so still it scared me. "Mama?" I said, and touched her shoulder.

"Go away," she said, jerking her head to the other side.

"I was only trying to help," I shouted, "and so was Jack. But you always ruin everything." I dropped the suitcase and manuscript on the floor beside her bed and ran crying to my room.

Jack came later to ask me what was wrong. When I said I had a stomachache, he brought me some of his paregoric-and-honey tonic.

It was that night after Stevie and I were in bed that Mama threw her manuscript into the fire. Jack was able to rescue most of the pages, but Mama burned her hand so badly — she'd tried to shove the whole thing under the burning logs without a poker, he explained later — that he'd had to take her to the hospital. It was a third-degree burn, he told us the next morning, and the doctor had said there might be permanent nerve damage.

Stevie and I fought over who would carry in the breakfast that Jack had fixed for Mama. I won, so Stevie ran into her room ahead of me. When I went in with the tray, he was kneeling on the other side of her bed beside her bandaged hand, saying a Hail Mary.

"I'm OK, sweetie," Mama kept whispering, "I'm OK."

"Good grief, Stevie," I said. "Mama's not *dying.*" Though she did look terrible, her face pale, her lips and eyelids swollen.

I put the tray across her lap and helped her sit up, then sent Stevie to get salt and pepper.

"Thank you, Beryl," she said, trying to smile. "I'm sorry to put you to all this trouble."

I went to Mama's closet to get an extra pillow to put under her bad hand. Then I saw the typewriter lying on the floor on its side. I stood staring a moment, remembering Mama's happy, excited face as she'd talked on the phone to Bernie.

Mama whimpered a little as I eased my fingers under her bandaged hand. Her eyes — darker than ever, almost black — fixed on mine. As I lifted the hand she gasped just slightly, but her eyes widened and I felt it with her, a scorching pain right through me.

For a while after that, Mama went to see Dr. Becker several times a week. She tried to get Jack to go, too, but he refused, saying, she told me, that he wanted no part of *that* dog and pony show; it was enough he had to pay for it.

"I wish you'd ask him, Beryl," she said to me one day. We were in a dressing room in Belk's, where I was trying on strapless bras to go under my new winter formal (I had cast my lot with Clyde). "He usually listens to you."

Mama was sitting in a chair in the corner of the dressing room, her bandaged arm in a sling.

"No he doesn't, Mama. He never listens to anybody," I said. Though we both knew this was a lie.

I looked away from her and adjusted my bra. I could hear

Mama take out a cigarette, fumble with her lighter — she had learned to do this left-handed — and inhale.

"Jack would do anything to get my goat, Dr. Becker says." I could feel her eyes on me as I undid the bra. I tried to keep myself covered — I hated the way she kept staring — as I picked up another bra, the black lace one I wanted.

"Do you realize that for all his driving me to write, Jack is actually very jealous of my talent?"

When I didn't say anything, Mama snapped, "You can't wear that black brassiere under a pink dress."

"Why not?" I said, turning to admire how it looked from the side. "It won't show."

"Because it's indecent, that's why."

When I spun around to protest, Mama said, "Look at you. You're spilling out of it anyway. Take it off right now." She left the dressing room and came back with a white wired corset that looked like something Grandmuddy might wear. It made me look pointy, but she made me get it anyway. Otherwise, she said, I could just forget the dance.

On the way home Mama said, in a dry voice, "By the way, I'm in the process of developing a fascination for those goddamn bees."

"That's great, Mama."

She turned to scowl at me. "Dr. Becker says Jack's obsession with those insects has to do with wanting to nettle me. He suggested that I take some of the wind out of his sails by acting interested — using my charm."

When I tried to hide my smile by looking out the window, Mama said, "I'll have you know, Miss Priss, Dr. Becker said I could charm the socks off any man."

———

The next time Jack brought up the subject of bees at dinner, talking about whether he'd restock with mail order bees or wild swarms, Mama said, in a voice I wouldn't have believed possible, "You know something that really interests me, Jack? What you've said about scent being part of the bees' dance language. Just how does that work?"

I was amazed that Jack looked surprised for only a moment, then said, "Well, it's quite marvelous. The dancer carries the nectar in her honey stomach. As she does the round or wagtail dance, she stops occasionally to feed the other bees her nectar. That way they can tell by the scent what flower to go to."

"This is fascinating," Mama said, spearing a piece of roast beef left-handed. Her right hand, though out of the sling, was still bandaged; it lay hidden in her lap. "Isn't it, children?"

"It certainly is," I said, in a voice that let her know I meant more than I said.

"I'm full," Stevie said.

"You may be excused," Mama said, keeping her eyes on Jack. Stevie rose, making a lot of noise with his silverware and plate.

"Bees really are fascinating," Jack said, raising his voice as Stevie stamped off toward the stairs. "I've never known *anyone* with an ounce of curiosity who wasn't interested in what makes them tick."

"I'm interested," I said. "Really."

"I know," he said. "I want to start teaching you some real beekeeping this spring, too."

"You can be interested in bees without actually keeping them, you know," Mama said. "So tell us more, darling."

"Well — where was I?"

"Scent," Mama said.

"Oh, yes. Apparently bees can distinguish many different kinds of odors, not just flowers. Each queen has a different odor, for instance, and that can spell real trouble for newly introduced queens. That's why you have to keep them in a little cage at first. And for some reason bees hate the smell of bana-

nas. Don't ever take a banana near a beehive if you don't want
to get stung."

"You know, speaking of stings, sweetheart" — I had never
heard Mama sound so Southern — "isn't there somewhere else
a lot farther from the house you could put the hives? If you
decide to go on with bees . . . ? Which of course I'd hate to ask
you not to do — but maybe just one or two hives down by the
road?"

Jack frowned. "They'd get too hot down there in the summer."

"Well, thanks a lot," Mama said, rising to clear the table.
"All I'm asking is that you think about it." She snatched up her
plate left-handed, her chin trembling as if she were about to cry.

"OK," Jack said, "I'll think about it."

But when she turned and walked to the kitchen without
saying a word, Jack looked at me and shrugged.

The next time Jack talked about bees, Mama had that phony
smile pasted on her face again, but her eyes were glazed; by the
end of dinner Jack was talking mostly to me. I got a nasty look
from Mama when she asked me to pass the salt, but I just gave
her one back. I was really interested in the fact that queens can
faint and that if you put your ear up to the hive and hear a
contented hum you've got a good queen.

"I wish we studied stuff this good in school," I said. "Don't
you, Stevie?"

Stevie had been staring at his plate. "Yeah," he said, without
looking up.

"Steven's trying to remember how many saints you can get
on the head of a pin." Jack said.

"For the last time — St. Bartholomew's has nothing to do
with Jesuits," Mama said. "As you damn well know."

"Why don't you do your research paper on little-known facts
about bees," Jack said to me. "You could put in this wonderful
old English custom — I wouldn't be surprised if they still do

this in the more primitive areas — of beekeepers putting holly on the hives on Christmas day. If they've been kind to their bees during the year, the bees are said to hum carols."

"Yours sure won't hum any this Christmas," Stevie said, looking up at Jack.

Jack stared back at him, speechless, then stood up and headed for the stairs.

"Come on, Jack," Mama said. "Stevie didn't mean anything."

"Like hell," Jack said, going up the steps.

"Gosh, you're so *sensitive,*" Mama called after him. "If you're going to be a beekeeper, *darling,* you have to learn to take a little healthy criticism."

Jack's study door slammed; Mama looked at Stevie and grinned.

Twenty-two

MAMA'S BANDAGE was taken off just before Christmas. When Jack brought her back from the doctor she came into the living room, where I lay on the sofa reading, and held her hand up for me to see: the skin of her first two fingers and a patch below them was white and very smooth. She stood silently, her hand trembling slightly, making me look.

Jack carried in the Christmas tree that had been soaking outside. "The doctor says there's no permanent damage. Isn't that great?"

Mama sat on a chair across from me, cradling her right hand as if it hurt worse than ever. "The scar's going to be permanent," she told me.

"That's right," Jack said, struggling to get the tree upright in the stand. "Accentuate the negative. Beryl, why don't you go up and get the decorations. Let's have a little Christmas cheer around this joint."

I went up to the storeroom next to Jack's study, stopping on the way to look in Stevie's room. He and Harry, his new friend from school, were making a tent out of blankets and chairs. Harry was going to spend the night; his sleeping bag was already unrolled on the floor.

Harry and Stevie followed me to the storeroom to get the

ornaments. They were in two big gray-and-white dress boxes from Montaldo's which smelled of mothballs. Stevie and Harry carried the heaviest box — the one with the lights and the crèche scene — and I carried the one with the shiny balls and the crocheted angels and stars that Mama and Jack had fought about last year. Mama thought Joanne had made them, so she'd tried to pitch them out, but Jack, who rescued them from the trash, said it just so happened his mother had made these precious things, the last Christmas before she died, but even if she hadn't, how dare Mama throw away something of his without asking? The crocheted ornaments had gone onto the tree, but Mama had sworn that next year we'd get new ones. As we went down the steps, I prayed Mama wouldn't make a scene in front of Harry.

We were halfway down — Stevie and Harry, in front of me, were going slow on the curves — when we heard Jack shout, "It wasn't me who threw your frigging book into the fire."

We froze. Mama said something I couldn't hear, then Jack yelled, "OK, I will. Same to you, sweetheart!"

There was a loud crash — something dropped, or thrown — then the sound of Jack's footsteps in the dining room. When he started up the stairs, Harry and Stevie put down their box and ran up to Stevie's room, slamming the door behind them.

Unable to move, I watched the top of Jack's head as he came up the spiral steps. He brushed past me without a word or a glance, went into his study, and locked the door.

I dropped the box. Balls, angels, stars, spilled out, falling between the steps way down to the dining room floor. I watched two balls bounce down several steps before they disappeared and made tiny smashes far below. I waited but no one came, no one called, "Beryl, are you all right?" so I ran to my room, got into bed, and cried. I cried hard, with my head under the pillow so Harry and Stevie couldn't hear, thinking how I hated Christmas, and how I hated them all, Mama and Jack and

Stevie. I thought of a long-ago Christmas when Stevie had broken my favorite ornament, a shiny blue ball with snowflakes on it, and Daddy had rocked me while I cried into his sweater. I remembered so clearly how the sweater looked up close — it was a red vest, with big fat stitches — and I remembered the crinkle of his Luckys pack in the pocket underneath and the warmth of his hand on my head. But now crying wasn't enough. I bit my pillow, bit my hand until I tasted blood, and then I cried so hard that they had to hear me — I could hear them hearing me — but no one came.

I was surprised that I had slept; I knew it only when I felt someone sit on the bed beside me.

It was Jack. "I'm sorry about the ruckus, honey," he said, stroking my hair. "Everything will be OK. Don't worry."

When I opened my eyes, he made a face that was supposed to be funny. "Just a normal part of marital bliss," he said. He kept smoothing my hair, tucking it behind my ear in a way I didn't like, so I sat up, shaking my hair free.

Jack looked around the room, trying to think of something to make me feel better, I could tell. "Why don't you read a while?" he said.

I shook my head no.

"Well . . ." He looked at my prom dress hanging on the closet door. "How about modeling that for me? I'd love to see it on you."

"OK," I said, even though I didn't really feel like it just then. He went out and waited in his study while I undressed. I did cheer up a little as I slipped the dress over my head; it was strapless, made of pink net with crisscross lines of silver sequins on the bodice. I also put on the matching pink high heels that Mama had had a fit over.

Jack was sitting at his desk. He turned when I went in and pretended at first to be struck dumb. Then he said, "Gorgeous is not the word. Turn around."

I turned in a slow circle. "Ravishing. Remember what I said about your swan potential? Well, the metamorphosis is complete."

"Thank you," I said, beginning to feel a little awkward. I crossed my arms and looked down at my shoes. "Mama doesn't think I'm old enough for high heels."

"Your mother needs to have her head examined. The only thing is . . ." He leapt up, came to stand behind me, and pulled my shoulders back. "Stand *up*. Be *proud*."

I straightened and breathed all the way in, feeling as though my dress might fall off, but when I looked down it was in exactly the same place.

"That's better," he said, rubbing his hands up and down my upper arms as though I might be cold. Then he turned me around and let me go.

"When is this shindig?"

"Two days after Christmas." I felt some of my sadness return, saying the word *Christmas*.

"What's the matter, honey?" he said, looking as if he really cared.

"I don't know. It's hard to explain."

"Well, you'll be perfect. All you need," he said, looking at my shoulders and chest, "is a necklace." With one finger he lightly traced where it would go: the side of my neck, a circle across my chest just above my breasts. I couldn't move: it was like having my back tickled, only I felt it all the way down the front to my feet.

He took his hand away suddenly. "Speaking of metamorphosis — come see what I've done downstairs." He turned and walked out of the room, so quickly that I felt a little shock. "Steven!" he called, sounding angry — at me, I thought. "Hey!" I heard him rattle the doorknob of Stevie's room. "Steven — Harry — open up. You boys get yourselves downstairs for supper right now. You too, Beryl."

"In this?"

"Sure," he said, hardly glancing at me, then hurried down the stairs.

I followed, walking slowly on the steps in my high heels.

"Beep beep!" Harry said, as he and Stevie went by, nearly knocking me over. I held on tight to the rail and stared down through the spiral at the patch of marble floor below: someone had cleaned up the decorations I'd spilled. My chest hurt the way it did when I needed to cry; otherwise, I felt numb.

The living room looked like Christmas morning. The tree had been decorated with the angels and stars, and colored lights that went off and on. Under the tree were piles of packages. A side table had been pulled out, covered with a white cloth, and set; a waffle iron was on another smaller table that was decorated with cedar and holly branches. It all seemed to have happened by magic, since neither Jack nor Mama was in the room.

"Wow," Harry said. "You all sure have a lot of presents." He tested one with his toe, and Stevie started pawing through the others to find the biggest. "For Beryl," he said, in disgust.

Jack and Mama came in, he guiding her by the arm as if she were blindfolded.

"I didn't realize we were dressing for dinner," she said, giving me a sour look. It seemed to me her gaze lingered on my chest, right where Jack had touched it.

Jack turned the lamps off so we could enjoy the fire and the tree lights. He tended the waffle iron while the rest of us sat there in the flickering rainbow of light, eating waffles and honey. We were mostly silent, and only Harry ate enough to please Jack. I had just half a waffle, Mama only a few bites. "You'd better eat up," he kept warning us. "This is the last of last year's honey."

——

Opening gifts from Jack always made me nervous. I was afraid my face wouldn't show exactly the right kind and amount of feeling. He tried so hard, with the serious presents, and there was always the possibility of a joke.

When Jack handed me the huge Christmas gift wrapped in silver paper, I knew it was either a joke or something wonderful. Holding my breath I opened the package and found inside a bee suit, helmet, and veil: I still didn't know.

I pulled out the bee suit. "Gosh," I said.

"You can't mean it." Mama said.

Jack looked disappointed. "If she's going to be my helper, she has to have protection," he said, handing Mama a small box wrapped in the same silver paper. "And that's the best gear money can buy. I had to order off to Iowa for it, too, to get a small enough suit."

"It's great," I said. I put on the helmet and pulled down the white netting. It was cozy inside, and smelled interesting, a little like smoke.

"I think it becomes you," Jack said.

"Oh, JACK!" Mama had unwrapped her gift: a small bottle of Joy perfume. She jumped up to kiss him. "Thank you, darling — but you shouldn't have spent so much!"

"Wear it in good health," Jack said, going to pick out three more presents from beneath the tree. These turned out to be ice skates for Stevie (that was my great passion as a youth, Jack said, when Stevie didn't say anything), a black cocktail dress for Mama which she went to try on right away, and for me a beautiful rhinestone necklace to wear with my prom dress.

"It's perfect!" I said. It was heavy and cool in my hand, a sparkling chain with an intricate fleur-de-lis in the middle.

"I kind of had a premonition it might be," he said as I put it on. "Looks especially fetching with that headgear."

Mama came back in the room in the new dress. "Too small," Jack said when she turned to show us the back.

"Well, I don't know where I'd wear it anyway," she said.

"Don't be silly," Jack said. "Just go exchange it. We'll think up somewhere to go."

Later that day when I went into his study to show him how perfectly the bee suit fit, Jack pulled another book off his shelf and gave it to me: Dadant's *First Lessons in Beekeeping.* "It's a good primer — everything you need to know. You need to read it by March, so you can help me when the new bees come."

"I think I'd rather just do the flyers," I said, but Jack didn't answer.

His own Christmas gift to himself, Jack was saying, was a course he'd signed up for which would make him an advanced journeyman beekeeper; this time he was going to do it right. He was thinking of doubling the number of hives from seven to fourteen. We'd have more honey to sell and we might also offer some bee by-products — beebread, royal jelly, beeswax — all very lucrative and fascinating to learn about, Jack said.

At dinner that night, Jack said, "Well, my assistant and I are expanding our honey business, doubling the number of hives."

"Doubling?" Mama said. "You said you might cut back."

"I never said that."

"You did, and you said you'd move them."

"I didn't say that either."

"Well, it's insane," Mama said. "You're just asking for people to get stung."

"I'm taking confirmation classes this spring," Stevie said suddenly. "Harry's mother and father want to be my godparents when I get baptized."

Mama looked at Stevie openmouthed.

"It's time to clear up some misconceptions about stings," Jack said. "Did you know that for all the paranoia some people have about bees, only twenty-five people a year actually die of beestings? And it would take two hundred and fifty to three hundred stings to kill the average person."

"All right, Jack," Mama said. "I don't care what you do with your idiotic bees. You can go out and roll in them, you can sell their shit, for all I care. But if you are bringing more hives onto this property, they have to be moved way away from the house. It's them, or me."

"Mama!" I said.

"I absolutely mean it!" She leapt up and ran to her room. Stevie stood up, too, looking uncertainly after her.

"I'll handle this, son," Jack said, and followed Mama into the bedroom. They didn't appear again that night.

In the morning Mama came upstairs to tell me and Stevie that Jack had promised to ask the Whitakers if they'd like to borrow the beehives to pollinate their clover, and furthermore he was taking her out for a very special celebration on New Year's Eve — he wasn't even saying in what city.

Twenty-three

CLYDE WAS SIXTEEN but didn't have his driver's license yet. We were driven to the dance by his father, a silent presence in the front. Clyde and I sat on opposite sides of the back seat, he yakking about his chess club, I holding to my armrest and dying of shame in advance as I breathed in the odor of the red carnations pinned to my chest (he hadn't bothered to ask what color dress I was wearing and didn't even seem to realize that red clashed with pink). I couldn't believe I'd agreed to go anywhere — much less to the dance, where everyone would see me — with this drip.

He was a terrible dancer — it figured — unable to jitterbug at all, so we sat out the fast dances. During the slow songs he held me stiff-armed and clobbered my feet. But Clyde turned out to be much less shy than I would have guessed. On the ride back to my house he sat wedged next to me, his damp hand squeezing mine. On the walkway, in spite of his father in the car, he put his arm around me; I knew he was going to try to kiss me at the door. I decided, out of curiosity, to let him. Just how would an egghead kiss? We walked past the large glass windows of the living room — there was Jack, in his chair with a book.

Clyde squinted up at the light over the door. "Would you

like to see our tennis court?" I asked. "Come on. There's a moon — we can see." We walked quickly and silently through the frozen grass to the court steps. The net was down for the winter, but the poles shone in the moonlight, and the lines on this side of the court were faintly visible.

I turned to look at him with my face turned up. "Well," he said, glancing over his shoulder. Then he kissed me. His lips trembled at first, but it turned out not to be such a bad kiss, especially for someone who hadn't had much practice. I smiled at him, and he grinned back. Though I couldn't see his eyes because of the way the moon shone against his glasses, I could tell he was thrilled. I decided to give him a real thrill, so I arranged his arms around me, pulled his face down to mine and kissed him the way Zeke had taught me. At first, when I outlined his lips with my tongue, I could feel how nervous he was — his elbows way out to the side, his fingertips barely touching my back — but then he relaxed, and by the end, his arms were tight around me. He took a loud breath, like he was coming up from under water. "No wonder you're so good in school," I said. "Fast learner."

He laughed and kissed me again, much better this time. I pulled open my coat so he could put his arms around me inside it.

I didn't hear Jack coming. The first thing I knew, his flashlight was shining on our faces. "The dance is over, boys and girls," he said in a flat voice.

Clyde jumped back. I couldn't see Jack's face behind the light, but I could feel his fury. "Get in the house," he said, gesturing with the flashlight.

Clyde and I walked in front and Jack behind, shining the light on our backs. "Well, good night," Clyde said at the door, not looking at me, and kept on walking, faster now, toward his father's car.

"Good night," I called after him.

Jack yanked open the door; I went in and started toward my room.

"Just a minute, young lady." Jack caught my arm and pulled me toward the living room, walking me so fast I kept stumbling.

"Don't," I said, trying to pull free, thinking he might whip me, like Stevie. I had never seen him so angry.

In the living room, he pressed me against the wall. "Look at you." He pulled open my coat, using the flats of his hands. He looked down at my crushed corsage and at the tops of my breasts going up and down. "You little. . . . Get on to bed." He gave me a push.

————

Later, when I had on my pajamas and was going into the bathroom to brush my teeth, Jack came out of his study. "I'm sorry," he said. He looked miserable, as if he might die if I didn't forgive him.

The tears started to my eyes then. "That's OK."

"Come here," he said, opening his arms, and I walked into them. I remember that it felt good to have my head against his chest and his arms around me. I cried harder, letting it all go. "I'm sorry, too," I said.

"Oh, Beryl," he said into my hair. "Beryl, Beryl. You're just growing up so darn fast — I want to make sure nothing bad happens to you, that's all."

"I know," I said, wiping my face on the sleeve of my pajamas.

He kissed my other cheek, the one that was still wet. "You're too sweet to cry," he said, and then, I am not sure how, the corner of his mouth touched the corner of mine, leaving there the taste of my own tears.

————

Mama had her bag packed several days before New Year's Eve. Though Jack still hadn't told her which city they were going to celebrate in, she was guessing Boston, since he'd mentioned several times lately he needed to meet with his editor there, or maybe New York on the way to Boston. She had planned what to wear on the plane and when she met the editor — the same tweed suit with different blouses — but the New Year's Eve dress was a problem. She had tried to exchange the black cocktail dress Jack had given her, but the store didn't have her size and everything else was too frilly or frumpy, she said, so she'd gotten a refund — much more money than she'd have dreamed Jack would spend! ("A lot" was all she would say, when I asked how much.) Her idea was to find a new dress in Boston or New York, if there was time (she was hoping for New York, as she'd always wanted to buy something at Saks), but just in case that didn't work out she was taking along her purple silk dress. Even though it was old, she said, it was becoming, and she had those beautiful amethyst earrings Jack had given her to wear with it. She arranged for me and Stevie to stay with Grandpa and Grandmuddy, and for Grandpa to take us to school on January 4, if they weren't back by then. But she told Jack none of this, and she kept her suitcase hidden: she didn't want to spoil his surprise.

New Year's Eve eve came and went, and Jack said nothing, not even on New Year's Eve morning, and I saw no sign of his having packed a suitcase. Mama didn't mention the trip, not even to me, but I could tell how worried she was. In the morning she wandered around the house, straightening things. At one point she poked her head in my room, where I was reading, and said, in her grouchiest voice, "This place is a pigsty. How can you live this way?" But her face looked more sad than angry, and when she went to lie down after lunch with a cold cloth on her head, I followed Jack up to his study.

"Where are you taking Mama for New Year's?" I asked, keeping my voice low. "I think she's beginning to wonder."

"Holy cow!" He clapped a hand to his mouth, then reached for the phone.

I went into my room and lay down on my bed again with my book. Through my open door I heard Jack calling restaurant after restaurant, all of them in Blacksboro. Finally he got a reservation at the Confederate Inn, not a fancy place at all — high school students even went there sometimes. After a while he went to tell Mama. "Get your high heels on, sweetheart," I heard him call to her down below. "We're stepping out."

Mama was wrong about the purple dress: it was not becoming. It made her skin look yellow, and her stomach stuck out below the belt. "I don't guess you've worn that in a while," I said, before thinking better of it, and then could have kicked myself: she sucked in and tried to smile, but I could see in her eyes how bad she felt about how she looked, and about New Year's Eve. I didn't ask her if she'd asked Jack about Boston or New York, and she never told me.

Nobody had asked me out that night, not even Clyde (I'd thought he might, in spite of what had happened with Jack), so I stayed home with Stevie, each of us alone in our rooms.

———

"Look!" Jack cried, holding up a page that fell into his lap and all the way to the floor. "Eight years of labor, finally in print!" He had called me into his study to show me the galley proofs of *Metamorphoses,* which had just arrived.

"That's great!" I said, limp-sounding words; I didn't know what would be good enough. "I mean that's really fabulous."

"I think it calls for a little celebration, don't you?" He jumped up and from a high shelf behind some books brought out a bottle of sherry and a teacup. He poured some for himself in the teacup and some for me in one of the tiny cups from the sake set Mama had given him.

"Skoal!" He touched his cup to mine, and I drank. I'd never had sherry before, or any alcohol except a sip once of Mama's wine. I hadn't liked that, but I did like the thick sweetness of the sherry, and the way it turned my face warm.

Jack refilled my cup. "What the heck," he said. "This is a red-letter day. Now, I wonder if I could prevail upon you for a moment?"

When I said sure, he gave me part of his manuscript — this would be a good story for me to start with, he said — and had me read aloud while he checked the galley proofs for dropped lines and typos.

It was about Daphne and Apollo, and how he turned her into a tree when she fled from his advances. Though I'd heard this story before from Jack, that could not explain how easily I read it. The lines seemed to rise up and flow through me like water; it must have been the sherry.

"Your voice is beautiful," Jack said at the end. His voice too seemed different — softer. "Will you help me again?"

"Yes," I said, feeling my face grow even warmer as he looked at me. "I guess Mama will want to help too."

"Maybe." He took the typed pages from me and put them back in the manuscript on his desk. "But maybe not. It might just remind her of her own difficulties."

We had several more proofreading sessions after that, usually after I got home from school. There was no more sherry, but Jack often served high tea — cocoa for me, tea for himself, and some exotic food like smoked oysters for us both. After we finished work, I would stay for a while longer, looking through bee catalogues and magazines Jack showed me, until Mama called us to eat. During dinner I often felt her eyes upon me, but once when I asked her what she was staring at she said she hadn't been.

One day after our proofreading session, Jack told me he was going to get started on the honey house. He intended to build it himself, in the far right corner of the yard, between the tennis court and the woods. He hadn't yet decided what material to use — though he was thinking of birch, the kind of wood real Finnish saunas were made from — but he did know the shape would be hexagonal, like a honeycomb cell, the most perfect architectural form in nature.

At Dr. Becker's suggestion, Mama took up knitting that winter. It would be therapeutic for her, she told me he'd said, to learn to do something with her hands. I wondered if he'd still think so if he could see her working on the long blue-and-white-striped muffler she was making for Stevie, swearing every time she dropped a stitch or miscounted, unraveling more than she knit, so that by the time she was halfway through, the white part was already dingy.

She was going to make me a scarf too (she'd already bought the pink wool), but I figured it would be spring before she got around to it. I didn't care, I had other scarves, but she went out of her way to tell me she was making Stevie's muffler first because she was worried about him, the way he was taking Lent so seriously — fasting, going out in his shirtsleeves and barefooted to run up and down the gravel drive. "Oh, Stevie's all right," I told her. He was always bragging to me about how he was building up his spiritual muscles. And I was happy for him to use my chores (he took over on my dishwashing nights, for instance) to count toward his Acts of Penance.

_____

January was cold, and the first weeks of February wet, so construction of the honey house was delayed. Jack said we might as well take advantage of the bad weather by getting to work on another flyer. Maybe I could write a poem this time, he said. I labored over a sonnet about bees, and gave up. Finally, using "Trees" as a model, I wrote:

> I think that I shall never see
> A creature lovely as a bee,
> A bee whose tiny wings are sped
> Down to his feet, above his head,

As daily through the clover or thyme,
He gaily gathers his nectar sublime.

When Jack read this, he laughed and said it was a publishable parody. I said thank you, though actually I'd meant it to be beautiful.

The only problem with my poem, he said, changing the *he* and *his* to *she* and *hers,* was that worker bees were female; he was surprised I didn't remember this from my reading. All that the males (or drones) were good for was mating the queen; they just lounged around all season, waiting for their one big chance. But that would make an interesting article, he said, which I could research and write myself, if I wanted to.

So I read with great interest about bee sex: how the queen mated just once with many drones, giving her a lifetime supply of sperm; how each drone used his endophallus to remove the last drone's mating sign from the queen's sting chamber; how, during copulation, the queen ripped out each poor drone's endophallus, along with part of his insides, and he fell lifeless to the ground. But the furthest I got with the sex article was the lead sentence, "How many parents who tell their children about the birds and the bees actually know how bees reproduce?"

Seven new hive boxes arrived one day by truck. Though Jack left them near the driveway, where they'd been unloaded, I began to worry about the eventual placement of the new and old hives. The seven original hives were still in the back yard in a row by the woods, where they'd always been. Jack hadn't once mentioned the Whitakers' pasture, where he'd promised Mama to move all his bees. I wondered if he'd asked the Whitakers and they'd said no, or — my real suspicion — if he'd forgotten, like he had about New Year's Eve. As the bees' arrival grew nearer — they were to come by mail in early March, to coincide with the maple bloom — I was several times on the verge of asking Jack about the hives, or of raising the issue with Mama. But I did not, and each time I did not, grew more uneasy.

Mama hadn't mentioned bees in a long while, but then Jack hadn't talked about them in front of her, either. Until one night he came home from Lester Hayes's beekeeping class excited about Dr. Tsintsin's longevity study.

Mama, Stevie, and I were on the living room sofa, Mama knitting, Stevie and I watching Milton Berle on TV in spite of Mama's protests that we should turn it off because of the thunderstorm.

"Stop the presses!" Jack said as he strode in, his raincoat and umbrella dripping. "I've got a great article idea," he said to me, taking off his coat in front of the fire. "And an inspiration about a new product."

Then Jack reported what he'd learned in class about Dr. Tsintsin, who had discovered that the oldest group of people in the world — the ones in the Russian Caucasus, famous for living to be 120 — were all beekeepers and their main food was honey. Not just any honey, but the honey scraped from the bottom of the hives, that part being considered unsalable. This waste honey contained pollen that had fallen from the bees' legs, and it was the pollen, Tsintsin concluded, that was responsible for the extraordinary longevity of his subjects.

"They've claimed that about yogurt, too," Mama interrupted.

"It's conclusively the pollen," Jack said. "Each speck of it, almost smaller than the eye can see, is an incredible storehouse of energy. Another guy did a double-blind study on mice to follow up the Tsintsin data. Those mice fed pollen not only lived much longer, they had a higher rate of reproduction."

"Then by all means, let's not give it to our mice," Mama said.

When I laughed, Mama gave me a surprised look and laughed, too.

Jack glared at Mama and said, "Soviet doctors are beginning to prescribe beebread for all sorts of things — anemia, nervous disorders, menopausal symptoms —"

"What the hell is that supposed to mean?" Mama said, laying down her knitting.

"So you were thinking we could sell it?" I quickly said, trying to give Mama a sympathetic look, but she didn't see it, for glaring at Jack. "Was that your inspiration, Jack?" I asked.

"Yes — not just in the usual way — but mixed with honey, like those Russians eat it. And the Greek gods, too. Do you know it turns out that's what ambrosia actually was — honey and pollen? So what do you think, Beryl? Maybe we could put our ambrosia in a small Grecian-looking pot, with a little printed explanation to go with each one?"

"Well, I have just one question," I said.

"What's that?"

"Well —" I waited until Mama was looking at me too. "Since the pollen is so tiny" — my heart was beating fast — "how will we keep it from flying all over the place when we bring it back from the Whitakers?"

"The Whitakers?" Jack said. He *had* forgotten.

I gave Mama a surprised look and shrugged.

She turned slowly to look at Jack.

"Now hold it, hold it, keep your shirt on." Jack held up one hand. "I know what you're going to say. Stevie's reaction, blah blah, if he gets blah-blahed. Now, I have given this a lot of thought. I've even discussed it with Lester, who thinks it's an excellent idea. What we'll do is get Stevie stung."

"What?" Mama and I said in unison. Stevie turned from the TV to stare.

"In a doctor's office, of course, in a pristine medical setting. That way, whatever his reaction is, they'll have all the necessary equipment to deal with it."

"That is the most lunatic idea I've ever heard," Mama said.

"This is actually very sane. Please, sweetheart, listen just a minute — let's not fight." Jack reached out for her hand. He really was trying, I thought. "Now, I don't know why someone didn't think of it before. After all, Stevie could be stung anywhere, not just here. It's better to find out ahead of time —"

"That is true," I said.

"You little bitch!" she said, whirling toward me.

"Mama! I've been on your side!"

"You've never been on my side in your entire life."

"That's not true — you've never been on *my* side."

"Shut up!" Stevie shouted, turning off the TV and jumping up. It doesn't matter, Mama," he said. "God isn't going to let me get stung."

"See what you've done to him?" Mama said to Jack.

"Me? I'm not the one teaching him all that mumbo jumbo."

Mama grabbed her knitting and fled from the room, Stevie close behind her.

"I take it this means no?" Jack called after her in a sarcastic voice.

There was the sound of a crash in the dining room. I held my breath.

"Such eloquence. Would you guess that to have been a Wedgwood no or a Spode no?" he said to me, then rose and walked into the next room.

"Don't hold me responsible if something happens to your precious baby boy," I heard him say. "You get on to bed, son."

"If those bees come on this property, you will be responsible as hell for whatever happens."

I heard her run to her room and slam the door.

"You're going to hell when you die, you know that? And I hope it will be soon!" Stevie shouted, then ran from the dining room and up the steps. Jack soon followed, his feet heavy on the stairs.

I listened, to make sure he went into his study and not into

Stevie's room. Then I sat for a long time, staring into the fire, wondering who I'd have to live with — because I felt sure it was over between Mama and Jack. Later I thought of this as the moment when Mama could have saved us by leaving Jack. That she could not took me a long time to understand, and forgive.

Twenty-four

AT BREAKFAST that morning after the fight, there was no mention of bees, no hint of packed suitcases. The talk was of school and weather. Stevie, with his missal by his oatmeal bowl, was memorizing as he read. I noticed that Jack did not avoid looking at Mama, though his gaze didn't linger on her either. Mama's face was arranged to look normal, but her eyes were flat. I kept asking her questions to get her to look right at me. I wanted to see in her face that she wasn't going to leave; that she would want me, if she did. It frightened me when her face didn't change, when her eyes showed nothing, not even irritation at my questions. Jack winked at me as he passed the sugar. At least *he* would want me: or would he? I realized I would probably have thought the same about Daddy.

At school that day, and in the days that followed, my stomach began to hurt during last period, before the final bell. My legs shook as I walked down the hill to the car, for I was expecting Jack to tell me — or Mama, who might be in the car instead, alone with Jack's goodbye note to show me — that they were getting a divorce. Then, as weeks passed and this did not happen, my worry gradually shifted to the bees.

Neither the placement of hives nor the proposal to have Stevie stung was mentioned again, at least not in my hearing.

Jack delivered no more bee lectures, not even to me. Though the subject of bees disappeared from conversation, Jack did begin work on the honey house — a plain square shed, however, not the original hexagon he'd planned — so I assumed the bees were still coming. They were supposed to arrive by mail, I knew, from a company in Sparta, North Carolina (chosen for the classical connection), sometime during the first two weeks of March — maybe on the Ides, Jack had earlier joked. I wondered what Mama was thinking — whether she had some secret plan to get Jack to move the hives or if she was just waiting for a showdown. And then — this was soon very clear — she began thinking of other things.

It started one morning at breakfast when Stevie announced he was going to say a blessing.

Jack whistled. "Shades of your grandfather. Well, make it snappy — we're already running late."

Stevie bowed his head; the rest of us did, too. Then there was silence.

"Bless us, for Christ's sake," Jack said.

"Jack . . ." Mama said in a tired voice.

"Remember not O Lord our offenses," Stevie began, "nor those of our parents . . ."

I saw from the corner of my eye Jack's head jerk up.

". . . and take not revenge for our sins. Let all my enemies be ashamed, and very much troubled; let them be turned back and be ashamed very speedily. Glory be to the Father and to the Son and to the Holy Ghost. As it was in the beginning, is now, and ever shall be, world without end. Amen."

Jack was looking at Stevie with his cheeks sucked in.

"Psalm Six — *Domine Ne In Furore*," Stevie said, looking back at him with a little smile. "One of the Penitentials."

"The cream pitcher is right in front of you, Stevie," Mama said. "Please have some and pass it on."

"I'm not eating," he said, folding his hands in his lap. "This is a fast day."

That brought Mama's face to life. "You have to eat! Especially breakfast — it's the most important meal of the day!"

"I presume we will be allowed to partake?" Jack said. "Would you kindly pass the cream?"

"You take some first, Stevie," Mama said. "Eat just a little bit anyway, honey. You can't go to school on an empty stomach."

"It won't kill him to miss one meal," Jack said. "You may be excused then, Steven. Go redo that messy math paper."

Stevie stood up slowly and pushed in his chair. "I will redo my paper with joy," he said, still with that smile. "February is the month of sacrifice."

Stevie looked so funny, I couldn't help laughing.

"I'll sacrifice you, Brother Steven, if you don't get your holier-than-thou derriere in gear."

"Shut up, Jack," Mama said. And, looking at me, "This is *not* funny."

After breakfast Jack sent me upstairs to get Stevie. He was hunched over his desk and did not turn around when I went in. When I walked closer I saw that he was pressing the sharp point of his compass against the palm of one hand.

"Stevie?"

He jumped and laid both hands flat on his desk.

"What are you doing?"

"Nothing." He still didn't turn around.

"Time to go. Jack said to hurry."

Silence.

"Well, come on. Are you coming?"

"Yes!" he said in a low, furious voice. "Butt out!"

"Holy moly!" I gave his door a good kick as I left.

No one spoke on the drive to school. I was in the back with Stevie, but I opened my Latin book and pretended to study so I wouldn't have to look at him.

The first stop, as usual, was Stevie's school.

"OK, buster," Jack said.

Stevie didn't move. I finally looked at him. He was staring down at his hands that were cupped, palms up, on his knees. Then I saw the blood, a bright red bubble at the center of each palm.

"Stevie!" I said.

His head snapped up. He looked around for a minute as if he didn't know where he was.

"Get moving, Steven," Jack said, turning in his seat.

Stevie pulled on the handle and jumped out, not quite shutting the door. When I reached over to shut it, I saw a trace of blood on the door handle. I wiped it off with my coat sleeve and said nothing to Jack: it would only make him madder. Besides, I thought, it was just another of Stevie's tricks to get attention.

Nevertheless, I thought of Stevie off and on all that morning at school — how he looked when I spoke to him in the car, like he'd just waked up. I felt bad that I hadn't been nicer to him at breakfast, and in his room.

But by lunchtime, after two pop quizzes I hadn't done well on, I'd forgotten all about him.

When I got into Jack's car that afternoon and he said, "Well, your brother pulled a real doozy today, claimed to have the stigmata, like Christ," my mind moved with some effort back to the morning, the blood on his hands.

"The miracle apparently developed during math class. So naturally he couldn't go to the board. But that nun got him to come clean. Or maybe it was that priest — your mother was so hysterical on the phone it was hard to get a straight story. Anyway, he finally confessed that he'd cut himself."

"With the compass," I said.

Jack glanced at me. "You saw this?"

"Yeah."

"Did he tell you what he told the priest, that he did it, boo hoo" — Jack made his lips quiver like he was crying " — because he's from a broken home?"

"He thinks he's the only one in the whole world who's ever unhappy." I felt mad as I said it, but then tears began to bunch up in my throat. "He's not the only one who had a father go off and leave him." I looked away, out the side window, to cry.

Jack was silent. In the window I could just make out the reflection of his head as he turned toward me several times. He put his hand on my knee. "Beryl? Look at me."

I turned and looked at him through a blur of tears.

"You've always got your Jack," he said.

When we got home, I went to Stevie's room. Mama was there, trying to spoon some chocolate ice cream into his mouth, but he kept jerking his head away. He was in bed with the covers up to his chin, watching "Leave It to Beaver" on the TV. Mama had moved upstairs for him. Ralph was under the covers too; I could see his nose sticking out beneath the blanket.

Neither Stevie nor Mama spoke or even looked at me. "Is he going to get to keep the TV up here?"

"Your brother isn't feeling very well right now," Mama said.

"Yeah, I heard he had the stigmata but got over it."

He gave me a most unsaintly look.

"Beryl . . ." Mama motioned with her head that she wanted me to leave the room.

Stevie took one hand out from beneath the covers — this so I could see it was wrapped in gauze — and reached for the water glass on the table beside his bed. Mama must have brought the table up for him, too.

"Well, looks like he's got the life of Riley now," I said.

"Get out," Mama said, her eyes burning at me.

I went into my room, sat at my dressing table, and started brushing my hair. My chest ached and tears slowly spilled from my eyes.

Mama opened the door and came into my room. I could tell from the crisp way she shut the door and from the rat-tat of her heels coming toward me exactly what her first line would be.

"I want to talk to you, young lady."

I want to talk to you young lady: I mouthed it silently in the mirror.

"What's going on with Stevie is very serious. Dr. Becker recommended he start seeing a child psychiatrist — Dr. Miller — three times a week."

"I always knew he was crazy."

"He is not crazy!" Mama's hands were on my shoulders, shaking me. "Your brother is desperate for attention."

"Well, the poor thing."

She spun around and marched back across the floor. I watched her go: her straight back, the seams of her stockings, crooked on the right leg.

"I wish I'd died when Daddy left." I said it loud enough for her to hear, but she didn't answer, just slammed the door and went back in to Stevie.

———

"Thank God," Jack said one morning, just as Mama and Stevie were rising from the breakfast table, she to drive him to Harry's. "March has come in like a shorn lamb. Lot to do today," he added, looking at me. To get ready for the bees, he meant, though he didn't say that out loud. "By the way" — this over his shoulder to Mama — "Bernie will be here for lunch. He's going to help me put the roof on the honey house."

Her only response was to slam the door hard, but she came back from town loaded with groceries, and by midmorning I could smell onion soup cooking on the stove. (Her onion soup, Bernie had once said, was the equal of that made at his favorite bistro in Paris.)

I was in my room, nervously trying on outfit after outfit. I finally picked out a soft lime sweater that made my eyes look almost green and jeans that were just the right degree of tight. When I heard his car in the drive I picked up my journal and ran downstairs. My plan was for him to see me but at a distance: not close enough to speak.

I passed quickly through the kitchen, armed with my excuse of an English theme to write, if Mama should ask me to help. But she didn't ask, just gave my jeans a disapproving look. I went on out the door and walked quickly across the yard toward my tree.

Climbing the tree, a little stiffly because of the jeans and because I was out of practice, I looked over my shoulder and saw Bernie and Jack still near the driveway. Though their backs were toward me, I could see that each of them had a foot propped on a beehive and that Jack was leaning forward on his knee, talking, explaining.

I sat on the platform for a long time watching them. I began to feel uncomfortable — the boards were cold and damp through my jeans — but I stayed there, sitting Indian-style, facing in their direction. When they walked across the yard to the honey house, they might see me if they looked up: there were no leaves on the branches yet. "What's that exotic flower in the Osage orange?" Bernie might say, just loud enough for me to hear.

But when they did finally walk across the yard, each was carrying a beehive, walking stiffly with the strain of it, looking down. I watched, holding my breath, as they carried the hives to the back of the yard and put them next to the old hive boxes. I kept watching, hypnotized, as Jack and Bernie set out the new hives. There was soon a long row of them, fourteen instead of seven. Feeling a flutter in my stomach, I slid down the tree and went into the house. Bernie and Jack had gone into the honey house and didn't see me.

Mama was at the counter, mixing something in a bowl. She was all dressed up — gussied up, Jack would say — in black high heels, a black skirt, and a white sweater so tight her nipples showed. She had on perfume and earrings — she called them ear bobs, a name I'd always hated. She had a record blasting in the living room so she could hear it in the kitchen, some screechy opera she was humming along with.

"What's that?" I said, covering my ears.

"*La Traviata.*"

"I mean that," I said, nodding at the bowl.

"Egg whites for chocolate mousse," she said, giving me a coy smile. Bernie had also raved about her chocolate mousse.

"They've set out the hives," I told her. "In the same place. By the woods."

Her face changed for just a second; she gave me a strange, quick look before she went back to humming. It occurred to me suddenly what Mama's plan was: for Bernie to save us, like Jack was supposed to have done. Now she was going to try to get Bernie to marry her, and move us over to his house.

"Mama," I said, "don't you know Bernie's queer?"

She thumped the bowl down on the counter. "I know Bernie a good deal better than you do, Beryl. And watch your language. That's a very rude word."

———

At lunch, Bernie sat across the table from me in Stevie's place. He smiled at me in the old way: he sure didn't act queer. "Whose heart are you breaking these days?"

"Nobody's." I could feel myself blushing.

"I hope you still like onion soup, Bernie," Mama said.

"Yes, indeed," he said, breaking his spoon through the thick cheese crust. "Mmm." He closed his eyes and inhaled.

"Well, we're making pretty good progress out there," Jack said. Mama didn't look at Jack; I had never seen her so strongly not look at him. "Beryl, you ought to come take a look."

"By the way, Bernie?" Mama said. "You remember my poor old book?"

"Sure," he said. "Nothing poor old about it, though."

"You were always so encouraging," Mama said.

"Well . . ." Bernie put a spoonful of soup in his mouth and managed to swallow. "It really is an excellent book."

I looked at Jack: he was staring at the wall with a distant

expression, as though he were trying to remember something.

"I'm ready to get back to work on it," Mama said. "Do you suppose I could have just a tiny bit of your time this afternoon to ask you a thing or two? I never did show it to you after those, ah . . ." she went on, still not looking at Jack, "revisions."

"Sure," Bernie said, turning his head in Jack's direction, but not quite looking at him.

Jack stood up. "Let's get back to it, shall we, Hoffman?"

"Sure thing." Bernie stood quickly.

"There's dessert," Mama said. "Chocolate mousse."

Bernie hesitated.

"Maybe later," Jack said.

"I tell you what, Bernie. We'll have tea," Mama said.

"OK," he said. "And we'll talk about your book."

That afternoon I went for a long walk. When I got back, it was nearly dark, but Jack was still on the roof of the honey house. Bernie was in the living room with Mama. Tea was in high swing, only it wasn't tea they were drinking.

"Port," Mama said, toasting me with it.

"Drink of the literati," Bernie added. "Come have a taste." And without asking Mama, he poured some for me into a small green glass. I sipped it: the taste was a lot like sherry.

On the coffee table, next to the half-empty bowl of mousse, was Mama's singed manuscript. When she saw me looking at it, Mama said, "Bernie can't decide which he likes better, the mousse or my book."

"No contest, no contest!" Bernie said, patting the book.

"And he thinks it's just awful," Mama said in a slurred whisper, "what Jack did to it." Giggling, she added, "we've renamed it *The Phoenix.*"

Bernie helped himself to more mousse, then gave me a big spoonful. We went on eating — me straight out of the bowl — until Jack came in.

Jack stood looking down at us, frowning, not saying a word.

Bernie stood up. "Well, I'd better be pushing along."

"Don't forget this," Mama said, putting the manuscript in his arms. "Jack, *he* thinks it's publishable. He's going to send it to his agent, after he has his secretary retype it."

"Hip, hip, hooray. Well, much obliged, Bernie," Jack said, one eyebrow lifted. "You're one hell of a roof raiser."

After Bernie left, Jack went to his room and Mama to hers; both began to type.

———

Mama had started a new novel, she announced the next day at breakfast. "Nothing like a little encouragement to make you feel really inspired."

"That's nice," I said to fill the silence, but she was glaring so hard at Jack she didn't hear.

Jack stood up. "I'll need your help today," he said to me, with such a stern look that I answered, "Yes, sir."

He headed for the door. When it slammed, Mama jumped up, went to her room, and with the door still open, started typing so fast and loud I thought of a machine gun.

I sat there looking at the mess I had to clean up — sugar sprayed on the table, Mama's spoon sunk into the remains of her oatmeal, a glob of jam on Jack's place mat — and began to feel sick. I ran upstairs to the bathroom, sat on the edge of the tub, and stared into the throat of the toilet, but nothing happened. After a while I went to my room and got in bed. My face felt hot; probably I was coming down with something. I put the pillows over my head and went back to sleep.

I slept all morning until Jack came and woke me. Later he blamed the long nap for my not being able to sleep that night — it was two A.M. when he saw my light still on and came to check on me.

But night after night — all that time before the bees came — I kept on not being able to sleep and I had a constant stomachache. Jack gave me his paregoric-and-honey tonic for both; it did help the stomachaches but not the insomnia. I lay staring up through the dark at the constellation of Pegasus that Jack had pasted on my ceiling when we'd first moved in: that seemed so long ago to me now.

Sometimes Jack would give me back rubs to help me relax. They didn't help, though I never said so. They were too rough, for one thing — Jack's fingers dug into the muscles to show them, he said, who was boss — and I did not like it when his hands went below my waist. Every time he rubbed my back I drew a line in my mind at my waist, willing him not to cross it; when he did go lower, I'd squirm but he'd say, his thumbs moving in deep circles on my pajama-covered bottom, "Hold still — this is where the problem is."

One day after school Jack gave me money to buy spring clothes, an entire one hundred dollars to spend on whatever I wanted. When we went home with all the boxes and I told Mama about the hundred dollars, she gave me a nasty look, then said to Jack, "I thought you were so damn worried about money."

He shrugged. "Just trying to even the score a little."

"What score?"

He didn't answer, but started upstairs with my packages; I followed.

"What score?" Mama yelled from the bottom of the steps.

He turned and shouted over me. "Headshrinkers don't grow on trees, you know. Private schools, either."

"You bastard." She was still shouting, but also beginning to cry. "Why do you have to be like this?"

"Why do you have to be like this?" he said, mimicking her voice. "You ought to see yourself."

I looked down at Mama — sobbing, with her head on the rail, her arms hanging limp by her sides — and for an instant imagined myself falling, my head bouncing down all those metal steps. But I turned and followed Jack up the stairs and into my room with all the new clothes.

That night when Jack was rubbing my back he pulled the

pajama bottoms down, jerking the elastic over my hips in one motion before I could say no. "Now," he said, beginning to rub, "isn't that better?"

"Uh-uh," I said. I tried to pull my pajamas back up, but he caught my hands. "Can't get *at* you through all that cloth. Now if you'd just sleep in your birthday suit like I do . . ." He went on rubbing some more, squeezing my buttocks, then running his flat hands all the way to my legs. My heart was beating fast, but I began to breathe deeply, as if I were going to sleep. His hands slowed down but did not stop, so I said, in a barely awake voice, "That's enough, thank you, I can go to sleep now." He stopped then, eased up my pajama bottoms, pulled up the covers, and tiptoed away.

I turned on my side and with my eyes squeezed shut began to think as hard as I could about my new clothes until I went to sleep. For several nights after that — all that time before the bees came — whenever I heard Jack's quiet footsteps on the stairs, I'd quickly turn off the light and begin to breathe deeply; sometimes I even snored a little. After he had listened outside my door — occasionally opening it, but not coming in — and then gone away, I'd think about clothes again, the image of myself in one dress after another blotting out everything else. So intensely did I do this that to this day I can still recall the color, texture, and smell of each of those dresses: a blue chintz cotton with a lace collar; a white shirtwaist scattered with shamrocks; and the one I saved for a special occasion but never got to wear, the scoop-necked dress printed with roses.

Twenty-five

THE BEES ARRIVED at the end of March, the Saturday before Palm Sunday. Stevie was at Harry's house, Mama was still in her room. Jack and I were at the kitchen table eating silver dollar pancakes he had made. I had syrup on mine; he — scorning my choice — Sweet Bee honey.

The phone rang. Jack got up and went to the counter to answer it. "Speaking."

All the way across the room I could hear the loud male voice at the other end of the line.

Jack listened, frowning. "If they — " he kept trying to interrupt. "If they — " Finally he shouted, "If they had been handled properly this wouldn't have happened — OK, OK, keep your shirt on, bud, I'll be right there."

He slammed down the receiver. "Ignoramus! Bees do not *bite!*"

Then he said, turning to look at me, "Well, they're here." Excitement was replacing anger in his face. "Go get suited up. I'll need your help when I get back."

"I can't," I said. "I need to sit out." This was what girls said in P.E. when they had their period. Though it wasn't true, I thought it might work: I'd heard Jack say the pip made bees angry.

But he had run to get his bee suit and smoker and didn't hear me. Soon he was out the door and on his way to the post office, where, he told me later, bees were swarming around cardboard package hives that lay beside the open door of a mail truck while the driver hid inside the post office.

While Jack was gone I went to my room and got into my bee suit, zipping it on over my jeans and sweater. Because my hands were shaking, it took a long time to roll the rubber bands up over the edges of the pant legs to keep the bees out, as Jack had shown me. I sat at my dressing table, put on the helmet, and pulled down the veil, tucking it into the collar all around. Then the gloves: some old white cotton ones of Mama's, elbow-length, that she used to wear to dances. I leaned toward the mirror, pulling the veil tight against my face. I remember how strange I looked — eyelashes matted down, nose flat, mouth stretched and with the mesh cutting into it — like something caught in a net.

When the car horn sounded in the drive, my heart began to pound. I wobbled down the spiral steps, holding tight to the rail, then across the dining room — my tennis shoes squeaking on the marble — and opened the door. I stood there, half in, half out, until Jack honked again. Retucking the veil inside the front of my suit, I began walking slowly toward the car.

Jack was pumping his smoker into the open trunk. There were so many bees zigzagging up through the white cloud that I thought at first he'd decided to carry them home loose, like a man he'd told me about once.

"Go get me a big paintbrush and a bucket of water," he shouted. "I need to wet down these boxes. Hurry — what do you think this is, a debutante tea?"

I ran, not knowing where else to look, to the kitchen and started searching through cabinets for something to put water in. Finally my eye lit on Mama's stockpot, still on the stove. I dumped out the broth, rinsed the pot, and filled it with water.

"Mama!" I shouted. "The bees are here. Where's a paint-brush?"

No response. I went to her room and opened the door. She was at her desk writing in the black-and-white-speckled note-book. She had on a pink quilted bathrobe and glasses.

"Where's a paintbrush?" I asked again.

"How the hell should I know?" She raised her left hand, and, shielding her face with it, went on writing.

When I went outside with the stockpot, Jack was on his way back from the honey house with a paintbrush and a pail of water.

"I'm sorry!" I called after him. "I tried," but he didn't answer.

I carried the stockpot to the car and watched from a distance while he took the cardboard hives out of the trunk and one by one brushed water on them; I saw how the bees had escaped, through the small holes punched on the tops and sides.

"There," he said, straightening, rubbing his back, "that will keep any more from flying out." He picked up two of the cardboard hives, stacking one on the other, and with the smoker under his arm started across the yard. I followed slowly, still carrying the stockpot.

Jack stopped by the first hive and bounced the cardboard box on the ground. "This will jar them to the bottom of the package," he said, glancing at me. "Would you go get the queens out of the car? They're in the small cages in the front seat." When I didn't move, he said, "Goddammit, you're no use at all."

He eased the cardboard hive open, puffed smoke inside, then dropped the hive lid on the ground. When a dark line of bees flew up at him, I couldn't help it: I screamed. "Shut up," Jack hissed. "You're making it worse." He set down the smoker and backed away. "Get on in the house, Beryl." I ran, crying, spilling water from the stockpot all down my front. I saw Mama at her window, then gone from the window: she was coming to me, I thought, to see what was wrong. But when I went in, the kitchen was empty, and her door was shut. Even when I cried harder and dropped the stockpot in the sink, making a big clatter, she still did not come out.

Later that day, Jack apologized. His behavior had been unforgivable, he said, but would I forgive him?

I was at my dressing table doing homework. I looked at him in the mirror. He'd been stung on one eyelid — that eye was swollen almost shut — and he looked so sad that I said, "Of course."

He bent down and hugged me; for a moment there we were together in the mirror, our faces side by side.

That day Jack had taken the tops off the cardboard boxes and put one by each hive, so the bees could find their way in. He had also put the queens in the hives, each one in her small separate cage, a hollow block of wood with screen on one side and a plug of white candy for the other bees to eat through.

The next day he asked me to come see the bees at work, freeing their queens — it was quite a spectacle, he said — and to help him put some sugar syrup in the hive feeders.

"I don't know," I said. "I still have more homework."

"Oh, come on, they've calmed down now. Remember, this is a business enterprise — and remember the Little Red Hen."

So I went. I remember crossing the yard with him, both of us in our bee suits, he holding my hand toward the end when I slowed way down. "You just need to get your feet wet," he said. "Then you'll be fine."

My heart was thumping when I looked in the first hive to see the queen in her cage. A knot of bees were nuzzling at the white candy. "See," Jack said, "they're too busy to worry about us." When he poured sugar syrup into the funnel-shaped feeder attached to that hive, bees began to cluster there. A few floated up around my veil but they seemed more curious than angry.

"I think they like you," Jack said. "Bees are famous judges

of character. Here," he said, giving me the jug of syrup, "you do the next one."

My hands trembled as I took it, and my mouth went dry, but I walked to the next hive and, with Jack steadying my elbow, poured syrup into the feeder. "So far so good," Jack said. We went on down the line, me pouring, Jack steadying, until — I am not sure how this happened — syrup sloshed over the edge of the feeder and onto the ground. Suddenly bees were rising up at me in one loud furious mumble.

I was screaming and hitting out at them before Jack caught my arm, and then — feeling a sharp stab at my neck, then another — I screamed louder and tore off my helmet.

Jack was pulling me along, trying to get the helmet back on, then covering my mouth with his hand. I felt sugar water spilling down my leg. Jack knocked the jug from my hand, picked me up, and ran toward the honey house; I stared horrified as the wet legs of my suit darkened with bees.

It happened so fast: outside the honey house, Jack ripping off my suit, my sweater, my jeans; then, inside, his hands all over me, checking for bees, touching me everywhere. He combed through my hair, then lifted it from my neck. I was crying. "Ssh," he kept saying, "you're all right, Jack's here." Gently, with one fingertip, he touched the stings on my neck, counting them — there were three — and then putting his arm around me and saying, "OK, steady, girl, steady," he scraped out the stingers with his thumbnail. "You hold your hair now. Jack will fix you right up."

He turned away, reached for the baking powder on the shelf. I stood waiting, both arms raised, and looked down: I still had on my underpants, but my bra was gone. There were my naked breasts, the nipples pink and tight. I did not move to cover myself, did not lower my arms; I felt my nipples tingle when Jack turned and looked.

He walked toward me, still looking, the baking soda in one palm. I could hear his breathing, and mine. I was no longer crying. He licked one finger, dipped it in the soda, dabbed it on one sting. When that wasn't wet enough he spat into his hand and mixed the soda into a paste. When he put the soda on the next place he stood closer, one arm against my breast.

He dabbed at the back of my neck. "It's that hair," he whispered, "that gorgeous hair." Suddenly his mouth was against my hair, his breath in my ear, and his hands were moving over me again, my back, my sides. Then one hand, gritty with soda, was squeezing my breast, and his mouth was on mine. My mouth was opening, my breast rising to his hand, then he pulled back suddenly.

"Jesus God, we've got to stop this." He stood staring at me; I stared back, looking at his red, swollen eye, the freckles standing out against his skin, ugly, the color of age spots. He unzipped his suit, stepped out of it, flung it back toward me as he left. "Put that on," he said, in an angry voice, then abruptly, he was gone.

I stared out the window at what was framed there: a slice of yard, hives in a row, the gleam of Jack's car in the distance. My neck was beginning to throb; otherwise, I felt numb. Not looking down at myself, I put on Jack's suit and stepped outside — there were my clothes covered with bees. I ran to the house, my heart pounding. The stings hurt, but not enough; I should have been stung all over, stung to death.

Jack and Mama were in the kitchen. She was sitting at the counter; he was rubbing her back. Jack did not look at me, but Mama did; she turned and stared. I saw her take in the too large suit, my messy hair.

She stood up, almost spoke, did not.

"She got a couple of stings, Beatrice, that's all — I had to give her my suit."

Mama started toward her room. I knew she knew, but she said nothing.

"Oh, for Christ's sake . . ." Jack said, "here we go again."
He turned and headed for the stairs.

Mama slammed her door and locked it. I expected to hear the crash of something thrown, but there was only silence. A silence that went on and on.

When Stevie came home, Jack appeared from his study to fix sandwiches and soup for us. He did not look at me; I did not look at him. He left the dining room and went back upstairs. Mama did not come out of her room and Stevie did not ask why. I did not eat; the smell of the soup made me sick.

Stevie and I went to his room and watched TV until it was time for bed.

I fell into sleep like a stone.

I thought I was dreaming. My bed seemed too small, and hands were turning me over, and then, when I tried to sit up, pushing me down. A voice in my ear: "I came to see if you had a fever." One hand on my forehead, the other unbuttoning. "Need to check those stings."

I lay still, my body waking all over.

"Poor baby," he said, kissing the stings, his hand moving to my breast. "Your Jack wants to take care of you, make you feel good.

"That's a girl, that's a girl." Sliding down my pajama bottoms. "Yes." Stroking my thigh. "Your Jack loves you so much."

When he touched between my legs I jumped. "Ssh." His hand cupped me there. "Precious baby. Precious." Then his thumb began to stroke. "That's right, that's right."

"No." I tried to sit up.

One hand was on my mouth; the other was pushing me down. "Jack is going to make you feel good." Then, his mouth on mine, small, gentle kisses, whispering, "Sweet baby, sweet, sweet baby," his fingers between my legs, stroking, pinching. "Oh, yes, Jack found it, didn't he, the sweet place."

I knew I was crying when he began to kiss away my tears, taking them from the edges of my eyes with his lips. "Sweet baby," he whispered, "ssh, don't cry." When I didn't stop, he said, "Hush, hush now, shut up."

His hand was against my mouth before I could cry out; then his weight was on me and his other hand fumbled between my legs. He pushed himself inside me. No! I tried to yell; his hand tightened on my mouth. He moved inside me, jabbing harder and harder. It hurt all the way up inside me, splitting me open; I sobbed onto his hand.

When it was over, he pulled up my pajamas and held me where I hurt. He was crying, too; his face was slippery against mine. "I'm sorry," he whispered, "I'm sorry." He put his arms around me, beginning to rock me. "Ssh, it will be all right. Jack loves you, go to sleep."

And then — it was of this that I was later most ashamed — I put my face on his chest and slept.

In the morning I jerked awake and lay still, staring up at the ceiling. I felt sick between my legs but didn't touch there. I lay with my hands by my sides as the weight began to gather on my chest, pushing me down. When I got up and went to school it was still there, a dark heavy stone where my heart had been.

In Latin class, I remembered the bed — I had not remade it, had not even pulled up the covers — and I fainted. I awoke in the principal's office, my head on the pillow of his couch. No one else was in the room. The bottom part of me felt cold, as if my skirt had been raised, but when I touched there, the skirt was over my legs. When Grandpa appeared in the doorway, his face stiff and pale, I thought it was because he knew.

But that was not why he had come to get me. He had come because of Mama.

Twenty-six

"YOUR MOTHER'S in the hospital, we have to pray for her." That's all Grandpa would say until we got to his house.

On the way we picked up Stevie. He tried to sit close to me in the back, but I turned away and put my face out the window, where the roar of air would fill my eyes and ears. I wished this moment would go on forever, so I wouldn't have to know. Whatever had happened, it was my fault: I kept thinking of Mama's face as she stared at my messy hair, the too large suit.

When the car stopped in the drive, I went cold all over. Somehow my feet worked: I watched them on the steps, following Stevie and Grandpa inside. Grandpa led us to his study and knelt on the floor.

Stevie and I knelt beside him on the green rug with the swirls in it. Stevie's hands were against his mouth, his eyes fixed on Grandpa. My head spun. I thought I might faint again.

"Heavenly Father." Grandpa's voice was shaking. "We beseech thee, we the family of . . ." He put his hands over his face; tears leaked out between his fingers.

"What happened?" Stevie grabbed Grandpa's arm and shook it. "What's wrong with Mama — tell us!"

"Stung." Grandpa's back began to shake. "All over. Hundreds of stings. They don't know if she'll live or not."

I saw Grandpa slump forward, crying, saw Stevie leap up, heard him run down the hall, heard the kitchen door slam. I had not moved.

I looked at my hands, still pressed together: same nails, same chewed place on the thumb. My wrists: familiar knobs of bone, tiny hairs, the black cord watchband. Stung: I let the word loose in my head. Stung: I felt nothing. I was not there.

I was standing, turning, my hands still together. I let my legs take me down the hall, past the hall table with the rose-shaded lamp, past the dining room, up the carpeted steps. I was beginning to feel them on my skin, hot places, stings. I ran up the steps; they were coming faster and hotter, inside my clothes.

In Grandmuddy's room, I tore off my dress and underwear and bolted into her closet. I buried myself in her clothes, scrubbing the sleeve of her old tweed coat hard against my face, gouging the teeth of the fox fur into my hand, stuffing the fox head in my mouth until I gagged. Then I pulled everything down onto me, coats, dresses, suits, piling them on top of my legs, my chest, my head. Everything.

Curled on the floor, weighted down by Grandmuddy's clothes, by the smells of wool and her body, I let my mind go down to a small place, smaller and smaller, like the shutter of a camera narrowing to a circle of light, then to a pinprick, and then down to nothing.

———

Someone was calling my name, far away. There was not enough air. I pushed against the dark weight until my head broke free.

"Beryl!" Jack's voice. Downstairs in the hall. I began to shake. "Beryl!" Louder this time. I leapt up, pulled Grandmuddy's tweed coat from the pile, and wrapped it around me. I was down the stairs before he could come up and find me.

He was holding on to the newel post, looking up the steps as I came down. When he reached his hand out toward me, I moved to the other side of the steps, came down leaning hard against the wall. With my eyes I made him take back his hand. He put both hands in his pockets and looked at the floor.

In the hall I backed up against the door, holding the coat tight around me, aware of having nothing on underneath. I could see from the way he kept swallowing that he had something to tell. I put my hands under the coat sleeves and dug my nails in hard.

Still not looking at me, he said, "She's going to be all right."

I felt my breath go out and my knees begin to give.

"She's still in intensive care, though. And when she's well enough she'll be going to the psychiatric ward."

He looked at me then. There was a long moment when I felt my eyes filling with tears and I thought from the way his eyes shone in the glare of the overhead light that he was about to cry, too. But when he spoke again, his voice was harder. "She should have been hospitalized months ago — I'm going to give Becker hell."

He took his hands out of his pockets, laid one on the other, and looked down at it as if he were checking his nails. "It's a lucky thing I went back to the house for a book, because she was already unconscious. She was lying by the hives . . ." He looked up, staring at the doorframe beside me. "Not a stitch on, bees all over . . . she was stung everywhere, even on her tongue."

I could feel tears sliding down my face and neck. "I wish I was dead," I whispered.

He pushed me against the door so hard my head bounced against the wood. "Don't *ever* say that. This is *not* your fault." His eyes drilled into mine. "She is a very, very sick woman, Beryl. She stirred those bees with a broom, for God's sake — I found it by the hives. She even" — his face twisted with something like disgust — "smeared her breasts with banana."

I could smell banana, sweet and stringy, could taste it. I felt my stomach rise. I pushed Jack so hard he staggered backward, then ran past him down the hall to the bathroom, slammed the door, and locked it. I knelt by the toilet but nothing happened.

Jack was outside, knocking on the door, turning the knob. "Open up, Beryl, come on, let's get you home."

"I want Grandmuddy," I screamed.

"She's at the hospital. I realize you've had a big shock, honey, but come on." He rattled the doorknob. "We need to get you home. We'll pick up Stevie on the way — I thought you could help me talk some sense into him."

"I'm not coming."

"He's refusing to leave, even though they won't let him see your mother. But if you're there — "

"I'm not coming with you, ever." I yelled, banging the toilet lid down over and over.

"Beryl. You come out of there right now or I'm breaking this door down."

"If you do, you'll be sorry."

There was dead silence. Then, "All right, Beryl. I tried." Another pause. "But you refuse to be helped — just like your mother."

I heard him leave then, going not too fast, not too slow, his feet steady in the hall, on the kitchen floor; heard him shut — not slam — the kitchen door. In the quiet before he started the car, I saw him walking to it, getting in, flipping on the lights, checking his watch, turning the key. As he backed the car out of the drive, I thought of his hands on the steering wheel. *He had tried. Just like your mother.* I jumped up, jerked open the medicine cabinet, and started pulling bottles out — Mercurochrome, milk of magnesia, Pepto-Bismol — and smashed them in the sink. Then, shaking, I looked down at the sink full of glass, the liquids running slowly together, and began to cry.

I picked up a piece of blue glass and held it against my wrist. Though I already knew I wouldn't use it, the possibility helped me cry harder, until I was exhausted.

I threw the piece of glass into the trash can and then, suddenly seized with the thought of Grandmuddy coming home and finding all the mess I'd made, I began furiously cleaning up:

scooping up the glass with a guest towel, carrying it outside to the garbage, then running back inside and upstairs to Grandmuddy's room. My heart raced, my hands shook, but I worked quickly, and by the time I heard Grandpa's car in the drive, everything in Grandmuddy's closet, including the tweed coat, was back on its hanger, and I was dressed and waiting on the living room sofa.

Later that night when I couldn't sleep I went downstairs to the kitchen. On the way past Stevie's room — the small room that had once been the pantry — I heard a strange noise, so I opened the door and looked in.

Stevie was kneeling against his bed. He jerked around as I turned on the light. His eyes were blazing, and he had his pocket knife in his hand.

"I hate him! I hate him."

"Put the knife down, Stevie. Here, give it to me."

He threw it at the opposite wall, flung himself on the bed, and began to sob. "I hate that bastard's guts."

I went to kneel beside him. He leaned against me and cried hard. I remember kneeling there beside him, hugging him with one arm, hugging him hard to let him know I was there. But with my other hand I was feeling the rips in the spread, measuring them with my fingers, trying to decide if I could sew them up. When I left I took the spread with me — fortunately it was an old one, and Grandmuddy never seemed to miss it — and put it in a box in my closet, under a pile of dirty clothes.

———

I never had to explain to Grandmuddy why I wanted to stay with her. She seemed to take it for granted that Stevie and I would live there until Mama was well.

We went to Jack's house once, later that same week, for Stevie and me to get our clothes, and for Grandmuddy to get some things she thought Mama would want.

Grandmuddy drove because Grandpa's heart was acting up.

Stevie and I sat in the front beside Grandmuddy and helped her look both ways at the stops.

At one stop her eyes and mine happened to meet; she looked at me for several seconds, her gray eyes steady, and I held my breath. I felt she was looking right into me. "One day at a time, honey," she said.

I could feel tears filling my eyes. Grandmuddy really loved me. I almost spoke: it was the closest I came to saying what had happened.

Stevie jammed his hands in his pockets and stared straight ahead. Grandmuddy put her arm around him, but he stayed stiff. She then reached out her hand and touched my arm. "You poor children," she said. Her eyes were getting watery now, and her face looked wobbly in a way that made me think of biscuit dough.

I leaned away from her and looked out the window, my heart beating fast from what I'd almost said. She would despise me if she knew. There was silence the rest of the way, except for Grandmuddy's occasional sniffling.

When we went up the drive, I was relieved that Jack's car wasn't there. I had had my fingers crossed that he would be gone. Ralph came running to greet us, his body twisting double in that way he had. Stevie pushed past me to get out. "Ralphie, Ralphie," he cried, as the dog jumped up he caught him in his arms and held him. "He's so thin," he wailed. "Grandmuddy, we have to take him with us."

"I don't think so, honey," she said, getting out of the car. "He'll be fine here for a while."

"He will not!" Stevie shouted. When Grandmuddy and I started toward the house, Stevie stood there a moment. I wondered if he was planning to put Ralph in the trunk again, like last Thanksgiving when he'd sneaked him to Grandpa and Grandmuddy's — but then he followed, carrying the dog.

As we walked toward the house I did not look at the bee-hives, but I could feel the weight of them at my left side. I could tell Grandmuddy was also not looking on purpose: she kept her head down, staring at the flagstone walk, and her fingers shook so much when she tried to unlock the door that I finally had to do it for her.

I glanced back at Stevie. He was still holding Ralph — the dog flopping under one arm — and staring at the beehives. His face was furious but so still that even the tears in his eyes looked carved there.

"Come on, Stevie." I touched his arm, but he did not move. As I went in the house, my head was pulled toward the hives; in one instant I took in the terrible white row of them, each with its single slit eye; the hive at the far end, nearest the honey house, was turned on its side.

Inside, I worked fast, dashing up the steps, pulling out my suitcase, and filling it with old clothes; all the new dresses I left hanging in the closet, jammed to one side. My bed had been stripped — by Mama, I thought. I managed to keep my eye from the mattress, striped black and white like prison cloth, and from the stains I'd find there, but I could hardly breathe: it was as if all the air had been sucked from the room. I put my journal, radio, and jewelry box into my suitcase, mashed it down, got it latched on one side, and hurried out of my room, carrying it in my arms so things wouldn't spill. I met Grandmuddy on the stairs. She was coming up to see how we were doing. When I said Stevie hadn't come in yet, she told me to go find him and meanwhile she'd start packing his things.

I went on down the steps, through the dining room, past the table with its chairs neatly pushed in, the empty silver bowl in the center, the cold light on the marble floor.

Outside I ran to the car, put my suitcase in the trunk, and began looking for Stevie. I circled the house, calling his name — looping through the front yard, around the side of the house, passing the tree where the Lathams had tied him up, then the tennis court, and the Osage orange tree.

I stopped at my tree and put my arms around it: my heart was beating so hard I could feel it in the trunk. I looked at the steps I knew so well, the blocks worn by my feet, looked up at the edge of the platform high in the new leaves, and I thought of climbing up, but I could not: my legs were too heavy. Remembering the smell of the platform with my face against it, the sound of leaves around me, I felt so jagged a pain in my chest I could not bear it. I rubbed my cheek hard against the trunk to make the pain go somewhere else. That helped a little. Then I broke off the tip of a nearby branch and squeezed an Osage orange thorn into my palm. It worked: I felt my chest smooth out as all of me went down to that one fiery point.

What I did next I remember as a sort of experiment: holding the thorn in my hand, walking deliberately across the back yard toward the hives, and when the pain came back to my chest, closing my hand tight on the thorn, jabbing it in. I discovered that even near the overturned hive, even near the honey house, even looking in the window where the box of soda sat on the ledge, I could, with enough pressure on the thorn, make myself go still inside. When I walked back past the Osage orange, I broke off a larger branch to take with me.

Grandmuddy came out of the house and called for me. Stevie still had not appeared. Grandmuddy said he must be hiding in the car to devil us, but he was not there.

It was late afternoon now, the loneliest time of the day. I remember how small our voices seemed, calling Stevie's name over and over into the silence. Grandmuddy was beginning to cry. I kept remembering Stevie's face as he looked toward the beehives: dear God, I prayed inside, let him be all right.

Grandmuddy said to get in the car, we'd go look for him, but her voice sounded like she expected the worst. Then, going down the drive, we saw him coming toward us.

Grandmuddy fussed at him as he got in the car, and I asked several times where he'd been, but he said nothing, just got in the back seat without looking at us.

"Where's Ralph?" I said.

He did not answer. We drove the rest of the way home in silence.

That Sunday was Easter. Just a week had passed since the arrival of the bees, but it seemed like forever. Stevie and I went to church with Grandpa and Grandmuddy that day. Only on the way home did it occur to me. "Stevie," I said, "you were supposed to be confirmed on Easter." And there he had sat, singing Baptist hymns.

"No," he said, looking out his window, "I can't."

When I heard him crying in his room that night, I went downstairs. In the light from the hall I could see him kneeling against his bed, sobbing, his rosary wrapped around his hands.

At first I thought he was crying about confirmation. "You can still do it," I said. "You can explain to Sister Mary Virginia and Father Gamber when you go back to school next week."

"Ralph!" he cried, his voice muffled in the covers.

I felt a chill as I remembered Stevie walking up the drive alone. "He'll come back," I said. "He always has before."

"No, he won't," Stevie wailed. "He never will."

I didn't want to know. "Be quiet now," I said. "You'll wake up Grandmuddy."

I went back upstairs, got into bed, and lay curled there shivering a long time.

Twenty-seven

ONE DAY AT A TIME, like Grandmuddy said. Somehow we got through the months when Mama was in the hospital.

Stevie and I went back to school. Those days passed in a blur for me: homework, classes, faces in the halls. The worst moment was when Eunice asked me, in a catty way, why we weren't at our house anymore.

"We've moved," I told her, calmly holding back my hair as I bent to drink from the water fountain. "It's such a relief to be out of the sticks."

We did not go to visit Mama, first because she was in intensive care, then — when she moved to another floor and we almost got to go — because she decided she looked too bad, and after that, because she was on the psychiatric ward, where no children were allowed. We did talk to her on the phone a few times. These conversations were filled with silences; I could hardly think of a thing to say, I felt too awful. Mama asked questions I could feel her straining to think of, like, "Well, are you studying hard?" and "Are you warm enough?" (even though it was at the time late spring). I remember her asking a question she intended as "Do you have everything you need?" only she said — or I heard — "anything;" "Do you have anything you need?" When I answered no, she did not respond.

Mama's brother, Paul, and his wife, Ethel, came from Seattle to see Mama. Grandmuddy was excited about their visit, the first one in years. For lunch she fixed what she remembered as Uncle Paul's favorite meal: fried chicken, corn on the cob, fried okra, cornbread, strawberry shortcake. I helped her with the shortcake and set the table on the screened back porch, using white mats Grandmuddy had woven and the best china and silver. But then when they came, it turned out they'd just eaten on the plane. They sat with us while Grandmuddy and Stevie and I ate; Grandpa wasn't feeling well and had to lie down. Aunt Ethel drank some iced tea, but Uncle Paul said it was too sweet, bad for the teeth (he was a dentist); he drank water instead.

Aunt Ethel was fat and squeezed into a shiny black dress with white piping down the sides; her eyebrows had been plucked and then redrawn in arches that gave her a surprised look. Uncle Paul was only a couple of years older than Mama, but he seemed more like a younger, smarter version of Grandpa. His fingers and fingernails on the water glass were amazingly clean, and I could easily imagine those fingers probing with a sharp metal instrument inside the mouths of his patients.

Nobody said much at first, then Aunt Ethel got started: the weather, the plane ride, Uncle Paul's dental practice, blah blah blah. She talked so much that afterward Stevie and I nicknamed her Aunt Ether; Uncle Paul ought to use her to put his patients out.

They went to see Mama after that. When they came home, they looked as if they'd been to a funeral. "Poor Beatrice," Aunt Ethel kept saying, when she thought Stevie and I couldn't hear.

Uncle Paul thought Mama should be moved to a psychiatric hospital in a big city where they knew what they were doing,

New York, for instance, or Seattle; there was an excellent facility in Seattle where he personally knew the director and could get her a bed.

"She'd be so far from the children," I heard Grandmuddy say. They were in the living room; I was outside, poised on the steps, where I could start walking up if someone came out.

"They don't see her, anyway," Uncle Paul said, in a voice like this was as it should be. "What about the children? You can't keep on taking care of them forever, Mother."

"We'll manage," Grandmuddy said, and I felt like running and hugging her; I thought this meant we were going to get to stay on with her, even when Mama got out of the hospital.

Uncle Paul and Aunt Ethel left, and nothing changed. May passed, then June.

After school was out I often went to lie in Grandmuddy's garden. Sometimes I took a book with me but almost never read it. What I liked to do was lie in the sun by the brick wall, where the plaques for her dead children were. I remember so well how that felt, my eyes shut, the sun hot on my face and body, thinking of how I was like one of those rocks in a Japanese garden I'd seen in a book of Mama's. Lying there with the hot sun burning everything away, thinking: Beryl lives here.

One day Mama came for a visit on a day pass. Grandmuddy told us that Mama was really all well, as good as new, brand new; she'd soon be getting out of the hospital for good.

Jack brought her; how vividly I remember that first sight of her as she got out of his car. How my heart raced — in excitement, but also in fear. What would she say to me?

There she was, brand-new! Brand-new, her haircut and permanent! Brand-new, her clothes! Brand-new, the way she jumped out of the car and wobbled for a moment on her high heels like a fawn on its first day, then held out her arms for me and Stevie together.

She kissed my forehead, then looked at me. Her eyes were not brand-new. They were the same, only dulled, the pain pushed back. She hugged us again, first me, then Stevie, one in each arm. "I sure did miss you kids," she said. I was so relieved that I began to cry: she'd forgiven me, she loved me again.

But on the way inside, Jack took my arm, held me back while Mama and Stevie and Grandmuddy went in to where Grandpa was waiting in the living room.

He looked right at me. "She's had shock therapy," he said. "Her memory is perfectly blank."

———

Not long after that, Grandmuddy called me and Stevie into the living room and told us we'd both be going to boarding school in the fall: he to an Episcopal boys' school in Richmond, I to an Episcopal girls' school there. That way, she said, her eyes watering, we could see each other on the weekends, and come home together at vacations.

Stevie burst into tears, and I — though secretly elated — acted mad. "I bet this is Uncle Paul's stupid idea," I said.

"I believe it was your stepfather's idea, and your mother's too. She thinks it will be the best thing for a while anyway, until she's completely herself again."

"I want to be with Mama," Stevie wailed, sounding like somebody half his age.

"Well, you will be soon," Grandmuddy said. "She's getting out next week — so you'll all be together for the rest of the summer."

"At Jack's house?" Stevie and I said it together.

"Yes, won't it be nice for you to all be together again? Your stepfather said to tell you, by the way, that he's gotten rid of the bees."

———

After Mama had been home for a few days, she and Jack came to get us. They didn't say we were starting over, but I could tell that was how he meant it to be. On the way out to the house we ate brownies that Mama had made and sang round songs, "Row, Row, Row Your Boat" and "Frère Jacques." I felt as if I were in a play.

We got out of the car and walked toward the house. I looked out at the yard: the beehives really were gone, but the honey house was still there. I felt a shock, seeing it as I stood so close to Mama and Jack. "Welcome home, kiddies," Jack said, holding the door for us.

There was new furniture in the living room, the comfortable sofa and chairs Mama had always wanted and several small Oriental rugs that she said were very expensive. There was also a harpsichord Jack had gotten so he and Mama could learn to play four-handed Bach together. She sat down at the harpsichord and demonstrated what she'd learned so far: a few chords, "Twinkle, Twinkle," and then "Chopsticks," to which Jack added a boogie-sounding lower part. I noticed that Mama was wearing the lapis ring Jack had given her on her right hand now; on the left was a ring I hadn't seen before, a band of diamonds.

"Isn't this great?" she said, turning around on the bench. She looked a lot older — maybe it was all the makeup. "You kids could learn to play, too. Jack is a really good teacher, it turns out." She giggled. "Of course, I already knew that."

"No thanks," Stevie said in a nasty voice that Mama and Jack acted as if they hadn't heard.

Jack started playing Bach by himself. Mama turned around to watch for a while, then went to fix supper.

That supper was like all the other meals we had there that summer, everyone very polite, passing dishes, passing butter; have some more rolls, dear? Mama and Jack, but especially Jack, kept the conversation going, mostly current events topics it sounded like they'd read up on just for this purpose. Jack waved Mama down whenever something was needed at the table and went to get it himself. Mama smiled a lot, but her eyes still had that dull look.

One day I wandered into Mama's room when she was at her desk, staring out the window. "I feel like a zombie," she said. "You can't imagine how terrible."

I stood there a moment, trying to think what to say or do. Then I turned and walked away.

That evening after supper the four of us sat around the coffee table in the living room and played Monopoly, one of the new games Jack had bought. There was opera music in the background — because, Jack said, it had been Mama's turn to choose, but every time the soprano sang high he put his hands over his ears and made a face. He and Mama were both drinking brandy. Because it was a special occasion, Jack said, he gave me and Stevie both a little sherry. When Stevie got both Boardwalk and Park Place, Jack toasted him. Then he said, his glass still in the air, "Gosh, this is fun — all of us together again, a real family again." With his other hand he reached for Mama's arm; I saw him squeeze it. "Isn't it, Beatrice?"

"It's fabulous," she said, a word I'd never heard her use before.

Stevie looked at me across the table, his expression both ironic and warm. I had never been so glad that he was there.

We went to bed early, as we always did during those weeks. Mama and Jack slept in the same room now; there was no mention of snoring, or sleeplessness.

That night, as usual, I couldn't get to sleep in my bed, so I dragged the covers and pillow out to the balcony. Stevie came out, too, and put his pallet next to mine. It felt good to lie there in the dark with him nearby, both of us looking silently up at the stars.

———

That first year when Stevie and I went away to school, we would sometimes meet for lunch at the Robert E. Lee hotel in downtown Richmond. There, in the dining room, being waited on by black men in uniforms who put the large cloth napkins in our laps and removed the silver covers from our steaming dishes, Stevie and I pretended we were British, that our parents had sent us here from England.

We were Sibyl and Bertrand.

"Well, Bertrand, I had a letter from Mum."

"Jolly good. How is dear Mum? And Pater too, of course?"

"Mum is tolerably well, but Pater, I'm afraid, is under the weather."

"What's the matter with the poor chappie?"

"Gangrene." The ladies at the next table had grown quiet. "Got pus oozing out everywhere."

"Scrofulous pus?"

"Veddy scrofulous," I said, beginning to laugh. Stevie was laughing, too, his face red, his napkin covering his mouth. "Oozing out his eyes and ears," I managed to say before Stevie and I both exploded, and biscuit spewed all over.

One Saturday Stevie was supposed to meet me for lunch but did not; the waiter came to tell me he was sick. I ate alone, then a man at a corner table asked me to join him for dessert. Later I told Stevie I'd had charlotte russe, but I did not mention the stranger with the pale blue eyes, his hands nervous on the menu, his leg pressing mine beneath the long red cloth.

Over the years what Stevie and I did talk about — always it was the central mystery around which our conversations revolved — was why Mama stayed with Jack, and he with her; why they lived on and on together, in continuing disharmony, for twenty-seven more years.

V

Twenty-eight

In 1986 Jack planned a family vacation — a reunion, he called it — at Kill Devil Hills, a beach on the Outer Banks of North Carolina.

I seldom returned to North Carolina. I had been in Chicago twenty years, first as a student, then as a curator of manuscripts and rare books at a small library frequented by literary scholars. For a while I'd looked for Daddy, haunting the jazz clubs, searching for his face in crowds, but I had long since given up. On my rare visits home — for Stevie's ordination as an Episcopalian priest, his marriage to Mary Lib, the birth of their daughter, Elizabeth, the funerals of Grandpa and Grandmuddy — I had always avoided Jack.

When Jack sent me the round-trip plane ticket, I called Mama to say I was swamped at work and doubted I could come. She begged me to reconsider. Jack was making no bones about his philandering now; during their recent trip to Greece she'd surprised him and his so-called research assistant in a hotel room and he'd hardly bothered to deny it. There was a follow-up call from Stevie. "Please come," he said. "It would really cheer her up." And I had to see Elizabeth, he said; she was twelve now and growing up so fast.

I told Stevie I'd think about it. I planned to wait a day or two, then send the ticket back with a regretful note.

But the ticket lay unmailed on my hall table. I began to have small accidents, things lost and broken, a kettle in flames on the stove. I was restless at work. The task of transposing the library's catalogue to computer — something I'd initiated — stretched endlessly before me. Even the devotional quality of silence in the reading rooms, formerly so soothing, now struck me as oppressive.

One day I left work early and went for a long walk along Lake Michigan. I passed two unshaven men sitting at a stone table, their heads bent over a game of checkers; a man and a woman arguing in German, lovers, I thought, from the intensity of their voices; a man in a blue uniform scooping dead fish from the edge of the water with a bucket. On a bench was an old woman who was wearing, in spite of the heat, a black sweater and heavy stockings; from a distance she reminded me of Grandmuddy. I stopped and looked out at the water, beyond the small gray waves and clusters of sailboats to the horizon. I *would* go. I hurried back to my apartment to call Stevie.

Jack had rented the cottage for a week, but I went only for the second weekend. I flew from Chicago to Manteo on a Friday morning.

I was surprised by how nervous I felt; it was a nervousness that seemed to have no particular content. I'd spent too much money on my travel dress — a black Italian knit that had been, I decided in the mirror of the airplane rest room, a mistake.

I went back to my seat, ordered a drink, and tried to read.

Stevie came alone to meet me at the airport. As I walked down the shaky metal steps of the plane, he loped toward me, his belly jiggling. I was startled by how much weight he'd gained, and by his ludicrous costume, a black clerical shirt and khaki bermuda shorts; my first thought was of an overweight postman in summer uniform. I was momentarily ashamed for him, and sad. But his eyes were the same; it was a relief to look into them, and to feel him recognize me. We hugged a long time without speaking. I closed my eyes, remembering the time in his room when I'd told him he might be sent off to school alone, how he'd held on tight like this.

It was a sweltering August day, so we rode to the cottage with the car air conditioning on. Stevie talked about Mama as he drove, warning me about how ill she looked, how depressed she was. As he told me, in greater detail, about the incident in Athens, I stared out my window, looking through the rows of houses for glimpses of the sea. I could hardly wait to hear the ocean, and smell it.

The cottage was a gray box on stilts with its name, "Sea Manse," spelled out on the front in imitation rope script.

Mama had held lunch. They were all waiting for me in the air-conditioned living room.

Mama had on an embroidered Greek caftan and heavy make-up. Her eyes watered as she held out her arms to me.

Over Mama's shoulder I saw Mary Lib, dressed in a pink shirt and green linen shorts. "Bear-ill!" she cried when it was her turn, offering me a powdered cheek and then her Altar Guild smile.

"You remember Elizabeth," Mary Lib said, frowning her daughter forward.

She was tall and gangly, and her hair was wet. She wore clothes I knew her mother must despise, cut off jeans and a T-shirt that said "The Grateful Who?" When she smiled dutifully and said "Hi, Aunt Beryl," I saw the braces.

"You've gotten so big," I said stupidly, and kept on staring. With her long, sleepy face, her slightly sullen expression, she might have been myself at twelve. Her eyes were different, though, brown like Stevie's, and more closely set than mine.

"Hello, Beryl," Jack said. He looked exactly the same; he even had on tennis clothes. I stared at his unlined face: the metamorphosist who does not change.

When Jack started to hug me, I held out my hand. He laughed, making a joke of it. "Charmed, I'm sure."

The contact with his skin shocked me; I quickly drew back my hand.

Elizabeth showed me to the room that she and I were to share, then I changed clothes and we all sat down to lunch in the living room.

We ate at a rectangular glass table, Jack at the head, Mama at the other end by the kitchen. Stevie and I sat cater-cornered to each other, just as we had at Grandpa and Grandmuddy's house. I was beside Jack and across from Elizabeth. Through the closed glass doors I could see, but not hear, the ocean.

The meal was Greek, all recipes Mama had learned on the trip: marinated raw squid, spanakopita with pastry toughened from waiting in the oven, salad with feta and black olives. To drink, there was retsina, bitter and medicinal-tasting until I got used to it. I drank more than ate, picking at my salad, rearranging the pieces of squid.

I told about the plane trip and my work, then listened to accounts of the week, the bad weather they'd suffered, first rain, now the heat, and this morning the ocean full of jellyfish.

I kept my head angled away from Jack. I could not keep my eyes from Elizabeth. Her hair was drying and hung to her shoulders in damp reddish gold waves. With the backdrop of the ocean, the effect was uncanny, so much like the Botticelli Venus that Jack had shown me in his art book. I remembered how Jack had moistened his middle finger as he lifted the tissue from that page.

I looked at Elizabeth's small breasts beneath the T-shirt, the pout of her lower lip. She flicked a glance at me: I was staring. I looked away from her, down at the table. I caught my breath, transfixed by the sight of our legs beneath the glass: Jack's freckled and bristling with red hair, Elizabeth's thighs sweet and firm, my own thighs pale and flabby, like large, shelled mollusks.

The conversation flowed on — the new wing on Stevie's church, some book Mary Lib's book club was reading. But I listened to the silence beneath the talk; it seemed to grow louder and louder, ringing in my ears. I watched Mama anxiously monitoring the slowly diminishing portions of food on the plates. My gaze returned often to Elizabeth, and to the legs, like magnified, nightmarish sea creatures beneath a glass-bottomed boat. Jack's right leg began to jitter up and down. Soon he began to outline the afternoon's agenda: first a swim, then a ride down to Ocracoke.

Elizabeth shuddered. "I'm not going back in that water again," she said. "Not with all those jellyfish."

"*Aequorae aequorea,*" Jack said. His face was turned toward Elizabeth. "I looked them up in the field guide. Many-ribbed Hydromedusae, quite harmless."

"Yeah," I said. "Just like your bees were harmless."

Jack swiveled toward me and tipped his head back slightly. "*You* are obviously feeling no pain," he said with a little smile.

"I think Ocracoke is a great idea," Mama said in a chipper voice.

"Shall we have coffee?" Mary Lib said, raising her eyebrows at Stevie. He got up and headed to the kitchen.

I poured myself another glass of wine.

"Better go easy on that, my girl," Jack said.

"You better watch your p's and n's," I said.

"You mean p's and q's," he said.

"I mean p's and n's," I said. "Pronouns and nouns — my man." I stood and looked down at him. My head was woozy, but there was a hard clear place inside me. For a moment everything rose up in me with terrible clarity.

"I'm getting the hell out of here," I said, and walked around the table to the door. I was unsteady on my feet. No one spoke, watching me go; the silence was like glass.

I tugged open the door and stepped out into the heat. As I

slid the door shut, I looked back in, but no one looked at me. No one had moved: a still life.

Kicking off my shoes, I went down the steps and toward the water, walking quickly across sand that scorched my feet. I climbed the small man-made dune with its pathetic fringe of sea oats and gazed out at the glittering blue ocean. *Feeling no pain.* Bastard. That bastard. That son of a bitch. Hot tears spilled onto my face. I ran down the dune and across the narrow strip of sand to the water.

I passed a blur of sunbathers and splashed into the water. I kicked against a small wave as I pushed out to the breakers. "Goddamn him!" I yelled, flailing my arms against a rising wave. The wave broke against my chest, pushing me back, drenching my shirt and face. I went back toward shore, then turned and began to run through the shallow water at the edge of the waves. I ran hard, crying, not caring who saw. Birds on the sand scattered and rose above me. I was soon out of breath, with a stitch in my side. I slowed to a trot, then a walk. Still crying, I walked across the sand and flopped down at the base of a dune. I put my head on my knees and sobbed until I was empty.

I wiped my face against my damp shirt and sat a long time, staring out at the rippled mirror of the ocean. There was a dull, heavy ache in my chest.

Walking back, I saw one of the jellyfish, a shimmering gelatinous mass washed up on the sand. I made myself bend down to look; through the transparent body the tentacles and organs looked like strands of torn flesh.

When I returned to the cottage, Mama and Jack had left for Ocracoke. The others were waiting to take me to the Wright Brothers museum with them. But I said no, thank you; I went to my room and slept.

I slept little that night, however, or the next. I was not used to having someone else in the room. As I lay listening to Elizabeth's quiet breathing, I could not tell if she was sleeping or not; perhaps she was awake, wondering when I would sleep.

After that first lunch, most of the weekend was uneventful. The others went on excursions, to see the fishing boats at Wanchese, to climb Jockey's Ridge. I spent most of my time lying on the beach, letting the sun bake me into the sand. The dull ache did not go away.

Stevie drove me to the airport, but this time everyone came along. The talk was determinedly pleasant; my outburst was going to be overlooked, and forgotten.

Mary Lib and Elizabeth were in the front seat of the station wagon with Stevie. I sat behind him, next to the window; beside me were Mama and Jack.

Jack was still wearing tennis clothes. Mama had on a bright turquoise sundress and too much of a cloying perfume that made me think of Evening in Paris; she fidgeted with her rings.

Mary Lib was going on about the church. They had eleven pianos now, they were so grateful. The latest one was a Steinway, you never heard such a tone, left to them in a will; the generosity of some people was incredible. . . . Poor Stevie, I thought. I rolled down the window and leaned my head out for a last breath of salt air. I shut my eyes. The wind against my face reminded me of the day we'd moved to Jack's house and I'd leaned out the window and thought about Daddy.

Mary Lib interrupted her monologue to say, "Bear-ill, it's ninety-eight degrees. We'll cook!"

I pulled my head back in and rolled the window up. Mary Lib went on yammering. "Stevie," I broke in. "Do you ever wonder what our lives would have been like if Daddy had never left?"

There was an abrupt silence. Then, in a carefully toneless voice, Stevie said, "I don't think about it."

"When are you going to grow up, Beryl?" Mama said.

"Good question," I said to the window. "When are you going to start giving a damn how I feel?"

Mama did not answer. There was silence the rest of the drive.

A few weeks later Mama called me at work.

"He's finally gone and done it," she said in a caustic voice. "Left me for one of his little chippies."

I stared at the computer screen. "The research assistant?" I managed to say.

She gave a bitter laugh. "It turned out he had a hotter prospect right here in town."

I felt for a moment as if I might scream out loud; I pushed the feeling down. "You'll be better off without him," I said. "It's just too bad you didn't make the first move."

"What do you mean, the first move?"

"I mean, Why didn't you leave him? I'm sure there were a thousand times you wanted to, all those fights about the bees — "

"I stayed for your sakes, goddammit, yours and Stevie's."

"Didn't it ever occur to you we might have been better off without him?"

Mama didn't answer; I could hear her breathing. Finally she slammed down the phone.

I sat at my desk with my head in my hands. I realized I had been shouting; behind me in the office I could hear the silence carved out by my words.

———

A few months later Mama was diagnosed as having breast cancer. Stevie called one night to tell me, waking me from sleep. I had gone to bed early, sick with flu. I listened numbly while he told me the facts: radical mastectomy of both breasts; the doctors were fairly hopeful; the operation was next week, a Monday.

I put down the phone and lay motionless in the dark. Suddenly it came upon me, like an image from a dream: Mama's breasts smeared with banana and dark with stinging bees.

I sat up and put my feet on the floor. Then I took off my gown and walked to the bathroom. I turned on the light and looked at myself in the mirror: my tired face, my heavy breasts. I put my forehead against the mirror and began to cry.

———

The operation was in Richmond, where Mama had moved — in spite of Stevie's protests — after Jack left her. She and Daddy had lived there when they were first married, and Stevie and I had both been born there: it was a city she now remembered with nostalgia.

I arrived in Richmond the day after the operation. Though I had a plausible excuse — I was just getting over the flu — I was relieved not to have to see Mama with breasts one day, without them the next. Everything had gone well, Stevie told me on the phone, the doctors said they had gotten it all, meaning the cancer, but I kept thinking of breasts.

She was at St. Mark's, a new hospital on the opposite side of town from the airport. On the way, I stopped at a florist's and bought a dozen red, long-stemmed roses. As soon as I got back in the taxi, I wished I'd gotten something else — a chrysanthemum, a gloxinia. In their green tissue and red ribbon, the roses looked like a lover's gift.

In the hospital elevator, going up to her room, my fingers grew damp on the tissue as I tried to think what I could say. I had forgotten to prepare.

The door to her room was cracked open; I pushed it wider and tiptoed in. There was Stevie in his priest's clothes on the far side of the bed. He was holding Mama's hand and praying; she lay with her eyes shut, receiving his strength through her arm. Except that they had aged, it might have been that time when Mama had burned her hand and Stevie knelt praying by her bed.

Stevie glanced in my direction. "Amen," he murmured.

Mama turned her head and looked at me.

"Hello, Mama." I walked toward her, surprised by how well she looked: normal, except for the bandage I glimpsed at the top edge of her gown.

"You're here at last." She reached her hand for mine. Tears came to her eyes.

As I bent to kiss her forehead, the sight of that familiar waxy part in her hair made my heart contract. "How are you feeling, Mama?"

"Not good." Her voice wavered and broke. "Not good at all."

"She's had a lot of pain," Stevie said.

"Poor Mama. I'm so sorry." I squeezed her hand, looking down at it: there was the burn scar, a white place running below the first two fingers like something spilled.

"Everything went well, though," Stevie said. "And she's been a real trooper."

"That's wonderful," I said, looking at her, trying to smile.

"Beryl's brought you some beautiful flowers, Mama."

"Oh," I said, "here," and held them out to her.

"Roses!" she cried, dropping my hand and Stevie's to hold the flowers to her chest. She bent her face toward them and inhaled deeply as though they had a scent.

"I'll go get a vase," Stevie said.

"How stupid. I should have thought of that."

"Don't be silly," he said. On his way out he stopped to give me a hug, then gazed straight into my eyes: the sincere pastoral look, I thought. "You look fine," he said.

"So do you," I said, though it wasn't true. There were pouches under his eyes and his face was pale and tired. "I'm sorry I wasn't here."

"That's OK," he said, giving my shoulder a pat. "That flu is nasty stuff. Elizabeth just came down with it, so of course she couldn't come, and Mary Lib thought she ought to stay with her — "

"I insisted!" Mama said. "There was no need for Mary Lib

to come all the way up here. Stevie was here to see me through it — and of course I knew you'd be coming soon."

There was a pause. "Well," Stevie said, "I'll go get that vase."

I pulled a chair up to Mama's bedside and sat down. She was holding the roses tight against her chest. She closed her eyes, opened them again, and stared up at the ceiling. I looked at the IV tube going into her left hand, the bag of fluid hooked to a metal rod above her. I hadn't noticed it before.

"You must be exhausted," I said.

"This is his fault, you know. I wouldn't be lying here right now if it wasn't for that bastard."

I felt a stab of anger so fierce I could not breathe. "You — " I began.

Mama turned toward me, her eyes smoldering, her mouth turned down in that sour angle I knew so well. "You — " I said again, and then stopped. She would not change. Ever. "It's just all very sad," I said.

Later Stevie and I had coffee in the hospital cafeteria. The large room was almost empty, just one group of nurses playing cards and an orderly mopping the floor; there was a strong odor of ammonia. We sat at a small table in the corner.

"She says this is Jack's fault," I said.

"Well," Stevie said, reaching into his shirt pocket for his Sweet 'n Low. "I see it all the time. People often get sick after a big shock, be it death or divorce." I watched as he tore the ends off three pink packages and dumped the contents into his coffee.

"She didn't have to stay," I said.

He shrugged. "She didn't think she had a choice."

"She did have a choice."

"Beryl . . ." Stevie looked over his shoulder, an embarrassed grin on his face. "You're shouting."

"OK, I'll shut up." I stared down at the coffee in my Styrofoam cup. "So," I said, "how's Elizabeth?"

"She got one of those punk haircuts. Mary Lib is fit to be tied." He gave a short laugh.

In the elevator going up to Mama's room, I said, "There are things you don't understand."

"What do you mean? What things?"

I shook my head. The elevator stopped. I stepped off and started down the hall ahead of Stevie.

He caught up with me outside Mama's room. With one hand he held the door shut, with the other he grabbed my arm. "I might understand, Beryl," he said in a low, angry whisper, "if you'd give me half a chance."

————

The next summer Mama's cancer returned, inoperable this time. In spite of radiation treatments and chemotherapy, her condition worsened rapidly. In October Stevie called to tell me she was dying, I should come right away.

The hospital was a small, old-fashioned one near Monument Avenue in Richmond. On the phone, Stevie told me he'd been upset at first that she was not at St. Mark's, but he was reconciled after seeing her. Nothing could be done for her now except to ease the pain. She was in and out of consciousness, on heavy doses of morphine.

When I got there she had rallied — for my visit, Stevie and the nurse both said. Stevie warned me that she looked bad. He and I went in together.

Her bed had been raised so that she was almost sitting. Her eyes were open; they turned toward me as I walked in.

Nothing could have prepared me for how she looked: a white cloth tied about her head to cover the baldness, her arms skeletal, her eyes hooded, desperate.

I tried not to cry as I sat down beside her and reached through the metal siding to take her hand. It was cold, and prominently bone.

"Hello, Mama."

She had to unstick her lips to speak. "Don't let my clothes," she whispered. "Don't let her get."

"What?" I looked at Stevie across the bed.

"Nobody's going to take your clothes, Mama," Stevie said. "You're fine here, this is a good place, excellent nurses."

"That bit — —, that bit — —" Her dark eyes sucked at me. Suddenly I understood: Jack's new wife.

"Don't worry, Mama, I won't."

She squeezed my hand with trembling fingers. Her left hand fumbled at the black-and-white-speckled notebook that lay in her lap.

"Mama's been writing today," Stevie said. "She's feeling a lot stronger."

"That's great, Mama," I said.

". . . hill of beans," she whispered. Her mouth dropped open, and she made a sound so loud I jumped; then I realized she had begun to snore. Her hand went limp in mine. I stood holding her hand a long time as she slept, listening to the long, shuddering breaths broken by jagged silences.

She lived three more days — the first, in and out of consciousness, the last two in a coma. That final day Stevie and I took a long walk down Monument Avenue past the statues of mounted Confederate generals.

We went into a restaurant and sat at a booth by the window. The waitress was talking and laughing with the only other customer, a man in work clothes at the counter. Finally she came and took our order, apple pie for Stevie, coffee for us both.

Stevie sat with his elbows on the table and rubbed his face. He had been sleeping very little. We were silent, waiting for the pie and coffee. When it came, Stevie dug into the pie. "Cardboard," he said, making a face, "but maybe it will revive me."

I looked down at the wooden surface of the booth, my untouched cup of coffee, my hand.

"How's Elizabeth?" I said.

"OK," he said. "Her grades are good. But I worry about her, Beryl. Things are so much harder for kids these days."

"Oh, yes," I said. "We lived in the good old days, Ozzie and Harriet in Dixieland."

He looked up at me. "I know — we had a hell of a time. I just thank God that Elizabeth has a normal family." He took another bite of pie. "But what I mean is the kind of stuff you and I didn't have to deal with — drugs, you know, and sex, all that pressure — "

"Stevie . . ." My heart was pounding. "Jack raped me."

Fork in midair, Stevie leaned forward, frowning slightly, as if he had misheard.

"Jack raped me."

Stevie's face, even his eyes, froze. He did not move, or speak.

"It was after the bees came — before Mama stung herself. I always felt like that was my fault." Tears flooded my eyes. "I never told anyone before."

Stevie put down his fork and stared, still struggling to take this in. "Where?" he finally said.

"In my room."

"In your *room?* With me right there?" Tears filled his eyes. He half rose, then pushed himself from his side of the booth and came to sit by me. When he put his arms around me, I let my head fall on his shoulder; then I cried and cried.

We walked back toward the hospital arm in arm. I felt exhausted but lighter. There was no ache in my chest this time.

We paused at a corner, waiting for the light to change. "That bastard," Stevie said. "I'd like to punch his fucking lights out."

"You sure don't talk like a preacher," I said, trying to get him to smile. "What if Grandpa heard you?"

"I hope he does hear me." He threw his head back. "Fucking bastard!" he shouted up at the sky.

A trio of teenage boys crossing the street toward us stared, then began to snicker.

Stevie's shoulders were shaking. "Come on, Stevie," I said, pulling at his arm.

"I hate Jack!" he shouted. "I've always hated him. I wanted to kill him . . . but I killed poor Ralph instead." Tears streamed down his face. "I killed him, Beryl, I choked him to death with my goddamn belt."

"Oh, Stevie," I said, and put my arms around him. He put his arms around me and sobbed, his belly heaving against me.

"I'm sorry," he said when it was over. He took a handkerchief from his pocket and mopped his face. "I know it's nothing compared to what happened to you. But it's what *I've* never told anybody."

We crossed the street arm in arm, walked a ways farther down the sidewalk, then sat down on a bench.

We were quiet a while, then Stevie said, "How did you stand it, Beryl, not telling anyone?"

"I don't know," I said. "I just got used to it."

He turned and stared at me. "God, that's terrible. That's the worst thing of all."

We sat looking at each other a few moments, then he said, "You've got to get it out of your system — it's poison."

"I told *you*."

"You've got to confront him."

"I can't."

"You can. I'll go with you."

"He'd just say I was crazy. Sometimes I wonder if I am crazy."

Stevie took me by the shoulders. "You are not crazy, Beryl."

"No."

"You are *not* crazy," he repeated.

It was beginning to grow dark. We stood and walked on to the hospital. We did not speak, but I had never felt closer to anyone.

There was a nurse in Mama's room, checking her pulse.

"How is she?" Stevie asked.

"No change," the nurse whispered, and tiptoed out.

We sat in chairs on opposite sides of the bed and watched Mama's still face until the room was entirely dark.

———

The call that Mama had died came at three A.M. Stevie and I went to the hospital in a taxi. The elevator wasn't working, so we walked several flights to her floor, the sounds of our feet echoing in the cavernous stairwell.

The door to her room was standing open. Stevie and I walked in. There was no doctor or nurse, only Mama, her head in the same position on the pillow as when we had left. Just like she's sleeping: that's how the nurse had described Mama in her coma. But when I tiptoed closer I was shocked by the change. Her mouth drooped open slightly to one side, and her face was empty. There was nothing behind those closed eyelids; she was gone. I felt a wave of dizziness. I caught on to the cold bed rail and held tight while Stevie began to pray.

Later, after the doctor had come and gone and Stevie and I had cried, we began to gather her things. I cleared out her closet, Stevie the bedside table.

"Beryl," Stevie said. I turned to look at him. He had the black-and-white-speckled notebook in his hand, holding it out toward me. He looked as though he might start crying again. "There's a message for you," he said.

I opened the book and looked through the pages: there was nothing but scribbling, marks I could not read.

"At the end," Stevie said.

I turned to the last page. There Mama had printed, in large, shaky letters, the only legible words: "BRYL, BURN MY CLOTHES!"

Mama had not wanted a funeral. There was a memorial service at a Baptist church she'd been attending the last few months.

There were five of us, all in the front pews, Mary Lib, Stevie, and I on one side of the aisle, on the other side Elizabeth and a friend of Mama's, a woman from the apartment building where she had lived.

I kept looking across the aisle at Elizabeth in her navy blue suit, the hat her mother had made her wear over her spiky, dyed-red hair. The shade of red reminded me of the Raggedy Ann I'd given her when she was a little girl. As she glanced over at me, I wondered what she saw. Not the girl I'd been, certainly. A middle-aged woman, dull, quiet, a little strange: no one who'd have something to tell her.

After the service I went to Mama's apartment to gather her clothes. Stevie offered to come with me, but I wanted to go alone.

Before I went inside the apartment building, I took a walk around the neighborhood, looking at what she must have looked at: rows of brownstones, spiked iron fences, a clutter of children's toys in one small yard, a planting of yellow chrysanthemums in another.

The black-and-white-speckled notebook was in my pocketbook. At a bus shelter I stopped and sat on the bench and took out the book. I looked carefully at each line, trying to make out any word, any clue of what she had been trying so hard to communicate those last days. Nothing was decipherable but those last four words. I closed the book and sat without moving, filled with the sadness of Mama's life.

I got up from the bench and began to walk. It was nearly dusk; lights were beginning to come on in houses. Through the windows I could see people in kitchens, people at tables. I walked fast, working my muscles, making myself breathe hard.

At the door of Mama's apartment house, I turned and looked across the street: the row of brownstones with lights on in the windows, the gold and scarlet maple leaves blazing in the last light, a girl in a red sweatshirt jogging down the street. Suddenly everything was in such sharp, brilliant focus that I held my breath. I will write about it, I thought, I will write about what happened to us. Exhilaration rose in me, filling my arms and chest and face; at that moment, anything seemed possible.

I walked upstairs to Mama's apartment, unlocked the door, and stepped inside. In her letters Mama had described her apartment as elegant, but it was depressing: a thin, mouse gray carpet, dusty venetian blinds, mismatched pieces of furniture that I remembered from Jack's house and before. In the bedroom was the rose armchair, its seat still sunken, that had been in my room. Above her bed on the wall was a gallery of photographs, a few of Elizabeth but mostly Stevie and me: Stevie in his Superman cape, Stevie on his bike, and the one of me grinning over my shoulder as I mounted the steps of the Osage orange.

I emptied her dresser drawers — socks, underwear, pajamas, sweaters, a soft bed jacket I'd sent her that was still in its tissue. From the closet I took suits, dresses, blouses; they made a huge pile on the bed.

I went back to the closet and cleared the top shelf. There were a few sweaters, some empty boxes, my old jewelry box, and the Blooming Leaf coverlet Grandmuddy had woven. I had not thought of it in years. I held the coverlet to my face a moment: it still had that scratchiness, that familiar smell.

I put the jewelry box and the coverlet on the bed, and went back for Mama's shoes. When I bent to pick up her shoes — they were jumbled together, lying at forlorn angles, all misshapen by bunions — it hit me: Mama was dead, her life was over.

I found the mask of the Japanese demon woman in the back of the closet inside a brown paper bag. I stared at the white face, the horns, the grimacing teeth, thinking of this mask above Mama's desk, remembering how its furious, deep-set eyes had seemed to follow me everywhere in the room. I put the mask on top of the pile of clothes, then called the airport to cancel my flight.

I rented a car and packed it with Mama's things: the coverlet, jewelry box, and a box of photographs on the front seat, the mask and the bags of clothes in the back seat. That night I drove from Richmond to Blacksboro. I slept a few hours in the parking lot of a Howard Johnson's outside Blacksboro, then went in for breakfast: poached eggs, sausage, English muffin. As I bit into the English muffin, I realized I'd ordered Mama's favorite breakfast.

I drove north into what used to be the country between town and Jack's house. Now there was mile after mile of strip development and clusters of housing subdivisions with names like Archer's Glen and Whispering Pines. The woods where Stevie had hidden from the Latham boys and where he'd killed Ralph were gone. A condominium complex stood there now.

As I sped past Jack's house I had a momentary flash of him crossing the road and myself behind the wheel of this gray, rented car, gunning him down.

The Whitakers' farmhouse was still standing but deserted; there was a shopping mall in what had been their pasture. I drove farther, down one road, then another, looking for the place where I had helped Mama throw Joanne's things and where I'd thrown Daddy's records and postcards. I had thought it might still be here, perhaps converted to an official county landfill, but I could not find it, could not even locate the place where it had been.

I drove slowly back over the roads along which I'd come. At the shopping center in the Whitakers' old pasture, I pulled in and drove down the line of stores — drugs, groceries, video rental, cleaners, K Mart — then around to the back. Behind the K Mart was a large green dumpster. I parked there, then walked to the grocery store and bought a package of dried black-eyed peas. I went back to the dumpster, took the bags of clothes from the back seat, and heaved them in one at a time. I saved the Japanese demon mask for last. After I tossed it in, I threw in handful after handful of the black-eyed peas: *oni wa soto, oni wa soto, oni wa soto.* It was done.

On my way back out of town, I drove past Jack's house again. This time I slowed, then pulled onto the shoulder of the road and got out of the car. Except that the trees were larger, the place looked just the same: the stranded battleship of a house, the tennis court. My tree house was still there: I could see the gleam of the tin roof through the branches of the Osage orange. There was no one on the court or in the yard, but there were cars in the drive — the brown one I remembered and a new one, bright red. It was a Saturday; perhaps they were sleeping late. I imagined going up the drive — walking so as not to alert them — then going to the house, getting the key from the hiding place, unlocking the door. Tiptoeing into the bedroom that had been Mama's. Saying it all while they stared open-mouthed. Or bypassing the house, walking across the yard, and climbing up to the tree house, where I would wait until they happened to look up and see me watching them. But as I imagined climbing up the tree, I had an eerie vision that made me shiver: I would find myself already there, cross-legged on the platform, peering solemnly down through the leaves.

I got back in the car and headed west. All the way across the country to Chicago I was haunted by the image of my face frozen in the leaves. It was then — in motels, in coffee shops, in rest areas, sitting in the car — that I began to write down things that I remembered: the chartreuse, pimpled skin of the Osage oranges and the sticky white juice inside; Jack in his bee suit, walking slowly toward the hives; and, long before that, myself jouncing along on Daddy's shoulders, looking back at the pony we never named.

Epilogue

TWO YEARS have passed, it is winter again. The branches on
the tree outside my window are covered with ice, but in my
room there are green plants everywhere, on shelves, in hanging
baskets, on a stand in front of the unshaded side window. The
begonias I've been collecting are by that window, drinking in
the late afternoon sun: some dark green, glossy as fine leather,
others a lighter green with markings that are red where the
light shines through. On my desk are a hyacinth just coming
into bloom and a cyclamen, its white, purple-tinged flowers
steady as flames.

A few days ago I roamed the city with my camera and took
pictures of all the places I had looked for Daddy: the Drake
Hotel ballroom, the jazz clubs on Randolph Street, the Lincoln
Park Zoo, the edge of Lake Michigan. This afternoon I put the
developed photographs in an envelope, sealed it, and wrote on
the outside: "Daniel Thibedeaux, 1918–1990." Then I took
down the pictures from my windowsill — the one of Daddy
with his face cut out, the one of me and Stevie with our snowman, the one of me climbing the Osage orange — and slid them
into another envelope. I put the Osage orange wood and the
thorn into a small white box, then placed the box and envelopes
in the bottom drawer of my desk.

I have finished writing this. There were times I did not think I would. I feel deeply tired but full: something like peace.

I sit for a long time at my desk, watching the light fade and the branches of the tree outside the window blur into the dusk.

When it is dark, I get into bed and pull Grandmuddy's coverlet up over me. Drifting to sleep I remember, as I often have these past two years, Grandmuddy in her winter garden, her whole wrinkled face smiling as she spoke the names of each fragrant branch I held out to her.